Time's Forbidden Flower

DIANE RINELLA

Copyright © 2013/2015/2016 Diane Rinella
Cover art copyright © 2013 Diane Rinella
Cover design by Indie Author Services
Original cover source art © konradbak/Fotolia
The model on the cover of this book, along with the photographer and the cover's designer, are in no way affiliated with or endorsing this product.
ISBN: 0615853021
ISBN-13: 978-0615853024

For those who love where the flowers grow.

ACKNOWLEDGEMENTS

To those of you reading this now, thank you. Thank you from the bottom of my heart for joining me on this journey. Lily, Donovan, and Christopher have become cherished parts of my life because of you. When I pressed the publish button on *Love's Forbidden Flower*, I had no idea I would meet so many amazing people. Thank you for bringing me into your lives.

My husband, Brian, who has been unfailingly supportive of my dreams and has never once complained when I locked myself away for "just a few more minutes" or spent "just a few more dollars" to complete this project.

Alicia and Tori, who are worth their weight in gold for giving valuable advice and insight.

Keith, for opening my eyes.

Carole, for friendship and support more cherished than she will ever know.

Trishalana, for being an amazing and tolerant person.

Lastly, and in no way least, the real life Lilys and Donovans who have trusted me with their stories. You are loved, supported, and respected.

PROLOGUE

Donovan's new fervor for life brought incandescence to every molecule of my being. Immediately after his release from Dr. Coe's care at the Harley Rehabilitation Center, I helped him move into a crowded dorm in Colorado where he began the completion of his bachelor's degree at Ramsey University. A year later, we settled him into the studio apartment where he would reside while continuing his studies.

It was a bittersweet dawn as the sun's golden glow slipped through the windows, bathing us in the glorious light of our new lives ahead. Relief, pride, and apprehension swirled through me as Donovan unpacked the last box. Ceremoniously, he placed four journals and his bachelor's degree on a bookshelf overlooking his apartment. Three of the journals he kept while abused. The forth marked his recovery.

Expanding his lungs to their fullest, he nodded his chin to the shelf. "Now we're done. It'll be a long time before I fill that shelf, but at least I know what will go there. Just five or six more years until the doctorate—give or take a little time for my thesis."

"I'm so proud of you for turning all the bad things that happened positive," I said, radiating with joy. Becoming a psychologist is brilliant."

Never before had his grip on me, or his life, seemed so secure. "It was all Lisa's idea," he credited in recollection of his phony high school girlfriend. The ruse was to make Dad think Donovan was being a macho stud while convincing Mom that he had lost interest in me. "Lisa reminded me that Carl Jung said, 'Knowing your own darkness is the best method for dealing with the darkness of other people.' "

Still, the Lisa situation perplexed me. "I don't think I'll ever get my head around your relationship with Lisa."

"We were just two people forced into the same bad situation," Donovan said. "Lisa's parents trying to cure her of being a lesbian isn't much different from what happened to me. Posing as lovers was our Hail Mary pass in hopes of relief. After all we've been through together, I'd be crazy not to trust her."

I placed a firm kiss on his cheek. "You are always my best therapist."

His eyes locked into mine as he granted words that left my longing heart free to act on what seemed an eternity of waiting. "Okay, Lil, I'm settled. Are you out of excuses now, or are you going to give me a new challenge to overcome at lightning speed so you can finish moving on? It would be much easier if you'd admit the truth. I forced myself to accept it a year ago."

This man is so frustrating when he's right.

"Are you sure about this?" I asked. "Because I'm ready—really, really ready."

"I promised to ensure that all your dreams come true. If you don't finally say yes to Christopher, I'm having you locked up. To have someone who loves you that much, whom you love just as dearly, and keep him hanging on a string, truly shows that you are crazy."

As my flight home prepared for landing, I slipped my trash novel into my carry-on bag in exchange for a flat, black box. My eyes turned glassy in memory of the day Christopher gave it to me. We had talked of marriage many times before, but with Donovan still pulling his life together, my insides were a mess, and Christopher knew it.

A year before, when we moved into our home in Westwood, California, I accidentally opened a box of Christopher's clothes. "I found your socks and underwear. What drawer would you like them in?"

Sheepishly, he slipped his hands into his jeans' pockets. "Kindly place them in the top drawer, please." Nestled under the socks, sat the box. "Open it," he said, hesitantly. Inside was a lovely pair of white gloves monogrammed LPE, the initials I would carry as his wife. "There's an old-world custom that a chivalrous man would give the lady he wished to marry a pair of gloves. If she wore them to church, he knew she accepted his proposal. I thought that maybe you would accept these and someday wear them as a signal to me. That way I won't always wonder if the time is right for you."

With a fluttery stomach I descended the airport escalator. Among the drivers awaiting their passengers, my adorable Christopher stood with a sign saying Beckett, along with a bouquet of sterling roses—the kind that remind him of my eyes. I raced over with a glow, both hands pulling my suitcase behind my back, and placed a sweet kiss on his lips. A surge of happiness zapped through me.

"You look adorable. Why do you have a sign that says Beckett? I thought you came to get me?" Christopher's jaw slacked as he cocked his head, his words failing him. "Hmm …" I mused, placing a gloved hand to my chin. His sky-blue eyes grew as wide as his gaping mouth. "I prefer the name Eccles. Oh, well. Let's grab my bag and get out of here."

The following evening I arrived home from work to find the house smelling of burnt chocolate. Christopher was frantically cleaning. "Umm… Do I want to know?" I asked.

"No! I must say you don't!" he brazenly declared. He dropped a pan into its drawer and slammed it. "I wanted to surprise you with dinner tonight, but I almost had to call out the fire brigade. I've made reservations at Pierre's. Run up and change. I'm bloody famished."

Christopher's desire to trade in his apron for a tux brought about my suspicion. Not only had his previous cooking mishaps always resulted in delivered pizza, reservations at Pierre's were never obtained at the drop of a hat without serious bribery.

With nervous jitters, I picked at my lobster, only to be startled by a *clank* as Christopher dropped his knife. It barely missed the melted butter; yet hit the fork that crossed his plate, thus catapulting an empty claw shell into the breadbasket. "How's your meal, luv?" he asked, fidgeting with the napkin in his lap.

"Wonderful. Are you still worked up from fixing dinner or has the bottle of Cristal gotten to you?"

"I'm fine. Will you excuse me a moment?"

Nervously I waited, knowing what was coming, yet also without a clue in the world what to expect. Christopher strode into the restaurant like a bandleader with the kitchen staff in tow. His dinner jacket had been exchanged for a slightly oversized waiter's coat, and a towel was draped over one arm while the other hid behind his back. Anticipation permeated my airway.

"Madame," he said. His Manc accent was more adorable than ever. "Seeing that you are by far the most amazingly beautiful creature that has ever graced this restaurant, a most exclusive dessert has been prepared especially for you." From behind his back, Christopher revealed a plate that was elegantly decorated with swirls of piped chocolate and silver dragèes. Its center featured a single cupcake—chocolate with pink frosting and colored sprinkles—exactly like the one he made for our first Valentine's Day years before—but with one exception. A ring with a diamond the size of the Rock of Gibraltar stood in the frosting. Christopher dropped to one knee and took my hand. My heart went the same route as my lungs and halted its function as well.

"Lilyanna, darling, I've never deserved you, yet somehow you've managed to love lowly me. I've experienced life with and without you, and I'm an absolute disaster when you are not around, be it for two years, a week, or only a few moments. Would you do me the honor of being my wife?"

My multitude of fantasies did nothing to prepare me for a moment so amazingly beautiful it would grace my dreams for a lifetime. Frantically I nodded. My arms jettisoned around him, knocking us both to the restaurant floor and drawing loud cheers from the refined establishment's suddenly lively patrons.

"I love you Christopher Paul Eccles, and I love my cupcake."

"It's exactly the way I wanted to give you one years ago."

ॐ

The petals on the sterling roses held in my hands fluttered like the butterflies in my stomach as I awaited the opening of the chapel doors. Christopher and I held the first of our two weddings in Las Vegas. While the wedding in England would be far more extravagant, this was the hurdle that needed conquering.

Donovan's words permeated when he asked why I was waiting for all of the amazing things I wanted when opportunity was about to steamroller over me. Since ceremonies were needed on both sides of the pond, I planned a simple vow exchange in The States and mapped out my future business while Christopher's mother, Grace, had a field day back in Manchester designing a wedding fit for royalty. We shared countless hours of video chats, and I sent photos and color swatches like crazy so she could ensure all of my desires were met. We loved every second of it.

However, it was in this quaint chapel that the big moment was upon us, the one that really mattered for so many reasons.

Despite the sparse surroundings of a room decorated by only a mural of a flower garden and two urns of fake red gladiolas, I felt regal in my flowing dress of white satin and French lace with a hand-beaded pearl and crystal bodice—my something new. A short veil, trimmed with rhinestone-embellished lace, framed my face as my chocolate-brown hair cascaded in swirls. The diamond earrings Donovan gave me, and my grandmother's pearl necklace, served as my something old. On my left wrist was an intricate gold bangle that belonged to Christopher's great grandmother—my something borrowed that Grace wore on her wedding day. My right hand still carried the pearl ring Christopher gave me five years prior. Inside my shoe rattled a polished British penny pressed in my birth year, a gift from Eric, Christopher's closest friend.

A lace handkerchief with a blue bow was grasped along with my bouquet. It served as a reminder of my discomfort. "Um, Lily," Donovan's girlfriend, Anna, had timidly said while handing me a box. Her formfitting, navy blue suit tastefully accentuated her every voluptuous curve. "I bought you a little something. My aunt had a similar one. Her marriage lasted thirty-one beautiful years, so I consider it lucky."

Anna's sweet gesture only added to my jitters. "Donovan, I'm so anxious that I can't hear myself think. Am I doing the right thing?"

His words were almost hypnotic, relaxing me into a near trance. "You're doing exactly what you're supposed to. You have a long and happy life ahead, and I'm going to always be with you making sure you don't blow it. I remember all you've ever wished, and I'm going to ensure we get *everything* we've ever desired. It's all just a matter of time. You ready for us to take that walk so you can put the shackles on your scrawny dreamboat?"

"You're such an ass. I guess you really are back to your old self."

"Did you doubt I wouldn't come out unscathed?"

After opening the door before us, Donovan kissed my hand one last time before walking me down the aisle. Once Donovan handed me off to Christopher, the universe ceased to exist as I looked into the peace of the blue-sky eyes before me—the only something blue I needed. In that sky I saw no clouds, no clutter—only admiration, protection, and a soul I loved boldly and freely. As we said our simple I dos, and his lips touched mine in interminable commitment, my heart soared above the heavens.

ℬ

"Ready for round two?" Donovan asked as we stood outside the entryway of Manchester Cathedral. My previous wedding attire now benefited from the addition of a cathedral length train and a sparkling tiara.

"Bring it!" I exclaimed. True wedding excitement filled me. The thumping of my blood was the loveliest melody I had ever heard. Again the happiest music had come from Manchester.

Donovan planted a kiss on my head that resounded in my ears as we rounded the corner into the gothic cathedral. The church's towering stone arches and soaring ceiling were not high enough to contain my swelling heart. The vicar's rambled words flowed over me. I couldn't be bothered with his formalities; I had eyes to stare into. Eyes of such a beautiful color I once said I wanted to bottle it so it could forever paint my heart. Those eyes had done exactly that, and I was completely lost in them when they suddenly darted to the floor and Christopher began his vows.

"It seems silly to take vows today. Vows are something you take from a moment forward, which would imply that what I feel is new. I've felt the same way about you for years, but I couldn't act on it when I wanted. When I finally could, my true vows began. I promised to be everything to you that you will allow, to stand by your side, to respect every nuance of you whether I understood it or not, and to share every bit of my being. You bring out the best in me, and I will remain faithfully by your side and by the sides of our future children for all of my days."

My heart had fallen into Christopher's words to the point where I had to be nudged to say my own vows. "I will never lose sight of the amazing and sensitive man you are. I will be your strength when life fails you, laugh with you in good times and struggle with you in bad, and be the best that I can for you and our children, no matter where life takes us or what challenges lie ahead. I will always love you, and I will

7

live in joy with you, for as long as God allows."

The floodgates of emotion crashed down for us. Christopher and I threw away pretense and sealed the words from our lips by bringing them together without the customary permission. We had each other, and nothing mattered but that and the road ahead.

After the main event concluded, I found the one thing I let Grace talk me into was well worth my caving. When she suggested we have the reception in the cathedral I thought she was insane. A wedding? Yes. But a full-on party in a church? Isn't that sacrilegious? However, we were in Manchester, a place known for music and life. The cathedral was no stranger to hosting raging parties and worked with caterers and event planners to turn the place into a hopping nightclub.

Christopher and I sat with Grace, Donovan, and the men Christopher refers to as his fathers. Christopher fed me a bite of hazelnut sponge cake with Williams Pear mousse. My taste buds sang while Keith continued one of his stories of their band's past.

"So Eric makes like the clappers and heads off stage only to trip on a cord and take a nose dive into the wings and straight into a guard. Lucky sod was then dragged off behind a curtain and waited out the crowd that ran by, screamin' their bloody heads off. Meanwhile, I'm trying to get out from behind my drums as the birds attack. Not only did they shred me new shirt, they took my cymbals! Those things cost a bloody fortune!"

"See what you've got to look forward to, Lilyanna?" the burley Derek laughed. "Now that you're the trouble and strife of a soon to be famous musician you'll have to fight the birds off your man."

Donovan was all too quick to catch on to the meaning. "Trouble and strife is right. That's a piece of slang that requires no explanation. She didn't need to become a wife for it to fit though."

"Gee, thanks," I said. "You're such a perfect joy at all

times, D-boy."

"Actually, tonight he has been quite the charmer," Grace said. Her bright blue eyes leered while she stroked the stem of her glass, looking a little too enamored with her new son-in-law. It was time to get her off the sauce.

Eric jumped to the rescue. "Come on, Grace. You owe me a dance."

Derek patted Donovan on the shoulder. "I'm off for some Britneys at the Ringo. Want one?"

"Okay, wait. Give me a second." Donovan looked like he had just enough alcohol for math to hurt as he tried to decipher the code. "Britney...Britain..."

"Think of the singer."

"Britney... Spears... rhymes with...beers... Ringo Starr must mean bar."

"Hey! There's hope for you yet. Want one?"

"I'm good, thanks. Hey, Christopher, mind if I steal my sister for a dance? They're playing our song."

Donovan hadn't referred to me as his sister in years. It sounded ... alien.

When we hit the dance floor, Donovan pulled me securely into his arms. I felt he was staking a flag into me.

"Our song? Since when do we have a song?"

His stupid grin was infectious. "Since years ago when every piece of sap that came on the radio reminded me of you. Basically, every song is our song."

The relief of the day nearing a close reflected in his eyes, or had he partaken in the open bar too much? "Have you been sampling the champagne?" I asked.

"A little, along with one or two other things."

"Please don't tell me you are trying to keep up with Christopher's fathers. They'll have you under the table with your pants up a flag pole in five minutes."

"Oh, no way," he said with rosy-cheeks. "I may not be the sharpest knife, but I'm not spending my one week of summer vacation trolleyed and razzing."

"Wow! Look at you! It didn't take you long to learn the

local vocabulary."

"With those guys, it's either keep up or shut up. They're a challenge. I'm going to miss them when I return home."

"And I'm going to miss you," I said emphatically. "Though this week had its awkward moments, I feel so much more complete when you're around."

The kiss he laid on my cheek released a resounding *smack*. "Me too, but I have a lot to accomplish. Give me a few years. If you still want me around, I'll be there."

"I'll never stop wanting you around."

His bold smile, that he had worked so hard to genuinely find, morphed into one of a man who had loved and lost. "I really hope that proves to be true."

∾

That November, Donovan flew to my home in Los Angeles for what would become an annual Thanksgiving visit. While I encouraged him to bring Anna, I wasn't prepared for the overwhelming emotions that flooded me when the doorbell rang. My mantra that had begun the night before—*You are happy with Christopher. Donovan deserves happiness too.*—brought me peace until that moment. This would be the first time my eyes rested on Donovan since my wedding. With the doorbell's chime, the reality of my feelings came back to bite me—thus I hid in the kitchen like a coward while Christopher greeted them.

There was no way I could face *them* together—*them* being both Donovan and Anna, and Donovan and Christopher.

Donovan immediately searched me out. He took the knife out of my hands and tossed it on the cutting board. He then pulled me into a bear hug and hoisted me off my feet, spinning me into a giggly fit. By the time my feet reconnected with the ground, my tension had dissipated.

While we were all having cocktails, Donovan pulled me into my home library, closed the door behind us and dragged me to the far corner. He whispered as if afraid the walls had ears. "Lily, there's something very important that I need to tell you before dinner."

"Is this going to be some kind of ridiculous joke about suddenly developing an allergy to tarragon and not being able to breathe around it? If it is, I'm going to let you pretend to be on the verge of death all night."

"No, Lily, I am *very* serious," he said, taking my hands in his and swallowing back emotions. "Something will be announced at dinner, and I want to warn you about it first." His eyes then diverted to my hands and he toyed with my engagement ring. "I, ugh … I asked … Anna and I are getting married."

My whole body hitched forward. Suddenly I felt plagued by a feverish stomach virus. He had every right to get married and deserved my blessing, just as he had given me when I married Christopher. However, what I knew should be said went against all that my being screamed.

"Lily, I … I'm sorry. Please understand that—"

"Why are you apologizing?" I tried to be noble, but I couldn't ditch the bitter taste of jealousy. "I want you to be happy like I am, but—Donovan, tell me the truth. Don't throw up any walls because I'll assume you are lying." My eyes shut, fearing the answer, because no matter what he said, the pain would squash my heart. "Yes or no, do you love Anna?"

"Of course I love her." He was so persuasive that my gut also crumbled. "I wouldn't marry her if I didn't."

"Are you *in love* with her?"

He cupped my hands in his enlaced fingers while pressing his palms into each other. Our hands became his focal point. "You mean like I am with you? No, I'll never be in love with anyone the way I am with you, but she does make me happy. When I'm with her, I feel like I have purpose." He drew his gaze into mine in a plea for understanding. "She gets me, Lily. She understands that I have a history I don't want to share and that I've learned from it. She respects what I am trying to do for myself by helping others, and she points out the validity of my past suffering. Lily, if I can't have you, I at least want to feel like a person of value. Anna helps me see my self worth."

Pain radiated through me, and I did a horrible job of disguising it with teasing. "So it's not that she's some hot chick that's good in bed?"

Donovan cocked an eyebrow. "Is she hot? I hadn't noticed." He smiled, and I lightly kicked him, unwilling to remove my hands from his to smack his arm. "Seriously, Lily, when it comes to my list of beautiful women there is only one entry." With seductive eyes he kissed my hand. I swooned and considered dragging him through the window to escape the world with me. His words killed my temptation. "However, when I look at myself and what I hope to accomplish in life, and then look at Anna, I see the same desires. I can make something of myself, Lily, just like she's doing. Everyday we both have challenges to overcome, and together those mountains of immovable stone look like mustard seeds. You know what they say: Faith the size of a mustard seed can move mountains. That is what I plan to do with her. Please, Lily. Please support this."

I snuggled my head into his chest. Defeat swept over me, and I choked on the last bit of acceptance I didn't realize I hadn't swallowed. "Of course, Donovan. Anything to make you happy."

After dinner I battled my emotions by sticking the guys with the dishes, then grabbing two glasses, a bottle of champagne, and Anna's hand. With a plastered-on smile I dragged her into the library, acting like old girlfriends instead of the near strangers we were. Despite being somewhat quiet, Anna was intimidating—hence my need of liquid courage. After my second glass, I was still struggling to know the fashionable woman who sat before me. She was tall, but her stilettos made her statuesque. Her deep brown, cotton-polyester dress accentuated every streamlined curve. Clearly she took care of herself, yet what attracted Donovan to this shy woman escaped me.

"That dress is amazing," I said of the form-fitting, yet tasteful, garment. "Where did you get it?"

Anna fidgeted with the rim of her glass. Though she had kept up with me regarding the consumption of champagne, she showed no signs of relaxation. "Taylor's," she replied.

I waited for elaboration, or a return question, but all was so quiet I didn't even hear crickets outside. I gave it another shot. "You have a lovely figure. How do you stay in shape?"

"Thanks. I hit the gym with Donovan a few times a week." She downed the remainder of her glass, and I poured her more. Still she did nothing to help with the small talk.

"To me a workout is sprinting into the bakery from my car when I'm late for work," I said. Anna took another sip. Her eyes searched the room, seemingly for something to grab her attention. Finally the champagne kicked in enough for me to lie while playing the friend card. "I totally get what Donovan sees in you, but what on earth do you see in him?"

Anna looked to her hands that nervously sat in her lap. Slowly a smile built, and her eyes rose like the light that had been turned on inside her was charged with adrenaline. "I trust him. For the first time in my life I have found a man who is gentle, understanding, and whom I completely trust. Donovan is one of those people that will never let you fall, no matter how precariously you put yourself out on a ledge." She sneaked a bashful peek at me, then again diverted her eyes. She spoke cautiously, yet her enthusiasm didn't falter. "He told me that he had some problems with your mom while growing up, and even though he hated himself for hurting you, he acted out of love to give you the best life possible. I've also been hurt before, and I've come to accept that those people had no concern for me. To have someone like Donovan is a gift. I've always wanted someone to love me the way he loves you."

Suddenly I understood. I had been the only one to ever really trust Donovan. With Anna he had finally found someone else who believed in him. While I still had my doubts about their relationship, the attraction made perfect sense. "I'm sorry that you had it so rough," I said.

"Thanks. I had to deal with a lot of illness in my family. Like Donovan, I wanted to take all the bad that happened and turn it positive, so I became a nurse. He's even inspired me to take it further and become a nurse practitioner. The more I help others, the more I help myself, much like what Donovan is doing. Sometimes when you are hurting, the only way to lessen the pain is to see the value in it; then it becomes a gift. I firmly believe that the suffering of one is a blessing to another."

With every bit of strength I had, I kicked my apprehensions and jealousy to the curb. Maybe, just maybe, Anna could be the blessing brought forth from Donovan's suffering.

1

An impassioned encounter with Christopher this morning gave me the salivating jitters of a sugar junkie entering a chocolate factory—which would be fantastic if I were not about to spend two nights alone with Donovan.

Backyards and footballs make for a foolhardy mix when I'm around. Stupidity prevailed when I saw how awkward, yet endearing, Christopher looked playing catch with our seven-year-old son, Graham, and our five-year-old daughter, Antonia. Embarrassment on Christopher's behalf compelled me to rescue the poor kids from their father's lack of grace. Seriously, while his muscles have nicely filled out from all the equipment he lugs, the Queen could lob a more masculine pass.

Who would have thought that me, Ms. Klutz On the Field, could throw a football better than her husband? That part was fine, but it was how I played coach that let the cheetah out of the worm can. It was nearly a replay of how Donovan taught me years before. However, not only did my actions have the follow through Donovan's lacked, my words almost revealed the sacred truth.

I strolled up behind Christopher. My left arm circled his waist while I pulled him close, twisting his hips as I went. "First, situate your body. Make sure you have a solid grip. Now pull back, like so."

That's when he clumsily bonked me in the face, exactly like I had done to Donovan years before. Warm flames of remembrance brought forth the desire to live out what I wished had happened then with the enticing man in my arms now. Again I pulled Christopher next to me, this time placing my cheek tenderly against his. Sadly, Christopher was all business, nearly assassinating my attempt to live out the fantasy.

Decorum fell to the sidelines when I nibbled on his ear, making him blush and shy away. My pulse raced when I exchanged my grip on the ball for a gentle cup of his chin and exploring Christopher's mouth with my own. The lust from our kisses melted onto my tongue as if a cooking torch were used on my hormones, causing them to sizzle like sugar being caramelized on Crème Brûlée. In complete surrender to the moment I grabbed his shirt and yanked him to the ground. Were my desires the result of the man above me or the memory of the one I had so desperately wanted before?

Christopher breathlessly uttered through his adorable Manc accent, that even after nine years of marriage still sends me to the moon, "Dear God, Lilyanna. I thought you were going to teach me like Donovan taught you."

That is when my hormones drove me smack into a concrete wall of stupidity. "Be glad I didn't show you how he taught me to give a guy a good sacking."

There's no possible way that could have sounded sisterly. Christopher's eyes, voluminous and frozen with shock, showed my assumption was correct. I switched gears by deepening his mortification. "Whaaat? Got yur knickers in a twist, eh luv? Lookin' a lit'le godsmacked, there ya is."

"Seriously, Lilyanna, one of these days I have to teach you proper Cockney. If you're going to botch an accent at least make it Liverpudlian. Then again, they already sound wonky without your well-intended help."

Ten hours later, my flight is touching down in Rhode Island where Donovan's flight from Colorado has already landed. My nervousness intensifies in memory of yesterday's call from Donovan, bringing about prayers.

Dear Lord, please guide us through the days ahead. Donovan's feelings of responsibility for the results of Mom's addictions are unfair. Instead of getting the help he advised, she became the victim of her own actions. As for everything else, you know the struggles Donovan and I face when together. Please ease the pain.

The flight lands, and Lilyanna Eccles turns into Lily Beckett. Donovan and I embrace our rare moments together, forgetting that our spouses exist—with one exception. Our wedding rings serve as reminders that cheating is unthinkable. While the area that defines cheating is gray, some actions are clearly off limits.

Outside of my terminal, Donovan sits hunched forward, scratching the back of his neck, and bouncing his knee. Seeing him nearly makes my heart beat out of my chest in a mad desire to collide with his. For the first time since the termination of our romantic relationship we won't have to sneak away to be alone. It's a welcome relief and nerve-wracking as hell.

Our meeting gazes stop me cold. He looks spectacular—his sapphires clear and bright, hair still raven-like, and skin aglow with the hues and luminosity of heath. Smug little glances exchange before we campishly search the room for eyes that might not be accepting of our impending actions. After jesting shrugs, we run into each other's arms—me jumping on him, wrapping my legs around his waist, and planting little kisses wildly all over his face. His head buries in my hair with a deep inhale, as if capturing a part of me. His words release with relief. "God, I've missed you!" Pulling back, he looks at me with a big, stupid curl of the lips. "It's about time we could do that without fear of facing a firing squad."

The joy of being in his arms is as consuming as ever, and it reflects in my words. "Let's go straight to the hotel. I don't want to lay eyes on anyone but you tonight."

2

Donovan and I sit facing each other on the sofa in his dimly lit hotel room that adjoins to mine, talking—not talking—sharing every thought. We see each other so little now it amazes me that we can disregard words yet be completely understood. It's a sad state. We were born not needing articulation, and our predicament has infringed upon our beauty.

Suppressing the emotions that could ruin everything we have both worked so hard for, my words interrupt our silent admissions of longing. "Now that it is easy to talk openly, tell me how you're really doing."

Donovan squirms. He knows he can't pretend I'm asking about his roof that was leaking. After a moment of uncomfortable glances, he confesses. "Not as well as I'd like. I still have moments where Dad invades my brain. I used to hear him calling me a loser, but for the last few years it's like he's begging my forgiveness for how he always treated me like a lesser being. It's really disturbing. I want to forgive him and Mom, but I just can't."

"Is that why we still deal with this madness and foolishly risk our families seeing her at Christmas?"

"I'm just trying to salvage something that died long ago. I might find forgiveness if Mom would confess why she lost it with me."

"You know, sometimes we need to forgive people, while other times it's best we don't." I toy with the sleeve of his T-shirt, running my fingers over the edge that caps his tight biceps and remembering how good they feel when around me. "Forgiveness can help us heal and move on, but lack of it can help us stay strong and true to ourselves." The realization that touching him is inappropriate makes me want to do it all the more. I retract my hand and slip it between my legs. The action brings forth the need to rotate my head and shift my shoulders in an effort to release newfound tension.

"Really, Lil," he says, eyes circulating, lashes fluttering. "I'm supposed to be the therapist." His orbs drop with a sigh. "I know it's irrational thinking brought on by the PTSD, but I can't help but feel that maybe I was the one who put them through hell. If I didn't have the feelings for you that I did, and still do, then—"

"Then I would be in this alone."

His grin is uncharacteristically bashful. Taking his hand to my hair, he captures a cluster of locks just below my temple and threads it through his fingers. "I'd hate myself, because I know that all enamored feelings aside, you and I would be precisely the way we are in other aspects."

"Do you ever wonder why that is?"

"All the time," he says with a sigh. He draws his hand away, but his eyes remain on my cluster of hair so that they now hold it captive. "The fact that we can share so much without even muttering a word is loony bin material in some people's eyes." He pauses. His eyes slowly shift back and forth. One lip moistens the other. They pop open when he speaks. "I have something to show you."

With a stiff back and broad shoulders he walks to the closet. He rummages through a messenger bag before drifting back, staring at a small tin and looking a tad shrunken. He pulls forth a chair and sits across from me. Does the contents of the container add danger to our proximity? "This is just for us," he says. He presses the tin into my hand and wraps my fingers around it. He then gives a squeeze signaling his own need for reassurance.

"What's inside? Why are you so nervous?"

"It's a flash drive containing a secondary journal I began while in rehab. I'm nervous from memories of the last time I shared my journals—when I told you the truth about what happened to me. This one is even more personal than those."

My stomach twists and feels pulled into a vortex. Those journals detailed years of abuse and stress that made him monstrous and eventually suicidal. "Donovan, what are you trying to tell me?"

"You're well aware of the way I'm haunted in my sleep, but not all of the ghosts are bad. Dr. Coe felt I should keep a separate journal for the things that haunt me at night, along with a new method of maintaining it—like sorting fantasy from reality. We would then review my nightmares and try to unlock more of my issues. The more I improved, the more often I had special dreams. Some were still frightening, but others were downright beautiful." He moves to sit next to me and slides his arm around my waist. His other hand is planted firmly on my leg, bracing me. "Remember how you said we're soulmates and eventually I started buying into that possibility?"

My eyes gaze up to his, longing to dive into them and become lost. "Yeah, it's when you gave me the infinity necklace I'm wearing. You said we traveled together before and we would again."

He nods in acknowledgement. "Shortly after accepting that idea I started having insightful dreams—some of them vague and others pretty vivid. What you hold are my journal entries of those dreams. Lily, I may really be crazy, but I think—no, I know we have traveled together before. I'm also pretty sure we are no strangers to conflict relationships. Would you be willing to undergo past life regression?"

My eyes expand and then try to refocus on the tin. I shake my head in hopes that doing so will grant clarity. "But you're a psychologist. Doesn't this go against your beliefs?"

"Sort of. Most psychologists see it as a crutch people use to avoid reality. Dr. Coe is a believer because he had patients who can describe details about shoes and clothing that are not in common history books but hardcore historians can confirm. All I know is when I look into your eyes I feel I'm having memories I can't see. If you're willing to undergo hypnotherapy, and our stories match, maybe we can understand why our connection is so deep."

Beholding the flash drive that may contain so many keys, intuition dawns: I've always been a butterfly trapped in Donovan's net. My heart knows Donovan and I traveled together before, yet I've never allowed myself to think of the logistics. If the more I pull back, the more I crave his enclosure, what happens if I learn my deprivation has been for centuries, or even millenniums? Is being an old soul why I have always felt and sounded older than my years? Why do I have the passions I do? How did I become me?

My insides become unsettled, and my words sound as hazy as my vision that blurs while staring at the tin. "For years I have tried to figure us out. Whenever you read about sibling consanguinamory there are crazy theories, like our family must have been dysfunctional, or we are perverted, or some other ridiculousness. Truth is, you and I just love each other.

"Here," I say, pressing the drive back into his hand. "I can handle it if you're wrong, but if you and I are fated to find each other time after time only to be pulled apart, how do I move forward knowing I am destined for pain?"

"Lily, I'm sorry. I never expected you to react this way."

"It's fine." My tightened grip emphasizes my words. "Really. Give me a little time to get my head together. When I can face the results, no matter what they are, I'll give it a shot." My hands reluctantly retract from his while forcing myself to look at him in a socially acceptable light because of my commitment to someone else.

"Hey," he says softly, pulling up my chin. Something in his eyes draws me in. "You okay?"

"Yeah, it's just late. I'm going to get ready for bed." I head into my room with the intention of later returning to say good night. When I exit the bathroom, the doors between our rooms are still open, yet Donovan's lights are off. It feels wrong for a married woman to enter the dark bedroom of a former lover as he lies in bed. The ring on my finger tells me to shut the door while the journal he keeps beckons me into his chamber. I crawl into my own bed, staring into Donovan's darkness, secure in his proximity, and knowing that though they feel wrong, my actions are correct.

ॐ

"Leave me alone! I swear I'll kill you if you come any closer!"

My cozy slumber is interrupted by the demons that haunt Donovan in the night. Grateful that I left the door open, I race into his room. My attempt to rattle him awake is interrupted by flailing slaps that escalate into forceful swings.

"Get off of me! I said I'll kill you!" he threatens.

Fearing the hotel's security will soon arrive, I grab Donovan from behind, attempt to restrict his arms, and scream, "Donovan, it's Lily! Wake up! Donovan, wake up!" I echo the chant to no avail. I cower from his swings. My nails pinch his inner thigh with a twist. Finally he wakes, jolting with a gasp. My back hits the bed in relief.

"Please tell me I didn't hurt you," he says, panting.

"Wow. You're concerned about me? This was way worse than when we lived together."

"Sometimes I get out of hand when I'm about to see Mom. Please tell me I didn't hurt you."

"No, I'm okay." However my pulse still flares and ebbs with each heartbeat.

Donovan bridges his back. His hands scrape through his hair. "Lily, I need to ask you something that may sound strange, and you have to give me an honest answer. Did I ever do anything to physically hurt you, or have I ever done anything to manipulate you into feeling the way you do?"

"No!"

Donovan remains hunched over, hiding from my impending answer. "Stop and really think about it. No knee jerk reaction. I need to know if I ever did anything at all, especially before this whole mess started."

My heart still races from Donovan's nightmare. I prop myself against the wall and take pause. Finally I address him in no uncertain terms. "Never. Not once have you tried to place any influence over me except to get me to not love you, but even then I saw the truth."

He peers to me so he can analyze my upcoming reaction. "Are you absolutely certain? What about that first day, when you tackled me, then I pushed you down and pinned you?"

My brain searches for a memory to confirm his false one. "Donovan, that's not what happened. After you sat, you helped me up and we went inside. You've never asserted yourself on me."

He lays back onto the bed and motions for me to curl into his shoulder. As his comfort settles in, so does mine, bringing forth guilt. For hours my brain deliberates the ethics of this moment of peace with myself versus the previous battle with frustration and temptation. Eventually comfort wins, and Donovan's heartbeat lulls me to sleep.

3

My head throbs as Donovan and I approach the hospital room of Lucretia Macevil. The jumbo bottle of aspirin in my purse won't be enough. Given whom we are about to see I should've brought Valium—or elephant tranquilizers.

Bags hang under my eyes that look like they are filled with dollar store rejects while Donovan appears well rested. He must be all too used to late nights, or maybe he's better at the makeup thing than I am.

Just outside the door, I grab his hand in need of support. Donovan smirks. "The Cirrhosis and Portal Hypertension aren't enough? Are you trying to give her a heart attack too?" The levity is desperately needed, yet it fails to sit well.

"Fine." I drop his hand like a dirty rag. "Forgive me for looking out for myself for once."

He scans me through aching eyes that are resigned to sadness. "Yeah, I need all the help I can get too, but she's going to flip if she thinks anything is going on. You can hold on to me all you want later, okay?"

My demure smile is accented with a subtle nod before we breathe deeply and enter at our own risk. Mom sits in her bed. Time, her disease, and the suffering she inflicted have all taken their toll. Her short, wavy hair, once dyed an age-appropriate chestnut is now misty gray. Puffy pillows reside under her blue eyes while fork-shaped crevices emit from their far edges. Her cheeks hang like petite jowls. She's awake, alert, and being her old self. "Oh, Lily! I never expected to see both of you," she says, nearly singing her words. Then she runs her eyes between Donovan and I, and her expression goes stiff. "Where are Christopher and Anna?"

You mean you hoped not to see both of us. We're a matched set, and you know it.

Wow. Where did that come from? Some days I surprise myself with the amount of animosity I hold towards this woman.

"Hello to you too, Mom," Donovan moans as he places a vase of Lilies of the Valley on her nightstand. The sag of his face reminds me of how the blooms hang. Why couldn't Mom have named me after a happier flower?

"Oh, thank you," she says to Donovan with scarcely a glance in his direction. Instantly she returns her sights to me. "It's just amazing that Christopher still works after inheriting all that money. I can't believe his father was Paul Eccles, the famous producer! Have you met more of his father's friends?"

Wow. Lying in a hospital bed with a deadly disease and she's still obsessing over the teen idols of her youth. Amazing! "Occasionally, but mostly we see the guys from Paul's old band whenever we go to England," I taunt.

Mom looks like she's about to faint. "I almost died when you told me who is in Christopher's extended family. I had such a crush on Eric Taylor. He was just so dreamy."

Seriously? She needs to get out of fantasyland. Time to mess with her—truthfully. "Oh, he's still pretty dreamy. I swear he's seventy-five going on fifty-five. That full head of hair is mostly brown and not from a dye job. He's single too. It's such a shame. Whenever we visit he and Christopher are almost inseparable."

Donovan shoots me a whimsical smile. I can hear his thoughts that say, *Oh, you're so bad!*

I flash a crinkled nose at him.

Mom sighs longingly, then schlepps herself back into reality so she can scrutinize the children who came to help her despite their reservations. "Is it really wise, you two being here alone? What do Anna and Christopher think, or do they still not know of your *past?*" Her tone implies we spent years under the guise of being The Kray Twins, viciously torturing and murdering people.

"No, they don't know, nor will they," Donovan says. His eyes remain calm, but his voice resounds with intimidation. Quickly he changes the subject to one far more difficult. Staring at his fidgeting hands, he makes no attempt to hide his pain. "Look, Mom, the doctor said your situation is very serious. We need to know how you want us to handle things, should they go in an undesirable way. Can we please focus on what we need to?"

Mom brings her gaze to her intertwined hands that sit on her stomach. "You really want to uphold my wishes, James?" she asks Donovan. "Even after all I've put you both through?"

James? My head cocks as I question Donovan. Why is Mom calling him by his middle name?

His brow crinkles. His eyes dart from side to side. With a questioning shake of his head he ignores her madness like it happens all the time. "Yes, Mom, we do."

How he can constantly deal with her, only to plunge forward and ignore the craziness, I will never understand.

೮

Donovan and I return to the hotel. Simultaneously we open the doors that adjoin our rooms, and I plop down on his bed. The circus of butterflies I sense performing trampoline tricks in his stomach make me wonder why I am willing to enter the lion's den. Donovan hovers nearby, picking at his nails. "Is this about the James thing?" I ask regarding his discomfort.

"Huh?" He peers up, and then returns his attention to his nails. "Sort of. I should be used to her crazy ramblings. It's part of the senior dementia that she probably fakes to taunt me."

He takes a seat next to me. Instinctively we kick off our shoes and face each other with our legs entwined at the knees. He grabs my hands and stares at my wedding ring before bringing his eyes to mine. "All my life I have tried to do the right thing—for you, me, Anna, my daughter, and Mom—but in doing that, I have lost so much. Everything about us feels wrong now. You being in my arms last night gave me the best sleep I had in years. I miss you. I miss you doing that," he says, pointing to my fingers as they play with a lock of hair below my temples. I was unaware of my actions. "You often twirl it when you look at me, and I've never seen you do it for anyone else."

"I do not!"

"You do! This cluster is mine, so is the one on the opposite side. If you ever cut your hair, you have to leave these clusters intact."

"Are you trying to possess me?" I ask, absolutely hating myself that it sounded hopeful.

He releases a shadow of a smirk. "No, just trying to treasure what I can. Easter at my place, Thanksgiving at yours, stressing out a few hours on Christmas with Mom while trying to keep her from blabbing our secret, and a week each summer in England is not enough, especially when we have to sneak off just to get a few minutes alone."

I twist the diamond of my engagement ring into my palm and toy with the stone. His honesty is getting to me. How did we let ourselves get this way?

"I don't want to leave you tomorrow," Donovan blazingly confesses. "The more I feel that time coming, the more I need to cling to you. Whenever we're alone, I'm on edge just trying to keep my hands to myself. Once I had my arms around you the threat disappeared, like I was doing exactly what I was supposed to."

"I felt the same way," I confess.

"With Mom being sick we will have to come out here occasionally. Do we take turns and suffer it out alone, or do we get frustrated and hide from ourselves? I want us, and I need to keep doing this," he declares while playing with my hair.

I miss him, too—his warmth, his drive, his scent, and

how he fuels me. Last I checked, none of those things were off limits. "Wait," I tell him.

Inside my adjoining room, I grab manicure scissors and cut a small cluster of hair from the nape of my neck. I bring it to him along with an envelope from the hotel stationary. "This is going to cost you a worn T-shirt." Donovan's expression slackens. He stares at the locks before slipping them into the envelope. "You and I let go of too much. There's nothing wrong with reclaiming a little."

Donovan lies back on the bed, tugging me down with him and wrapping a halo around me as my head buries into his shoulder. His voice is so soft it's almost seductive. "How do you always know what I need?"

My eyes close off the world. I hadn't planned on this intimacy, but he's right. Physical contact is but a moderate concern compared to the threat lying in our pounding hearts that yearn to burst out of our chests and merge into one— not for the night, but for eternity. The urges of my femininity can be conquered, but the drive of my soul is a different beast. "Then let's stop fighting and be honest. It is far better to embrace rare moments like these than to sit on our hands and let frustration rule. Whatever keeps us content and faithful is all we should be concerned about."

His inspiriting scent causes me to dissolve into his embrace. With a velvety touch he pleads into my ear, "Please, Lily. Don't ever let what's left of us go."

"I can't. I'll always love you."

"And I'll always love you," he says.

Blanketed by the security of Donovan's devotion, my consciousness drifts under the Sandman's spell.

4

"Grandpa Eric!" the kids cheer as Christopher's life-long friend appears in the doorway of the family manor near Manchester, England. Sadly, our annual summer visit is the only time we see this sweetheart of a man that Christopher refers to as one of his fathers.

When Eric crouches down to greet the kids, his tall, trim frame is knocked onto its bum by the power of their embraces. It sends his hair bouncing and brings about laughter with a dazzle in his blue eyes. This is exactly why I wanted a family, and why I chose a life with Christopher.

Once recovered, Eric gives Grace and I kisses on the cheek accompanied by lengthy embraces. He then takes Christopher by the shoulders and looks at him with a booming gleam in his eyes. "Your family is amazing. I'm so happy for you." The resulting hug is one of fatherly pride, just like the rest of Paul's old mates always give Christopher.

We enter the elegant drawing room, and Graham is already tugging on Eric's arm. "Is that a guitar?" he asks about the contents of the long, battered, vinyl case Eric carries. My curiosity appears to be along the lines of a seven-year-old, as I'm equally intrigued.

"Of sorts." Eric sets the case on the coffee table and gently lifts the lid. He resembles a timid little boy on Christmas morning. "Go ahead, but be careful," he says to Graham. "She's very old and frail."

Christopher's eyes become aglow. "I haven't seen one of those in yonks."

"Umm … if it's frail, should he really handle it?" I ask Eric while looking at Graham but considering my uncoordinated husband.

"Aw, sure. She's family, just like he is. Speaking of which, I was very disappointed when Donovan called to say he wouldn't make it this year. How is he?"

"We've spoken surprising little since I saw him three weeks ago," I say. "He's suddenly so busy that I can't keep up with him."

"That's a shame. We talk frequently, but I haven't heard from him since your mum took ill."

Antonia tugs on Eric's arm and points to the instrument he brought that Grace now holds. The fluid that blurs Grace's vision reeks of longing. With trepidation, Eric strolls to Grace and touches a hand to her shoulder. "Remind you of someone?" he asks softly, sharing her focus on the instrument.

Grace swallows heavily, and my eyes share her sorrow as she speaks through a knotted throat. "I haven't seen one of these in years. Paul's is in the attic. I fell in love with him that day I saw him playing it on the street corner, though he didn't notice me until years later when I was old enough to lie about my age and get into clubs."

My eyes scrutinize the primitive looking contraption that appears to be a wooden cigar box with a broomstick stuck onto it. "What is it?"

"It's a cigar-box guitar—the first instrument I ever had," Eric says. "My cousin gave it to me when he got a real guitar. It inspired me to save every penny I could. For Christmas one year, I asked my parents for a guitar provided I could pay half. We found a cheap, used one that sounded horrible but got me started. If it hadn't been for this thing, I never would have gotten started in music and likely would have stayed poor me whole life."

"That plays music?" my daughter asks while rolling her deep blue eyes. "Not possible."

"Oh, it's possible." Eric beams. "Let's give it a go." Eric motions Graham to sit with him in the middle of a maroon velvet sofa. Together they apply the knowledge Graham already possesses to the foreign object.

The moment is a window to the past, allowing me to envision a time when Christopher was little and Eric showed him the things on a guitar his father couldn't. My mother would love this moment. This was the type of family life she always wanted—the type we used to have. The fact that I'm with one of the idols of her youth, watching him smile as he educates her grandson, only adds to the sadness.

Things could have been so different, Mom. You weren't protecting me; you were lashing out against something greater—something I hope to never understand. If you had merely talked to us and seen the truth, if you had gotten help for whatever madness drove you ... The decisions Donovan and I made had nothing to do with you. Christopher and I still would have met, and you would be here now, thrilled beyond belief instead of sitting alone and miserable. You made your choices long ago. How I wish I could change them.

ॐ

There's a wild gleam in my eyes as I grill Grace during our annual tea date in Manchester proper. For a decade we have come to this whimsical palace that embraces the imagination of Lewis Carroll and couples it with true English class. White crown molding, resembling triangular cascades of lace, drip from a soft pink ceiling that crowns the room with both magenta and sea-blue walls. However, the room is far from garish. White d amask doilies trimmed in lace adorn rose tablecloths, muting their vividness. The chandelier hanging above brings an air of regality. It somehow blends beautifully with the pillars throughout the room painted with harlequins and the cresting sign above a display of teas that says, "Drink Me."

The room is as fresh and young as the woman who sits across from me. By birth, Grace is my mother's age, yet by vivaciousness she rivals me. Her attractiveness has little to do with her sunny blonde hair in its updo, her well-kept figure, the ability to wear clothes of a woman half her age, or the brightness of her tasteful makeup accenting her big blue eyes and cherry lips. I can only attribute it to the fact that Grace is … Well, Grace is Grace. She doesn't futz with self-imposed restrictions; she just lives.

"So, tell me more about the guy you've been seeing," I ask. "Justin, right? Are we going to meet him?" Christopher and I have yet to meet anyone Grace has dated. I'm dying of curiosity. Knowing her, she can probably still attract some wild boy toys.

With pursed lips, she raises her brow and tilts her head, knowing I'm on to her. Justin may even be younger than me. "Oh, I doubt it," she says with a brush of her hand. "It's nothing serious, and even though Christopher is a very open-minded person, Justin is not exactly the type he wants to see me with. Actually, he's not the type I want anyone to see me with. He's a passing fancy. I'd like to find someone to make me happy, but I can't seem to find the right man, let alone fall in love with him."

Yep! The cougar has nabbed new prey. Good for her. Yet it's also sad. I try to hide my own kaleidoscope of emotions toward the subject. "It must be difficult after you had such an amazing relationship with Paul. I remember your words about how he was both the love of your life and your soulmate."

Grace sets down her cup. Its rim holds her focus. "He was. Paul and I were freakishly in tune, almost as much as you and Donovan. I could never top my relationship with Paul, but that doesn't mean I can't be happy with another. I don't need an enrapturing romance with happily ever after, I just need happy. It seems more and more that I need to wait until I see Paul again for that."

What odd words. Does Grace see through Donovan and I? Her intuition and knack for being relevant never fail to amaze me. "Are you talking about in heaven or in a life beyond this one?"

Grace's blush-enhanced cheeks cave as she processes the question. Her words drive a cool sadness through me. "I've known since the day he passed that it wasn't the end. While

Christopher called the paramedics, I begged Paul not to go. I stopped pleading long enough to take a deep breath, and a moment of comfort came over me. I looked to Heaven, and I felt our eyes lock one final time. I knew then that our story wasn't over."

My insides quiver. "Do you think you may have known him before?"

"Like in another life? I've wondered that." A bit of color drains from her face. "Decades ago we went to India, and a Hindu sage said we would have many problems because our past carried into our present. We needed to discover what they were and fix them now so we could be at peace in the future. I thought it odd as we really didn't have problems then. Later, when trouble started, I wondered if the sage was on to something. I should have insisted we look into it, but Paul and I were good at ignoring things, much like the pact you and Christopher hold of not speaking of your two years apart. We never should have ignored it. It concerns me for what may lie ahead."

With a shrug that escalates into a shiver, she takes a sip from her cup, then quickly places it back down. Her vivacious hue returns as soon as she changes the subject. "So, as a woman, I think it only fair that I warn you of something. You mentioned before that you were considering another child. Are you still headed in that direction?"

The question takes me aback, and I shift my vision from her eyes to the miniature sandwiches before us. It's not that I mind talking about personal things with Grace, it's that she never pries. While by most mother-in-law standards this is mild, for her it is intrusive.

"Actually, yes," I admit. "We've been trying, but my body isn't cooperating. Frankly, I think part of it is psychological. The thought of being pregnant again makes me squirm. Wait, why are you asking?"

Grace grabs a petit four. "Christopher's cousin, Glenda, is pregnant and is dead set on an abortion. Apparently he went over there this morning to talk what he considers to be sense into her. You might want to prepare yourself for a big question."

Grace forgoes placing the confection on her plate and using a fork. Instead, she bites in.

"You think he wants to help?" I ask.

"Oh, definitely. I'm sure you know that while my son may be very liberal, abortions are not something he ever considers to be an option." Grace takes pause, then gives a sudden jerk, like she's shaking off a bad memory. "So, where we shall shop tomorrow?"

Oh no. With how confused my head is, the last thing I should do is bring another child into the picture.

5

Exquisiteness and effervescent beauty have filled my day—and it's only two in the afternoon. Since our return from England three weeks ago I have barely seen Christopher due to obligations surrounding his band, Fragile Cherry, and studio work. For weeks I've gone to bed alone, then woken to him being nearly comatose until long after I've left for the day. However, this morning he woke me with kisses that flowed like maple syrup and butter down a tall stack of hot pancakes—and he brought me coffee. He then snuggled me in his arms and presented the lovely idea that we rendezvous for a very early, extended lunch.

I should have known it was entrapment. The moment I walked into the house I felt wisps of discomfort swirling in the air. Once Christopher got me in the bedroom and loaded me up on champagne, the moment Grace warned me about finally arrived.

"You know how we're sponsoring those children in Togo?" he asked while lying next to me and resting the weight of his head in his hand. He was so nervous that his eyes locked onto my ear. "It's got me thinking we could do better."

My eyes darted around the room in search of a buttering up present.

"Since you had it rough with Antonia, and since you are so busy now ..."

If he commented about me not wanting more stretch marks, or how badly my legs swelled to the point where I could hardly walk last time, I was going to let him have it.

"It just seems that maybe we should consider ..."

"Seriously, Christopher, you suck at this," I erupted with

a chortle. Finally his eyes jotted to mine. His face froze. "This is the worst buttering up session in the history of mankind. I thought I'd at least get a necklace out of it. What did you sign us up for with your cousin? How deeply you got me involved will be reflected in the price of the jewelry I buy myself on your behalf."

He scampered back to sit on his calves. "Well, blow me!"

"No way, buddy. You're supposed to be buttering *me* up."

"How on earth did you know?"

"I'm a woman, therefore I know everything you sneaky men do. Now, how screwed am I?"

Christopher closed his gaping mouth and turned serious. "I've offered to pay all expenses, make monthly financial contributions, and put the child through school in exchange for Glenda not getting an abortion. It's all coming out of Dad's money so it doesn't involve you at all."

"Are you saying we can no longer afford my jewelry?" I asked, teasing.

"Darling, I know it's a lot of money. Are you all right with this?"

"Christopher, of course I'm all right with this." Actually, I was damned relieved! I really though he was going to suggest we adopt the child. "You'd have a hard time living with yourself if we didn't help her."

He enrobed me tighter than in years. "An innocent child should never suffer because of someone's selfishness."

His voice had taken on an eerie tone, reminding me of the distance I feel every time the subject of our two years apart comes up—the two years of which we vowed to never speak. Quickly he snapped back into the moment, focusing on me and pouring more champagne. Despite the guise it was presented under, and although all I ingested was exquisite chocolate and Dom Perignon, the lunch was nicely fulfilling.

Relatively.

Okay, a little unadventurous but satisfying—like vanilla

ice cream.

Lord, how I'd kill for some chocolate mousse.

Now I'm headed back to my shop, Pâtisserie de l'Amour, in Westwood, confident that nothing has crumbled in the hands of the cast of characters referred to as my staff. I am blessed with the most talented, loyal, and kooky artists on the planet. Their eccentric creativity has resulted in crazy desserts that none of our competitors would dare try, like Tequila Lime Tarts with an Orange Cilantro Glaze. Pâtisserie de l'Amour has a killer reputation for the eclectic, and I owe it largely to my comedy troupe.

My cell phone vibrates before I enter the back door. I look at the caller ID and already regret taking a call from the person I should have responded to weeks ago. "Hi, Mom," I groan into the phone. Oh, a brain hemorrhage would be so welcome right now.

"Hi, Lily. How was England?"

"Wet."

"Did you see Eric?"

Lord! That's a new speed record. "Yes, Mom. We always see Eric."

"I don't know how you hold it together," she practically pants. "If I were even in the same county as that man, I would go to pieces."

Which is one of the many reasons why I will never let her near him.

"Doesn't Peter Noone live near you?" she asks. "Has he come into your shop?"

Dear God! "I'm not sure where he lives, Mom. If he comes in, I promise to tell you." Someday I'm going to get over my hang-up about lying. I'll tell her he strolled in, took one look at me, and pinned me to the back wall before kissing me passionately and saying he would bet I have a gorgeous mother. "Hey, Mom, I'm sorry, but I really need to go. I had a lunch meeting and have been out of the store for the last three hours."

"Okay, bye dear. Oh, wait. I got that article you sent me

about how well your shop is doing. I'm really proud of you honey. I never told you this, but the night you talked to your father and me about going to pastry school and wanting to open your own shop he said he knew you would be successful. He would be very, very proud."

I give myself a moment to mourn the loss of my father and his good side that so rarely showed. Suddenly I feel a little stronger for having known him. "Thanks, Mom. I'll talk to you soon."

"Okay, dear. Give Christopher a big kiss for me."

"Will do. I'll kiss the kids for you as well."

"Oh, yes. Of course. Them too."

"Bye, Mom," I say, chuckling. She may have lost her marbles when she overreacted about Donovan, but she's still the same daydreaming, wannabe teenager.

I slip through the back door on the approach to my locker and start to take off my rings. My favorite baker, Cindy, with her fiery, pixie-cropped hair dyed a deep red, accosts me. "I know it's none of my business, but since we all love Christopher, I insist you keep your wedding ring on."

My head cocks as I look into her deep green eyes. Just as I'm about to ask why, Jenny, my petite, over-enthusiastic counter girl, runs in looking star struck. "Did you tell her? He's still out there!"

"Tell me what? Who's out where?"

Jenny gushes like a thirteen-year-old whose favorite teen idol has just bowed in her presence. Even when her king idol, Johnny Depp, drops in she doesn't get into this kind of an uproar. Jenny's brunette ponytail whips with her bounces. "Seriously, he has got to be the most handsome man I've ever seen."

"Who?" I ask, wishing she would just get on with it.

Robert, an amazing decorator and the most flamboyant of my staff, races up. His wavy carrot top, lime eyes, and pale skin make him and Cindy look like disgruntled siblings. "Did you tell her about the stud who keeps munching on the pastry? Boy do I have something he can munch—"

Cindy shoves Robert aside and gives me the scoop. "Some blistering guy has been waiting in the store for over an hour. I've no idea who he is except he's incredibly hot, has amazing blue eyes, and brought you a gorgeous bouquet of white roses."

My eyes won't stop widening in hope. With morbid curiosity, the fan club follows me as I whip through the kitchen. Peering out the swinging door to the shop, my heart skips a beat at Donovan's sight. Will it ever stop doing that? I turn to the adults who have regressed to groupie girls and hope my look is of sisterly disdain. "I thought you said it was some hot guy? That's just my jock brother."

My eyes roll, Donovan style. I push the door open with my heel and spin into the shop, only to hear Robert yell behind me, "A jock? Does he play football? Tell him I'm great at conversions."

Inside the bustling, aromatic shop the mid-day sun shines warmly through the two, white trimmed windows that enliven the outside wall that resides across from the kitchen door. A beige ceiling hovers above medium forest-green interior crowned with white molding. On each side of the door to the kitchen are antique, walnut and glass cases that sit before matching shelving units, topped with swirling Art Nouveau framework that form flourishing loops extending over the door. The remaining walls sport hefty, gold trimmed mirrors and shelves of pre-bagged cookies.

Among the walnut tables and antique chairs that fill the shop, Donovan rises to greet me. A lump of disappointment hits my stomach as he hugs me in the necessary, brotherly fashion. I beam at him, sounding giddy. "What are you doing here?"

He hands me a bouquet of white roses as we sit at the table. "I have a surprise for you."

"I see that." My heart barely stays in my chest. I'm so excited to see him that I grab his coffee cup and take a sip just so my lips can touch where his once were. "I never pegged you for a mint mocha person."

"Mint is sort of our flavor," he says in reference to years before when I finally had a break through with both training his palate and getting him to face his emotions. "I drink mint mochas all the time. It makes me feel closer to you."

Taking the cup, he places his lips in the same place that once touched mine and sips. He follows the action with a wink acknowledging the lack of coincidence. "My surprise has nothing to do with the visit or the flowers. It's much better than that." The grin he flashes is wicked and his eyes gleam in mischief—toying with me as only he can.

I pull back and scrutinize him through a squint. "You're here to stay? Really? Don't mess with me, because this isn't funny."

His snicker grabs my heart. "I'm teaming with a psychiatrist friend here in Los Angeles—sort of. I just secured an office. Can you sneak off and help me house hunt this afternoon? I fly out late tonight, and we need to be fully settled in less than two months."

"Are you serious?"

"As a mental breakdown! Happy?"

"Are you kidding? This is the greatest news ever!" And it's the most awkward. The only time he and Christopher are in the same place is when we gather at holidays, which makes it easy for me to deal with my dueling emotions. Now my need to separate Lily Beckett from Lilyanna Eccles is greater than ever, else I won't be able to stand myself.

After hugging Donovan with a force that nearly knocks him off of his chair, my feet practically gallop to the back of the store with glee. Donovan's fan club attacks me before I can retrieve my purse from my locker.

"Please, please tell me your brother isn't married!" Jenny mercilessly begs.

"Please, please tell me your brother isn't straight!" Robert adds.

"That's it!" Cindy flails her hands as she walks off. "I'm done with both of you."

"Oh, he's married all right! To a tall, gorgeous, exotic brunette. Seriously, Anna is one of those women you kind of want to smack."

Boy is that ever true. The woman has the perfect figure, and it pisses me off! Her lean muscles make for sensuous curves. Add in her high cheekbones, deep brown eyes, and glamorous, chestnut mane and she's nothing short of luscious. The thought of her with Donovan always makes me feel I have poison ivy wrapped over athlete's foot.

Donovan and I enter my car. I'm almost afraid to ask where we are headed. Donovan's successful, but doing well by many standards is starving in Los Angeles. He could be lucky to live in Fred Sanford's old junkyard in Watts.

"I assume you'd like to live near your new office. Where is it?" I ask.

"Brentwood."

My eyes just about detonate out of my head. "Are you nuts? Do you have any idea how expensive it is there?"

"I never said I was moving there," he says with a chuckle. "I'm just joining a group of colleagues. I swear Lil, since Anna and I made this decision, the universe has handed me a silver platter with a seven-course meal served by hot girls in bunny suits. Hopefully I can get my license to practice in California quickly. I've already had my EPPP transferred and took my CPSE a few weeks ago. This was after I finished cramming in the ten contact hours California wants in aging and long-term care training."

My brain spirals just listening to him. "Wait. You took a test a few weeks ago? Here?"

"Yeah, while you were in England. Seriously, Lil, I deal with some pretty jacked up people and there seems to be a ton of those here. Most of them are more normal than they realize, but some are into things that give me the willies. The term 'sexual deviant' covers a lot of ground. When I decided to become a specialist in what I was accused of, I had no idea how great the demand could be for me."

How this man has taken all the bad things that happened

and turned them positive has truly brought about my idolatry. "Have I told you how proud I am of you?"

"Every time we talk. Don't stop. It helps me sleep at night. We both know I need all the help I can get there."

Low and behold, we close out the day with him putting an offer down on what is defined in California as an affordable, two-bedroom fixer-upper in Venice with a large enough yard so Anna can have the garden he promised. His mini-Camelot is in need of a bunch of minor repairs and some electrical work, but it's only fifteen to twenty minutes away from his new office, which is about ten to twenty minutes away from my shop in Westwood. It's not much further to my home. Even with LA traffic, at any given moment we'll be less than an hour apart.

6

The sounds emanating from Christopher's basement studio pound through my head like a tribal war chant gone awry and pressed onto a scratchy old record. It's possible that my tastes are no longer progressing, but I find this new sound to be atrocious. When the band trudges up from the basement, all looking heavily knackered, I'm certain they just suck.

Frustration is the likely culprit. They recently lost their affordable rehearsal space, which has left them cramped in the basement. They strive for self-sufficiency, but independence is difficult for any group when starting out. Dennis makes far more money as a barista than as a musician. Only Fred and Christopher, who often work together during their day jobs at Anthem Records, do well enough in that arena to support a family.

"How's your head?" Christopher asks as he enters the kitchen where I'm finishing the dishes. "Mine's pounding."

I force a smile and give him a quick kiss on the cheek. He heads to the refrigerator. "That sucked," I whisper. "It's nice to have you home for once, but Lord, have you all hit the sauce?"

"I should be so lucky. I'll probably be on the piss five minutes after I toss these blokes tonight. The new guy, Mike—he's not working out so well. Tonight is the new low of lows."

No shock here. There's something about Mike that invokes feelings of spiders doing the salsa up my back. He seems physically clean, yet he has the persona of someone who never bathes or washes his clothes. Maybe it's because he's always in ratty jeans and a T-shirt with the sleeves cut off, and his mousey-brown hair frizzes out of a ponytail. He appears frail, like he does too much coke. The guy is so damn creepy my muteness regarding the discomfort he brings may soon cease.

"Hey, mates," Christopher calls to the group as they file into the kitchen. "You want something to drink with that pie?"

"Is this for us?" With his bright green eyes, Dennis looks like a teenager as he sits at the table and smiles through soft pink lips. His well-groomed, medium length honey-brown hair reminds me of a nineteen sixies surfer. Sadly he eats many of his meals off of the fast-food dollar menu. How he scrapes for pennies yet always looks hopeful is admirable.

"Can I trouble you for some coffee, Lily?" Fred asks as he takes a seat. His long hair, beard, jeans, T-shirt, and big smile make him look like he stepped out of a Doobie Brothers' concert.

"No trouble at all," I respond. "Dennis, Mike, would you like something to drink?"

"Do you have any juice?" asks Dennis. "Any kind is fine."

"Do you have anything to get juiced with?" Mike follows.

I'd like to brain him over the head with a juicer. "Two juices and a coffee coming up," I assert.

"Pass," Mike says. "I've got another energy drink downstairs."

"Dude, you've already had two," Dennis minds him. "Your heart is going to explode."

"Nah, I need the energy, and I'm too poor for coke."

Great. Well, that's some kind of comfort. The others seem all too used to Mike's alleged humor and ignore him.

The pie is almost demolished before I can even get the drinks on the table. Dennis brings the plates into the kitchen, and I receive a round of thanks as the guys head downstairs. Mike lingers behind and follows me to the dishwasher. "Thanks for the tart," he whispers in my ear before strolling off. His hot, slimy breath on my neck brings revolting visions of him rubbing warm palms covered in filthy motor oil up my back and over my breast.

Christopher won't tolerate Mike for long. If he does, I may risk a little tension from putting my nose in his business. Something is not wired right with him.

7

Two months after his hypersonic visit, Speedy Gonzalez, his wife, and their four-year-old daughter, Sunshine, have closed escrow and have started a ritual of joining us for Sunday dinners.

At dusk, Donovan and I sit on the flagstone patio overlooking my yard. The grass has lusciousness akin to a golf course, yet the roses that border it need shaping. Antonia passes a football rather haphazardly to her brother, wobbling it into the flower patch containing a bench that is rather unsafe to sit in right now. A cobblestone path leads to the fairytale-styled guest cottage that is so rarely used I often forget it exists.

Donovan and I sip Scotch while watching Sunshine attempt to catch a ball. "Ugh. My pants are too tight," he groans about his overeating. "Thank God I didn't have to wait until Thanksgiving for an amazing meal that didn't come from an overpriced restaurant. Even just having food with flavor is a welcome change."

My warning is hushed. "Don't let Anna hear you say she's not perfect. No woman wants to hear that." Anna may have me beat in the looks department, but when it comes to anything emerging from the kitchen I'm Marilyn Monroe to her Phyllis Diller. Her food is so insipid that even Christopher, the man who only enjoys food blessed by the Queen's Royal Scepter of Blandness, wants to grab a snack before we visit. "So how weird is it that she and Christopher share a passion for soccer?" I muse.

"No kidding! And both going crazy over Manchester."

"Manchester United," I correct.

"Right, never Manchester City, and never, ever

46

Liverpool." Donovan shoots me a conspiratorial wink. He raises his glass with me mirroring his actions before drinking.

I can't believe I offered to do this but, "I'm taking Anna shopping for some stuff for the house this week. Are you sure you don't want us to help with decorating the office too?"

His head smacks back into the chair, and he looks to heaven. Since when did he acquire my flare for mellow drama? "God, I've no idea where to start. The lifestyle here is so different than what I'm used to. I don't know if I should line my shelves in books or Faberge Eggs."

"Oh, no way!" I say. "Books, yes, but you'd better let me pick out some shelf filler from a local artists."

His guttural groan is almost comical. "I have too much to do. I've already started my charitable work at the health center." His gaze on the children resumes. "Wow, is it terrible that I think Graham can throw a pass far better than I ever expected Christopher's son could?"

I give myself a little pat on the back—literally. "That's because his mother showed him."

Donovan raises an eyebrow to me, to which he adds a heart-melting smile.

"What can I say? I learned from the best. What charitable work?"

"When Dr. Coe wrote my letters of recommendation I promised to assist those who can't afford counseling. It's actually more grounding than when I see my own counselor."

Donovan releases a hearty drag of air, releasing tension brought on by the sight before him. Graham is the spitting image of his father; soft brown hair, sky blue eyes, a slight upslope to his nose, trim frame, and a chivalrous personality. Antonia looks exactly like Donovan—same sapphire eyes, raven hair, chiseled features. She's nearly a perfect clone, just like Donovan is of our dad's father. It's cosmically weird.

"She's really missed her Uncle Scooby," I say of

Antonia's love for Donovan.

Donovan's focus on her is unwavering. "I love how she calls me that. We're so much alike. If I didn't know better…"

My mind starts confessing; *Often she makes me dream of what could have been.*

Only radio static is perceived in response. It is like Donovan is no longer in-tune with my thoughts.

Donovan, can you hear me?

He turns to me, just like any person would. "Mind if I grab a little more Scotch?"

"Help yourself." *Bring the bottle, along with some ice.*

A moment later, he returns with the bottle and his glass filled with ice. After adding a few cubes to my glass, he pours some Scotch, shoots me a smile, and returns to his seat before his eyes again avoid me. "I heard you, Lily. I'll even say it out loud. I screwed up, and it sucks that I can't change it."

My hand shoots to his arm. Suddenly everything about my life feels completely wrong, and my ability to be Lilyanna Eccles swirls with the bitter truth: I'm perfectly happy with Christopher, but ignoring the pull of my soulmate is impossible.

"Don't say anything. Just let it go," Donovan tells the bottom of his glass before jettisoning the liquid from it.

My jaw drops in an attempt to form a hesitant reply, only to be slammed shut by the opening of the sliding glass door from the kitchen. "Is this the same bloody dessert you made last week?" Christopher yells.

A small chuckle escapes Donovan, and he heads inside. "This should be a riot."

Entering the house plops me back into my universe. Christopher hands me a plate of dessert, and I follow him into the family room—feeling compressed despite the large, open surroundings. Anna curls up to Donovan on one sofa as they share a piece of mousse cake, while Christopher and I snuggle on the sofa kitty-corner from them. Anna takes a tiny taste then abandons her fork on the plate. I'm jealous of her willpower and the body that comes with it.

"This is great, Lil. How'd you nail it?" Donovan praises over the dessert. The question snaps my focus onto the plate before me. I'm developing a Lavender-Lemon Mousse Cake and almost have the formula refined, but the proper amount of lavender paired with the strength of the lemon insert is a subjective balance. This is lost on my husband, whose taste buds lack finesse, yet Donovan totally gets it.

Somehow my words sound foreign. "What you said about it having a tinge of bitterness played in my brain. The amount of lavender wasn't the problem, it was the infusion time. I reduced it by five minutes and bam, Bob's your uncle."

Christopher gives me a peck on the cheek. "That's the first thing you've uttered when tasting something that I've understood—not the business about reducing and all, whatever that means."

Training Christopher's palate is like teaching a slug to use a hula-hoop. "Can you at least tell the difference between last time and now?" I buoyantly ask.

Christopher's head turns downcast. He raises his eyes with a sheepish grin. "Say yes," Anna whispers.

"Can you?" Donovan asks with a raised brow.

"Yeah," she replies in her naturally timid voice. "I only know the lavender was stronger last week and that I like this one better, but there's a definite difference."

All eyes jot wordlessly to Christopher.

"Oh, bugger! Maybe if I had them both now I'd know the difference."

"Bloody well doubtful," Donovan says with an eye-crinkling grin. Truthfully, I concur.

"Blimey! How long did it take you to learn this stuff?"

"A few years," Donovan replies. "She's been your problem for—I mean, you've been married to her for almost ten years now. You're kind of out of excuses, pal."

Christopher releases his angst in a display of vibrant hand

gestures, pleading to God for mercy as we chuckle. "Again you think my misery is a riot," he says, slightly miffed.

"No, it's just sad that you can't tell the difference between two-percent and whole milk," I cheekily inform him.

"I—" Christopher halts, knowing self-defense is futile. "Can you?" he pleads to Anna in hopes of salvation. She nods with her lips suppressing a laugh.

"That's it!" I pop up from the sofa and yank Christopher's hand.

"Oh, this should be entertaining." Donovan says. He and Anna follow us into the kitchen.

Christopher reluctantly sits at the table and moans to Donovan, "How do you get off looking so smug? You're supposed to be me male support."

"I've served my time under Lily's wardenship. You're on your own."

"I'll take the plunge with you." Anna drags a chair around the table and sits kitty-corner to Christopher, then peers up to Donovan with an eager smile. Donovan would be thrilled if this encourages her to cook better than a hash slinger without the benefit of the grease.

I place two samplers in front of Christopher and Anna, including two-percent, whole milk, cream, and impromptu half and half. I point to their whole milk. "Start with this, then grab any other glass and tell me the difference." Anna takes tiny sips, then reorders the glasses according to fat content. Christopher appears lost, peering at Anna's glasses and seeking a pattern. "Stop cheating!" I accuse before turning to Anna. "Well?"

She slips her hands into her lap. "I wouldn't know exactly what they were off the bat, but I ordered them according to richness. Did I get it right?" she asks as if she will win my approval for existing if correct.

"Perfectly." I try not to address Christopher like he's a small child. "Can you label them according to fat content like Anna did?"

He looks so lost I want to curl him in my arms and tell him how much I love him despite his obvious fault. "Oh, you're just trying to wind me up," he rants. "You should be bloody ashamed, putting me under the cosh like this!"

"Really, Christopher? Your seven-year-old son could do better," Donovan playfully scorns. "Graham! Would you come here please?" The doorbell rings.

"Oh, come off it," Christopher complains. "The guys are arriving now."

Of course they are. Yet *another* rehearsal. Heaven forbid that I get a night with my husband. "Not our problem!"

Donovan reorders Christopher's glasses accurately by sight, then smugly clears his throat. Christopher's head meets his hands in defeat.

Anna practically drags Donovan toward the door as I open it to Fred and Dennis asking, "Hey guys. Want to try some Lavender-Lemon Mousse Cake?"

"Careful, it's a trap!" Christopher yells.

Mike brings up the rear just as Donovan and Anna slip out with Sunshine. Anna flinches when Mike brushes past, barely skimming her arm. Donovan stops and shoots him a look implying he knows Mike's ways all too well.

"Hey," Mike nods to Donovan.

"Hey, yourself," Donovan condescends while throwing an arm around Anna. His eyes turn to me, penetrating my thoughts. *Lily, stay away from this guy.*

Clearly it's not only me who feels Mike's slither.

8

Ambition is a word known by those who have not had too many early mornings and too many late nights dozing off before their husband is home from his new rehearsal space that practically resides in the next county. Unaffected by the double espresso guzzled on the drive over, I enter the back door to the bakery with a groan, tired and wishing I had slept in and seen my husband when he wakes in oh, four more hours.

I lunge my purse into the cubbyhole of a locker, and it hits the back with a bleak *thud*. My fingers shut the door with such aloofness it gently reverberates and drifts back before I begrudgingly slam it shut. With a muffled whine, I shuffle toward the kitchen. A small fire emitting from the decorating bench causes me to shriek. The lit, tapered candle reminds me of a tiny funeral pyre. Slowly it rises to Donovan's face as he sings "Happy Birthday" so off-key it makes me shudder.

Flipping on the overhead lights, the room turns a glow at the sight of Donovan sitting on the baker's table in his suit—tie off, top buttons undone—and surrounded by graduated pans that he has set upside down to form half a dozen metallic tier cakes. Each one has vibrant red, orange, and yellow Gerbera daisies tossed onto it, making the display all the more garish. Next to him resides a bouquet of white roses.

I advance toward his mirthful grin in amazement. "You scared me so much you damn near killed me." Suddenly the hamster that runs the wheel in my brain wakes up. "Wait, my birthday was two months ago. Do I need to call Dr. Coe and tell him you're having some kind of episode and that I'm shipping you back?"

He propels himself off of the metal table, takes my hands in his, and draws my gray-violet eyes into his oceanic sapphires. "Happy *Seventeenth* Birthday."

My eyes roam over the display. One of the faux cakes has the number seventeen poorly scribbled on the side in pink icing. A flutter overtakes my heart as the meaning of the spectacle sinks in. Donovan always kick-started my birthday in the most obnoxious ways, that is, until he was forced to stay away from me. His only contact for my seventeenth birthday was a card containing a sterile sentiment and a pastry book wrapped in the same paper my parents used to wrap their gift. It was so unlike Donovan that I should have known he was forced into being someone else. Instead, I foolishly assumed he had forgotten about me. Later I learned that my mother wanted to examine the contents to ensure he hadn't enclosed a message.

"Why now? Why my seventeenth birthday?"

"Because it was the first birthday of yours that I ever missed. We've been robbed, and I want back what we lost."

Dear God, so do I. "It's been a long time since you did something like this. I've missed it. I've missed you." My arms slide around him with my face glowing in happiness.

"Since Robert was the one who slipped me the extra key, I was afraid he'd come in early, and I'd be the one with the surprise," he muses, rocking me in his arms. My favorite scent—the blend of his cologne with his pheromones—coupled with the music of his heart, cause my soul to latch onto his essence and try to retain a drop so that I may forever cherish it. God how I wish I didn't feel this way for a man who is more off limits now than ever.

"Yeah, right," I snicker. "You'll cave to that the day he goes *into* the closet." I pull back and feel flush at the glorious display, now noticing more of his attempt at decoration. Bright icing ribbons scroll and splatter throughout the pans. He even tried piping a heart on one of the cakes, but it looks more anatomically correct than iconic. "Speaking of which, wow, you really don't have a gay molecule in your body. This is incredible."

"Sorry, it's a bit of a disaster."

I try to disguise the depths of emotions that reside in my words. "Honestly, I've missed you so much that I don't mind the tsunami of icing." While keeping one arm securely around him, I run a finger through a sugary ribbon then stick it in Donovan's mouth. I relish in his eager glow, only to be struck by a wave of remorse for the action that occurred without premeditation.

"I'm starving," he claims. "Let me take you to breakfast. I almost grabbed a fork and started attacking everything in the fridge. I'd kill for some chocolate mousse right now."

Dear God, he's not the only one. Sadly, what I define as exquisite chocolate mousse is wearing a suit and is completely off limits. He needs to fasten those alluring top buttons.

Forcing my eyes off of the drool-worthy man they return to the display of aluminum confections. "I shouldn't. I didn't schedule time away, and to leave people with this and have to compensate for my not being here is unfair."

"Come on," he pleads. "It's your do-over birthday." His hand rises to my cheek, his thumb gracing just under my lashes, as if wiping away the tears shed the day I turned seventeen and felt abandoned.

I nod to him and force an excuse to pull away. "I need a picture of this before we go."

"Here," he says, pulling a phone out of his back pocket. I press the on button, and the screen illuminates with an extreme close-up photo of his daughter sporting a silly, and slightly spitty, smile.

"You old softie," I say with a chuckle. He poses in front of the counter. "Oh, no. You need to sit up there among the carnage."

"You're not going to yell at me? Your rant from six Thanksgivings ago still rings in my head. 'Get off of my counter! I don't know where your filthy butt has been, and I don't want to know!' "

My eyes narrow despite my amusement. "Shut up and get up there. You being able to quote my past is both endearing and annoying as crap." He bounces up and I snap a quick shot before his smile becomes too posed. I then step back to get the full glory in frame, but the array of destruction is too wide. "Hey, slide that one on the end toward you a bit."

"Why?" he asks.

"It's not in frame."

"You don't need it to be. Take the picture, and let's get out of here."

"Fine! I'll do it myself!"

Donovan jumps up to protest, putting his hand out and waiving me to retreat. "It's fine, Lil. Just take the picture."

Crap. There's a reason for his laziness. I go for the pans and find my attempt to shove the tower is futile. "You *glued* my pans to the counter? You rat bastard!"

His eyes crest, "I'm diabolical, not cruel. I used industrial-grade high tack."

"Dear God, how much did you use?" I ask, trying unsuccessfully to get the stack to budge before moving on to the next one and encountering the same problem. I push harder, then shake the table. Nothing happens—not even a flutter.

"Umm ..." Donovan runs for the back door, just like he did when he was twelve and stole my diary. "Meet you at the car."

I grab a bag of icing and run after him with the intent of pin-striping his suit. My lips call him a jerk, yet my heart is thrilled over having my Donovan back.

9

Anna is an enigma. Our forest of distance has roots that extend beyond the awkwardness felt regarding her relationship with the man who is a complex part of my life. Today I hope to yank up a couple of trees.

We detour by an eclectic coffee shop while searching for Donovan's office decor. Before we order, I pull a twenty-dollar bill out of my wallet and place it on the counter. "On me," I insist.

"Oh, it's fine. I've got it," she rebuts.

"Nope. Let me take care of my sister. Order away," I say with a flourish of my hand.

Her lips part upon hearing the word, sister. She then gives a little nod before turning to the barista. "One large cup of hot water."

I fight the urge to rattle my head in confusion. The barista hands her a steaming cup like the request is common before he nods to me. "A regular Borgia, please," I order. As the barista makes my drink, I watch Anna take her cup to a table. Her head taps like she is humming to a silent beat while she extracts a hand-filled tea sack from her purse and plops it into the cup. I understand wanting to stay skinny and the health food kick, but bringing her own tea bag seems a little nuts.

While grabbing my coffee, my eyes catch sight of a yellow piece of paper on the floor. I swipe up the enrollment form for Anna Beckett in Intermediate Taekwondo lessons, listing her rank as blue belt. "Hey, Anna, you dropped this," I say, handing her the slip. Her face firms when she sees the paper, then pulses a smile while cramming it into her purse. "I enrolled Sunshine in a Karate class. Donovan's going to kill me if he finds out," she says like it's a secret, shifting her eyes and hushing her tone. "He thinks his daughter should be dainty."

I fake a smile. "Don't worry, I saw nothing of the like."

We head across Melrose on our way to a shop filled with objects by local artists. As Anna steps into the sunlight, her modest and billowy white dress sways in the breeze, pressing against the curves that hide beneath. I have always been jealous of her luscious figure, but today I turn catty, thinking she is too skinny and wondering what the hell Donovan sees in this woman who has a body type for which he has always expressed distaste. I don't like that my jealousy is on the rise, and I force it out of my mind as we enter the shop.

"Hey, check this out," I say, holding a vase that was upcycled from a discarded Scooby-Doo lunch box thermos. "Donovan would love it."

"Hmm …" Anna raises a finger to her lips, seemingly taking a moment to think of a polite way to tell me the idea sucks. "If your therapist had a vase like that, would you feel comfortable because he has a sense of humor or ill at ease because he may be wackier than you?"

"Point well made." I'm totally coming back later and buying that for him. "Any word on your California credentials coming through?" My eyes wander the shop. "Wow! Check out this glass box with a bat skeleton. I'm going to bury it in the bottom of his drawer just to mess with him."

"Yeah, now that I've secured a job it's just a waiting game." Anna's deepened voice, hard-tapping foot, and staring at the rows of shelves before her like they are one giant blur tells me she's bored out of her skull. "The break gives me time to get the house settled and find daycare for Sunshine."

"Oh, I mentioned to Donovan that, since you'll be working near my house, you should consider adding Sunshine on to my part time nanny. Then, if you get stuck at work, Christopher and I can lend a hand."

Anna turns to the table of wares between us. She caresses the edge of a rose quartz geode with diminutive strokes. Suddenly she seems gentle and timid, like the Anna I'm used to. "Did Donovan like the idea?"

"Yeah, he thought it was great."

"Okay." She subtly nods. "Donovan always knows what's best."

Finally I brave the question I've wanted to ask for years. "Sunshine is a very pretty name. How did you decide on it?" God, I hope that didn't sound flippant, but really, Sunshine? It's like they were destined to live in Los Angeles.

Anna's eyes drift over a display case. Her boredom has returned. "She made me aware that no matter how bad things are a new day always dawns. You know, that Scooby Doo vase would be perfect," she claims like she just saw it for the first time. "Let's get that and head home."

The enigma continues.

10

"Duck!" Robert yells as he passes with a tray of yellow Princess Cakes. He nearly brains me.

"Damn it, Robert!" Cindy chews him out as she marches behind him to open the door of the walk-in.

"Well, she was in the way," he snaps.

"You could have dodged her or asked her to move by politely saying, 'Excuse me.' I swear, one of these days your laziness is going to lead to someone's demise!"

Lord! How is it that I can have a kitchen staff of eight, yet The Bickersons make all the other players fade into the background?

My mind again drifts in anticipation of the lunch that lies ahead. I've been dying to go to Osteria Rossi for months. Apparently they have the best Venetian food in all of Los Angeles County, and I finally have someone I don't work with who is willing to dive in.

"Excuse me, *please*," Robert huffs as he again blazes past while glaring behind at Cindy. He's so busy being Mr. Bickerson that he bumps the now empty tray into a speed rack whose wheels have been locked. The tray flips up and smacks him in the forehead, making me almost wish the cakes were still on it.

I try to focus on going about my day as a buzz emits from the breast pocket of my chef's uniform. Pulling out the phone, Donovan's face pops up on my caller ID. "Hi," I answer brightly. "Give me a second to get to someplace less ridiculous." Dashing off past the far end of the kitchen, deep into the storage area where my desk resides, my butt plops into a chair with such enthusiasm its wheels send me sliding.

"Hi," I repeat into the phone.

"You're in a good mood. I must have caught you at a great time," Donovan says.

My feet loft onto my desk. "Anytime you catch me is a great time."

"You have no idea how happy that makes me." I sense his smiling, and then his grin crashing. "Listen, Lil. I'm sorry to be the bearer of bad news, but I need to postpone our lunch date. A new client is having some major issues. I now have someone coming in from twelve-thirty to two, which annihilates almost our entire slot. Can I make it up to you?"

My gut sags at the news. It may just be the cancelation of lunch, but I feel as if I'm a rotten fish being gutted. "Of course you can," I force with a brave voice. "Tomorrow is wide open."

"Unfortunately, it's not for me," Donovan laments. "Neither is the day after, but Friday works."

It feels like forever since I saw him at dinner on Sunday night, but the least I can do is not add to his guilt. "Friday is fine. In fact, it's actually a little better. Same plan?"

"Yeah. Thanks, Lily. I'll see you then."

"Bye, Donovan." My face droops as I say it.

"Bye," he says, and then pauses. "Oh, hey, wait." A beat of silence passes. "I'm really sorry."

I lightly snicker. "It's fine, Donovan."

"Yeah, but—it's going to be a long three days. I'll see you later."

His image on the phone's screen fades as the call ends. It's not going to be another three days. We've already been absent from each other's lives too long. Missing people sucks.

Clutching a large, brown paper bag, I abruptly halt just shy of grabbing the knob to Donovan's office. My heart shouldn't be revving right now. If all I am doing is bringing lunch to a friend, why do I feel so much anticipation? My head drives me in conflicting directions between departure and staying in hopes of learning how to live with this situation. After ditching my glow of infatuation, I place my hand on the doorknob, hoping Donovan hasn't already taken off to grab a sandwich. To my delight, the knob turns. Again my heart revs.

I breeze into the vacant lobby. Donovan's muted voice emanates from his office. Not knowing if it is safe to interrupt, I take a seat that is nestled near the corner on one side of his door. My knee bounces and my lungs exhale deeply. I fight the urge to check my makeup, reminding myself this is my friend and there is nothing to get worked up over. Finally, a hand touches the doorknob. The jingle rattles my anxiety. Donovan pushes the door open to let the visitor out.

"Love you, too," he says. My heart sags. "Thanks for lunch."

Anna emerges, and suddenly I feel like a nine-year-old fool who has a crush on the most popular boy in the senior class and stupidly brought him cookies in hopes of getting his attention. I start to scamper under the reception desk but realize the futility as soon as my feet take flight. Instead I act like the situation is perfectly normal. It is, right?

Anna heads for the door, barely noticing me. However, I caught Donovan's attention the second he stepped out, stopping him dead in his tracks. His eyes shoot to Anna.

"Oh, hi, Lily," is what Anna says through her feathery voice, but my guilt hears it as a crass, "What the hell are you doing here?"

"Hi, Anna. I heard Donovan was stuck working, so I thought I'd surprise him with lunch." My hands point to the bag, proving my words.

"That's really sweet," she says, gently smiling. Her body dips as her fingers ripple out a little wave to Donovan. "Bye." She repeats the cute gesture. Her tall figure peers down at me, yet her eyes don't meet mine. "Bye, Lily."

I wave back, but her eyes are focused on the door. My hand goes down as I surrender to being ignored, and it accidentally brushes against her. She flinches at my touch, and I feel like I'm scum. "Sorry," I utter.

Donovan follows and shuts the door behind her. Spinning back, he looks out of the corner of his eye, and color blooms in his cheeks. His focus wavers between the door and me. "I—I'm sorry," he utters, scratching his head before looking to his hand then dropping it. He no longer seems to know what it's for. "I had no idea you were coming." He gives up and sticks his hand in his pocket. "Anna called right after we talked and was afraid I wouldn't have time to pick up anything so she, uh—"

Why is it so hard for him to tell me his wife brought him lunch? "What did she bring you?" I ask, scrunching my eyes and scrutinizing her actions.

"Tempeh on wheat," he groans, "hold the flavor."

Retrieving my contribution, I stroll to him with it behind my back, then pop it out with a bounce and the gleam of a toothpaste spokes model. "Lamb Korma, Vegetable Biriyani, and fresh Naan."

"No way!" he exclaims. I nod vibrantly. He opens the bag with the urgency of it containing a bomb he has mere seconds to defuse. "God! It smells divine! You're amazing!" The dazzle of his rising gaze almost blinds. "Come on," he says, grabbing my hand and tugging toward his office.

"Don't you have to work?"

"We need to eat quickly. I have a client arriving in twenty minutes."

"I wasn't planning on staying. I just brought enou—"

"Lil-y." His eyes smile into mine. "Come on. Join me."

With a little bop of my head, I follow him into his office, praying his appointment falls victim to a miraculous recovery.

11

Like a wannabe ninja, Antonia stealthily slips her napkin out of her lap, pretends to wipe her lips, and spits broccoli into it. Per the rules of motherhood, I bust her. "Seriously, Antonia. Where did you learn to do that?" Duh! "Never mind, it's in your nature. You need to eat your broccoli. Tell me how to make it better next time."

"Bury it in the neighbor's yard," she says. The retort is so Donovan-like I let out a snort.

Christopher tries to play the proper father. "Apologize to your mum. She worked hard to make that for you."

"Sorry, Mom," she sings half-heartedly.

Christopher chuckles. "What do you mean, 'It's in her nature?' Don't tell me you used to do that?"

"Nope. Guess again." I roll my eyes and blink them for dramatic effect.

"Blimey! Those two really are alike." Christopher looks at Donovan's clone with amusement. "I hear you two had quite the time the other night. Did you have fun at Pizza Playland?"

Antonia's brows scrunch, and I solve her mystery. "Daddy means last week with Uncle Scooby and I, honey."

"Last week? Really?" Christopher ask. His eyes wander back and forth, searching for lost time.

"Yeah," Graham says, beaming. "I won two stuffed animals and gave them to Sunshine and Antonia." My snicker causes him to look at me as if puzzled. "Did I do something wrong, Mum?"

"Not at all. You are just like your father. I'm very proud of you."

"Dad, if I'm like you, who are you like?" Graham asks.

Dear Lord, Graham has no idea what kind of creepy-crawlies squirm in the can he's blown open. Christopher scratches his head. "Well, I'm exactly like your grandfathers back home. They and your nan taught me everything I know, so I guess I'm just like them."

"Do you look like your dad?" Graham asks.

"Not at all. I mostly look like me mum, though not much really. I probably look like me ancestors."

I try to slam the lid back onto the can. "You know, Graham, sometimes people who are related look nothing alike. Uncle Donovan and I don't look alike at all, and he looks nothing like our mother."

Christopher fidgets with his glass of wine. Quickly he changes the subject. "Have you children decided how to dress for Halloween?"

My eyes close as I grunt. It's the first night in a week Christopher has snuck in dinner with us and he just sabotaged me. It's October, and we've been making pumpkin desserts like crazy. How have I neglected Halloween costumes?

Christopher looks to me with an apologetic cringe as the kids spout out their dream costumes. "Tell you what," he says to the children. "I'll take you shopping, and you can choose anything you like. We can go next weekend," he says with resolve, only to retract his statement. "No, wait, I'm fully committed. Next Wednesday night … No, can't do that either." He looks up and sees my exasperation.

"I'll take them over the weekend. I've nothing else going on except for Sunday dinner with Donovan and crew. Will you be here?"

"No, I …" Christopher tosses down his napkin in disgust with himself. "Of course I'll be here, right after I take the children shopping." He shoots me a smile that begs me to tell him he did well in saving the day.

"Thank you," I say while the children go wild with ideas. Thank God he's remembering the rest of us exist.

&

At four in the morning, I discover Christopher sitting on the floor of the family room, drinking tea and pouring over old photos. He's been like this before, but never to this extent.

I sit next to him and snuggle my head into his shoulder. He wraps his arm around me while staring at two collages he's created. One of them consists of generations of Grace's family, the other of Paul's. "You know, you have three choices," I tell him. "Talk to Grace, accept that not everyone looks like their relatives, or let this bother you for eternity."

"I'm one of five sons," he laments. "All me brothers look like Paul Eccles—tall, blonde, and built like your brother. They even act alike. The only thing we have in common is blue eyes and pale skin. Our hands, ears, all of our features are completely different."

"Wow, you really are delving in this time. Why don't you just talk to Grace?"

"Because how the hell do you ask your mum if your dad is really your dad? I'm not adopted. I've seen snaps of Mum pregnant around the time she would've been with me. She had some rough times with Dad, and he and I were like chalk and cheese, but that doesn't mean she did something she shouldn't. Besides, she's repeatedly told me I'm named after me father, and I do hold Paul as my middle name. You're right. Look at Antonia. She looks exactly like Donovan who looks nothing like your mum."

"Christopher, you've been pouring over your brothers, but you've yet to get a good look at your daughter. You two practically have the same ears. Donovan barely has any lobes and mine aren't much bigger. Yours are perfect, and because of it she can pierce them like crazy and wear all kinds of wild jewelry that I can't."

"Oh, thanks loads! That's what I needed to hear!"

"Her hands are also like yours. Donovan struggles with his guitar. I bet in a few years Antonia could have him beat, and she can already sing. Donovan couldn't hit a note if you epoxied it to a punching bag. Also, she may have his facial features, but she has your natural build. There isn't a muscle on that girl." I shoot him a sly grin. Truthful toying is the best toying.

"Ah, nice! So me daughter can be a pierced, scrawny rock star. I liked her better when I didn't see the resemblance."

"Face it Christopher, with what she's gotten from you and the way she can be sly like Donovan, we're going to have our hands full when she hits puberty."

"Aw, pants!" Christopher gathers the photos and tosses them back into their box. "I'm going to bed before you tell me one of the children resembles my Great Aunt Georgina, the sideshow performer."

"What was she known for?"

"Something I'm glad Antonia didn't get from me."

12

Finding a reputable hypnotherapist in Los Angeles that suited my needs was far easier than expected. LA County is filled to the brim with people who give advice on how to sort out your brain. Of the ten people I spoke to, only one didn't hesitate to fulfill my request of avoiding outside influence as much as possible. Thus, when I entered Susan's office it was already dark. To me, Susan is a guide, not a person, and is therefore best faceless. Her voice is as comforting as snuggling into an old sofa with a soft blanket and warm cocoa made of fine chocolate.

I've finally braved the courage to delve into my soul's distant past, yet skepticism and apprehension cloud the beginning of my journey down a spiraled stairway. Its thirty stairs represent my thirty years of life. At various ages, I'm asked to stop and reveal my experiences. Happy flashes of childhood sprinkle my mind, but a blank screen resides where I expect a movie to play.

Susan guides me to the bottom of the stairway—the moment of my birth. Still the movie won't start—not even a trailer. What if my mind creates a false antiquity? What if my discoveries match Donovan's? Can we handle yet another curlicue in our saga?

Before me lies a deep, inky hallway containing numerous doors at various intervals. Inside the first portal I expect to see a movie. Instead, an alabaster brilliance swallows me into an alternate, three-dimensional reality.

"Where are you?" Susan asks.

"I—I don't know," I reply, feeling disoriented.

"Trust your instincts," Susan instructs. Her voice is delicate and distant. "It will soon become clear. Is it day or night?"

"Night. Inside." The facts are known with no understanding of how.

"Do you see anything?"

My film appears to be at intermission.

Susan continues, "Look down and tell me what you see. Can you see your feet? What covers them?"

The image before me is detached yet so real—like I'm possessed by a dream. "A desk—wooden, battered. A single lamp burns—I think."

"Trust whatever information comes," Susan assures. "Things will clarify as you progress. What is on the desk?"

"A letter."

"Is it dated?"

My hand quakes as I pick it up. Its contents are a smattering of words, scarcely revealing themselves through a giant haze. "I can't read it."

"Is it in a language you don't understand?" Susan asks.

"No, it's typed in English. I just can't make it out."

"That is fine. Tell me what you are wearing."

The vision of my garments is unclouded, making me fear the contents of the letter. "An apron—tattered. It has little pink roses on it and ruffles that are starting to fall off. My hands are dry and chapped." Unexplainably the reason becomes clear. "My nails, they're jagged and dirty from scrubbing floors."

"Good. Keep going," Susan persists. "Do you see anything else in the room?"

"A young girl of eleven, asleep in the bedroom we share. Emily, my little sister." Why does this girl feel so familiar?

"What is your name?" Susan asks.

"Rose."

"How old are you?"

"I don't know. Maybe eighteen?" Where is this coming from?

"Let the judgment in your mind fall aside," Susan unhurriedly leads. "Now, what year is it? Where are you?"

Again the answers sprint out. "1918. Kansas."

"At the count of three you will be able to read that letter. One… Two… Three… What does it say?"

My voice stutters as I speak the words before me.

July 28, 1918
Dear Mr. and Mrs. Hanover,
We regret to inform you that your son, Jonathan, was killed in the line of duty yesterday near Paris, France at the hands of the enemy.

"Oh, my God," I utter.

"Do you know who Jonathan is?" Susan asks.

A hazy image of white roses appears. My vision raises to a youthful man with medium brown hair and playful, yet virtuous, green eyes. "My boyfriend. No. Wait. My brother. No, stepbrother. My mother married his father when I was seven and she became pregnant with Emily. He was drafted. He tried to apply for CO status through the church, but Mom burned his papers instead of mailing them."

Oh, Lord.

"Where are your parents?" Susan inquires.

"Dead—from a car crash a few weeks ago. I've been trying to get the army to bring Jonathan home so I don't have to raise Emily by myself. I've no idea what I'm going to do." My earthly being trembles. How will I ever support her?

"Just stay calm and relaxed. Is there anything else on the desk?" Susan asks.

My mind turns to my hands and reveals I hold more than a typed document. Underneath it is a handwritten letter from Jonathan. Instinct tells me to withhold the words from Susan.

My Lovely Rose,
Again you fill my thoughts. Before I left, you tried to tell me something precious. I was foolish for not listening. Now that moment feels so distant I question if it ever happened, or if what you expressed was merely a falsehood in my mind. When I can finally see your face

again, I will tell you all I feel inside.

I have no right to request this, but please, postpone your wedding. William is a wonderful man but—Please do not make any decisions until my eyes behold you again.
All my love,
Jonathan

A chill creeps through me. That sounded like the notes Donovan wrote under the faux identity of Alex. My lie races out. "I—I don't see anything else. I need to stop now."

"Okay, let's take you forward a few years," Susan requests. "Bring yourself into the daylight. Feel the sun on your face. Can you feel the sun?"

My memory shifts to a drizzly spring day. "No, it's raining."

"Where are you?"

A dim reception area with walls of concrete surrounds me. It's a frigid version of hell. "Walking into a jail," I say, quaking from the chill. "Emily is holding my hand. There is a guard who greets me. Once a week he slips me a dollar, I have no idea why except that he must feel sorry for us. He seems so familiar, just like Emily, but I can't place them."

"Who are you there to see?"

"William, my husband. He stole vegetables off of a truck to feed us. Emily accidentally knocked over some fruit, and the scene caused him to get caught. They are making him do hard labor to help the war effort. I worry for him."

"What does he look like?"

The mist forming in my earthly eyes turns to sobs as my mind sets its sights on an alternate version of Christopher. "Sandy hair, medium height. Weak from not eating, just like Emily and I. I'm so scared for him. He was only trying to help us."

"Okay, Lily. Let's return you to the present. At the count of three, let your mind release the image. One. Two. Three. Do you see yourself floating away from your body?"

The view ebbs, but the pain and despair felt while

looking at Christopher in that jail cell linger. Just like then, I have lost Donovan, and Christopher would do anything for his family.

The second I step out of the hypnotherapist's office, I call Donovan.

"Hey, Lil. How'd it go?"

"World War I," I say matter-of-factly, expecting him to completely understand the gutting I just experienced.

"Ugh." His groan reinforces my misery.

"You found it too?"

"Yeah, Rose. That I did."

"Send your notes to my personal email address. I'm coming to your office with the recording."

The depression that fills me like flavorless jelly in a stale donut makes my drive feel ceaseless. When I finally reach Donovan's office, I check my email for his notes in preparation of what lies ahead.

WWI - Jonathan H. Hanover

Tried to escape the war by claiming CO status. Had the completed the paperwork signed by my pastor. I thought my stepmother had mailed it, but when my draft notice arrived she confessed to burning it, claiming I should stand up for my country like a real man.

Dad works in a steel mill. Saw my two sisters, Rose and Emmy. Emmy is much younger. Long, dark brown hair. Innocent brown eyes. Always a sweet smile on her lips when she sees me. It scares me to admit I think she is Anna.

Rose is my treasure. Her green eyes glisten like the sun. Her auburn locks cascade in soft waves around her face. Her skin is like the petal of a flower—soft, smooth, fragrant. When she moves I hear a melody. I write her letters all the time. I don't send them all, fearing it is creepy, though I know she feels the same. She tried to tell me before I left—the last time I ever saw her. The memory of that moment, the tingle that lingered on my cheek from her kiss, graces me still.

Rose and Lily are one and the same. Mom is still Mom. She sabotaged me. I died because of her.

I enter the room, and Donovan halts his filing. With hardly a hello I head to his computer and search ancestry.com for Rose Hanover in Kansas. Nothing appears. "Look for Albert Hanover," Donovan says. His words carry weight.

The revised inquiry reveals The 1910 U.S. Census listing Albert Hanover, his wife Mary, and their three children, Jonathan, Rose, and Emily. I turn to Donovan, and the suffering in my eyes is a reflection of his own. "Even then you wrote me notes. You gave me white roses before you left."

"The neighbor let me cut them out of her yard." Donovan's voice is appropriate for a confessional in a Catholic church. "I chose white because I wanted you to know my thoughts were pure. The look on your face when I gave them to you was the final image in my mind as I died."

I close my eyes and replay the moment just remembered. Though he stands before me, my longing for Jonathan lingers.

I rush through my front door, anxious to throw my arms around the current incarnation of William in appreciation of all that we have now. However, though Christopher and the kids should have been home an hour ago, silence greets me.

My cell phone shows three missed calls from the nanny. A message revealing Christopher has failed to arrive frays my nerves. Finally, he answers my forth call, just as I arrive at the nanny's house. "Darling, what's wrong?" he asks. His voice is laced with concern. "I just saw all the missed calls."

I am uncertain whether I am relieved he is safe or upset he has uncharacteristically forgotten the children. "Christopher, you neglected some important people today." Disappointment rings in my voice, but not as much as it does in his moan as he realizes his error. My tone of forgiveness is forced as I take up the slack, again.

An excuse to tell my children why their father stood

them up is forming when my phone plays the Looney Tunes theme. "Hey, Lil," Donovan says upon my answer. "Anna's sick, so I'm taking Sunshine to see the original *Incredible Mr. Limpet* at The Egyptian in forty-five minutes. You and the family want to join us?"

His timing couldn't be better. The angels have blessed me with the perfect diversion for the children, and myself, from their father's neglect. "Donovan, the wonders of you never cease to amaze me. We'll meet you there."

13

The universe has locked me away from my husband and tossed the key into the Bermuda Triangle. The one free night Christopher has falls on an evening when we snagged a last-minute, high-profile wedding cake. Why can't celebrities plan like normal people instead of suddenly getting married when Cindy has been called out of town and the rest of my staff is MIA?

I'm stacking a set of tier pans into their home base when everything goes dark via a pair of hands covering my eyes. My thoughts flash to a surprise visit from Christopher. However, an exhilarating scent sells out the true culprit. I tilt my head back and snuggle into Donovan's chest. "What are you doing here?" My question sounds like a moan of want.

"Are you complaining?"

"Never," I say, turning into his embrace.

"I brought you something. Admittedly it's a trite excuse to see you. You know how I'm always bringing stuff from your shop to colleagues? Well, today one of them tried to return the favor." Donovan grabs a box that sports the imprint of Belle Boulangerie de Jour, a flashy, over-priced rival in Beverly Hills who is known more for its address than its goods. When their innovation does manage to one-up us, it pisses me off for weeks. "It's perfectly fine," he continues, "but you could do better."

Donovan grabs a fork as I peer inside the box. "Are you going to tell me what I'm getting into, or is this Russian roulette?" I ask of the orange-colored tartlet. "Knowing those guys it could be anything."

"A very good, but uneventful, mango with a little passion fruit." He leans in to whisper, "Tonight, we both need your

74

magic." His breath warms my neck, then slinks down to thrill my breast. Tenderly his fingers glide my chin upward, drawing my eyes into his. He feeds me a bite, then traces my lower lip with his thumb. The curiosity on his face is far more appetizing than the tart.

"You're right," I utter with heated breath. "Meet me at the baker's table."

"How many prep bowls?" Donovan calls as he heads off. My eyes wander down to his hips, and I wish to forgo the bowls and spoons for the curve above his ass and my tongue.

"Three," I holler, darting for the fridge. Its chill helps me regain my focus, which quickly shifts back to his ass as he straddles a stool at the counter. "Use seventy percent mango, thirty percent passion fruit." I hand him the purees and dash off for some juice and spices. God, I can't get my mind off of how tightly his butt cheeks curve in. I fight a memory of him taking me on a table while I watched in a mirror as his hips pounded against me.

"Are you ready?" he asks.

Boy, am I ever.

After we've prepped the last bowl, Donovan motions me to sit next to him. Drawing our stools tightly together, he wraps his legs around mine. The urge to forgo my stool and straddle his waist nearly overwhelms. "Which way would you like it first?" he asks. My eyes flash up as he reaches for a bowl containing puree and lime juice. "How about this?"

Donovan's eyes shine into mine as he raises a spoonful. My mouth drifts open in anticipation. My breath shallows. The spoon glides over my tongue, and a drop of the puree slides onto my chin. A feather's touch sends my heart soaring as he caresses it off with his thumb, licking it with an enchanting smile. "You should have avoided the middle man," I tell him. Suddenly I'm self-conscious and fidget by touching a napkin to my lips.

He leans in, and I relish in the fluttering of his lips on my ear. "I take it you didn't like that one as much as you could have. It's not what I wanted, either."

His hand goes to my knee, then slides upward, sending my heart racing. I turn my sights to the puree and our original mission. Eagerly I grab the second bowl and sweep a spoon into the mint mixture. My mouth slacks as I raise the utensil to him, and my eyes rendezvous with his. His grin morphs into a pleasure-awaiting vessel. His lips clamp down with a moan, and my insides warm and tighten in delight. Languidly I withdraw, then flip the spoon into my own mouth—my tongue worshiping where his once graced.

My voice comes out deep and sultry. "What do you think?"

"Better, but I need something more."

"So do I."

His hand extends to the back of my head, his fingers stroke my scalp and taunt me with gingerly tugs to my hair. Softly, his lips reveal, "You haven't tasted it yet."

My eyes dart to the bowl. Quickly I grab a spoonful. As the cool puree and mint slides over my taste buds, Donovan tucks his favorite cluster of hair behind my ear. The act pulls my attention back into his beckoning eyes. "You're right. Much better, but we're not there yet," I say while craving his hands on my breast.

Donovan brings forth the last bowl. My breath turns deep and soft. My mouth widens in anticipation of mango and lemon, wishing I had the courage to cast the spoon aside and taste him. Suddenly he yanks it away and thrusts it into his own mouth, bringing forth my groan of jealousy. It's me his lips should clasp on.

"Wipe that smirk off your face," I scorn. My voice turns breathless. "Actually, please don't. It's rather captivating." His teeth tug at his lower lip, and I become jealous of their capture.

"Fun, but still not what I crave."

"What do you crave?" I ask.

A dirty grin crosses his face. "You, and the way you used to make me feel." He feeds me another spoonful. "Be sure to savor it this time."

Reluctantly, my brain shifts its focus from the man to my taste buds. "Hmm ... the best flavor was when there was nothing left on the spoon but you."

His eyes fill with a blaze that causes my insides to melt down, and my legs squeeze together. If he doesn't touch me soon, I think I may die.

I shouldn't be doing this.

I try to snap myself back into our project. Jetting my hands out, my fingers flail toward the bowls as my eyes lock their focus, but Donovan doesn't let me back down. "Casting a spell?" he asks.

"Stop it. You're making this hard."

"No, that's what you're doing," he says, derailing my thoughts.

Again I strain to focus on my job, not an alternate universe where I've been tossed onto the counter and am matching every one of his hard thrusts with my own downward lunge until swirling colors dance behind my eyelids.

With a forced snap, my flavor affinity skills kick in, and I take the bowls containing mint and lemon, mix them together, then head off to add a speck of pepper.

"Try this." I slip a spoon of the puree into Donovan's mouth, the only passion exhibited being culinary. The flavor slaps him back into reality.

"Yumm," he utters. "That's fantastic!"

I taste it, this time remembering to put some on the spoon. "Wow, you're totally right," I tell Donovan as Jenny enters the back, bringing the day's remaining desserts to the refrigerator. I completely forgot we weren't alone. Actually, I almost forgot a lot of things.

"Oh, hey, Donovan. I didn't know you were here." Jenny looks down at the display before us as she blazes past. "What are you two up to?" she calls while opening the door to the walk-in fridge.

"Donovan had an idea for a new dessert," I yell before

turning to him. "Thank you. I needed this creative boost." *Actually, I need you.*

"Sure thing, Lil." Rising from his chair, he grabs the napkin that once touched my lips and slips it in his pocket. He eyes Jenny as she dashes to the front before he addresses me. "You free for an extended lunch day after tomorrow? I thought we could try that new restaurant that opened down the street from my office, if you have time."

"I always have time for you," I tenderly moan before realizing my tone and squishing thoughts of him licking puree off of my breasts out of my head. He places his hand to the back of my neck and draws me in so he can kiss my forehead. The kiss lingers a beat, sending a feeling of pixie dust spiraling down around me.

"Bye, Jenny," he calls to the front. My eyes cling to him as he departs. It's going to be a long two days.

I gaze at the spoons on the table and wish one still had his taste so I could savor it again. It's been years since I've had that much fun being creative. Donovan fuels all of my passions.

Jenny returns with a tray of cookies and places them on the counter before heading off for some plastic wrap. "It's amazing how well you and Donovan get along. Most married couples aren't as connected as you."

"Boy, isn't that the truth," I muse. "We're pretty odd."

"Odd? If we all didn't know better, we'd think you two were dating."

"Huh?"

"I'm sorry. That sounded really bad, huh?" Jenny rips off a sheet of plastic wrap with a flourish. "It's just that with how Donovan pays you little visits, brings you trinkets, and takes you out, if we didn't know he was your brother, we'd think he was Christopher's rival."

Rival?

I have a boyfriend.

Oh, crap!

ॐ

After a restless night, I accept that Lilyanna Eccles and Lily Beckett have collided and merged. As Donovan exits his office for lunch I bolt into his lobby, stick my hands out in front of me and push him back inside, shutting the door behind me. My hands touch my temples then bounce out in revelation as my words jabber forth. "I can't take it anymore."

"What, Lily? What can't you take?" He rolls his eyes at knowing I'm about to blurt out something utterly ridiculous. My sleep-deprived brain should take it as a warning. Sometimes how well he knows me really sucks.

"I'm having an affair, and I can't stand myself," I blurt.

Donovan shows he wants to throttle me as he smacks the files in his hand onto his desk. "You're what? With who?"

"With you," I reveal. Suddenly realizing my stupidity, I squeeze my lids as if the act will make me invisible.

Donovan's hands go to his hips. His head turns into a maraca. "Are you crazy? Look Lil, we all know I have moments where the obvious escapes me, but I'd be well aware if we were cheating on our spouses."

"We're not cheating. We're having an affair."

"Wow! You have really got me this time." He drops his hands in surrender before approaching me. His tone changes from shocked to passive, yet sturdy—like I'm a toddler needing a reprimand for an innocent mistake. "Okay, Lily. Tell me about this affair and exactly how I'm involved."

"Um, well, you're kind of my boyfriend."

His blinking eyes match his stammering words. "Your—your what?"

"We're dating!"

"Lily, we are not dating," he asserts.

"No? Think about it. All the lunches we have, the way we interact like lovers—"

"Lily, you're my best friend, not to mention that we have been through hell together. Of course we lean on each other."

"Best friend? Are best friends constantly on the verge of throwing themselves at each other?"

"Some are."

"Oh, please. How about feeding each other—seductively. What about the playfulness and the innuendos? Damn it, Donovan, if you weren't off limits, last night I would have thrown you on that workbench, used you as a bowl, and licked you clean."

"I think there's some mango yogurt in the fridge."

"I'm serious! Does this not faze you, or were you playing me all along?"

His sapphire eyes close off the world as the truth of my words sink in. "I'm not playing you, but the idea of what was going on had smacked me in the face before. I suppose you want to stop."

I step closer and look him squarely in the eyes, wishing a lie would come forth. "No." I hate myself for feeling this way.

His hand caresses through my hair, stopping at the back of my head. My chin raises. Suddenly my lips are in need of moisture. "Neither do I," he confesses. "How close are we going to allow ourselves to get? I really want to be the dutiful husband, but…"

My eyes blink away their forming pools. "There is no way I will cheat on Christopher, but since you've come back into my life I've gone from happy and relatively satisfied to excited and passionate. You fuel me like no one else is capable. I hate to admit it, but being like this is so much more honest than ignoring the truth we don't want to hide from."

With a touch to my chin, his words grant blessing for the release of my tear. "Please don't hide from us. We fought so hard to accept the truth. I can't bear to ignore it again."

"Okay, no hiding, but we need to remember there is a line before we cross it."

14

The car's *bop* into my driveway reflects eager anticipation. Christopher called requesting I come home early and not worry about the children. An enticing surprise may await me. Well, vanilla ice cream enticing. Sadly, for the last ten years my daring sexual adventures live in an alternate reality. I'll happily take it though. After last night's encounter with Donovan, I'm hungry for anything that pumps life into my marriage, which is inching toward failure.

Inside, I find my family gathered at the kitchen table. Antonia sits on Christopher's right knee with Graham in a chair to his left. All of them are staring at a laptop's screen. This can only mean one thing—and dessert has nothing to do with it.

Eric's image transmits over video chat. A slinked smile hides my disappointment. "Hi, Eric!" I crouch behind Christopher and kiss his cheek. Residing next to the laptop is a note pad decorated in scribbles. Christopher's handwriting indicates he missed his calling as a doctor. All that is legible is "6 weeks, 21 stops."

"You're looking lovely, Lilyanna. How are you, dear?" Eric asks.

"Wonderful, thank you. You sure are missed. You've been dangling hope of a visit in front of us for a decade. Don't you think it's long past time?"

"Be careful what you wish for, luv. Keep me posted, Christopher. You did right by firing that yob. Cheers."

"Cheers, mate." Christopher says before closing his laptop.

Antonia jumps for the television with Graham scrambling behind. Christopher rises from his seat. His grin is hard to contain yet a little twitchy. "Fire?" I ask, wrapping my arms around Christopher's waist. He gives me a lovely kiss that leaves me dying for more.

"I fired Mike."

Oh, thank the Lord! "I'd ask, but I think I know why."

"He was simply out of control and completely unprofessional," Christopher asserts while throwing the pen in his hand onto the table. "That and I know he was making you uncomfortable. It was big of you not to say anything. It's a good thing I did it last night too," he declares.

"Because the big news that came through today is?" My lips curve in anticipation.

"It's getting harder to keep anything from you."

I give him a little flash of my eyelid. "Good. That makes it easier to keep watch on your antics."

He looks to my work shoes. His grin is sheepish yet reserved. "You know how I've been making friends with promoters and offering to play poxy, last-minute gigs in an effort to boost interest in the band?"

"Umm hmm." Boy, do I ever! We've had some great moments interrupted and family plans flipped around by bad, last-minute gigs.

"It finally paid off. We've been offered a twelve week, cross-country tour opening for Spiral Lamb, whose album just went platinum."

"Christopher, that's fantastic!" And it's horrific! Twelve weeks? Instead of vanilla ice cream I get cow dung. The last thing I need while being tempted away from my husband is for him to leave for three months. "When is it?" I ask. My breath is trapped in fear he'll leave tomorrow, yet I also want this over with so I can have my husband back.

"That's the cracking part. Since it's a major tour and the band specifically wants us, we actually get notice. We leave in the middle of January."

"That's perfect! That gives you months to prepare." My face contorts into an overplayed smile with full moons for eyes. Christopher's blanched expression and sagging body tell he sees through my charade. "Why don't you look happy?" I ask. "You've been waiting years for this."

"All that preparation means I'm going to be away a lot more. You're not all right with this, are you?"

"Is it that obvious?"

"It certainly is. You really want to let me have it right now, and you've every right. Today I heard of the children's recent adventures. Donovan's become their surrogate father."

"Christopher, we shouldn't be expected to wait like neglected puppies who are grateful every time you brush past and tap us on the head. You already have a full-time job at the studio, not to mention all of the rehearsal time with your band. I know you can't do it all, but please try a little harder. We all need to enjoy what we have a bit more. Okay?"

He snuggles me into his shoulder. His voice is soft and reassuring, but his body is tense. "More than okay. I won't let us slip away further. I promise."

15

Cindy and I cower in the dark recess of the kitchen, afraid someone will discover the delectable Mascarpone-Pear mousse we created and we will have to share. It's so luscious we're giggling as if intoxicated. Visions of using it in a mousse cake with a pistachio crème insert accompanied by a glass of wine swirl in my head. "Moscato is perfect with the pear and Mascarpone, but given the pistachio this needs a strong red."

"Yeah," Cindy agrees with idolatry for the mousse. Her eyes flair. "Like a good Cab."

My head tilts back, and my knees dip with an excited bounce, relishing the thought. "Oh, totally!"

Jenny softly interrupts, suspending my taste buds from their happy dance. "Lily, Donovan's here. He needs to see you." Her expression is pained to the point where my grin instantly crashes.

"Why didn't you send him back?"

"He, um—he warned me that he needs to take you on a walk. I think something's really wrong."

I chuck my spoon into the sink and bolt to the front of the store where Donovan trudges with angst. Halting his tread, he turns to me with a shrug of emptiness, thus selling out the source of his misery. I drag him through the kitchen, past the lockers, and out the back door. Once we reach the lot, I touch my hands to his cheeks like I'm saving his head from plummeting to the pavement. "What did she say to you? Do not let her do this!"

His eyes close with a whimper. "Mom's Cirrhosis has turned into liver cancer. They're starting chemo, but with everything else, odds are she won't be around much longer."

A wave of vacancy flows through my gut. I hate the thought that the woman who raised me—who tried to be my best friend and often came close to succeeding—is suffering, but it doesn't eradicate how I detest her blasphemous handiwork. My loving heart and the animosity in my head cancel each other out, leaving me anesthetized.

ॐ

Like the Doublemint Twins, Donovan and I enter our adjoining hotel rooms and open the set of doors that separate them. I fling myself backwards onto his bed. My flair for melodrama surfaces as I flail my hand to my forehead and utter breathlessly, "I feel faint. I don't think I'll be able to make it tomorrow. Just tell Norma Desmond I said hello."

"No way, Marion Davies. You're stuck," he snaps while tossing me the room service menu. "As you have told me many times, some things we're still in together." He nods to the menu. "What do you want?"

While doing my best Scarlett O'Hara I agonize, "World peace, the end of poverty, and a ride to the airport." Donovan's glare demolishes my fun. "Geez! Lighten up. You turn into a fireball of testy when you're about to see Hanniballa Lecter."

"Can you blame me? The woman ruined my life."

Wow, after a decade has he finally figured that one out? "Hey, Baby Jane." I prop myself on my elbows and motion for him to sit next to me. Donovan crinkles up a side of his nose and turns away, flicking his hand at me. "Hey," I say. "You okay? Did I do something to upset you?"

With rigid muscles his hands rest on his hips. His lips tense, and his head oscillates while he stares at the wall. His head drops before turning to me. "I'm sorry. It's the stress." He sits in slow motion, like he's attempting to stretch every muscle.

"Your life is far from ruined," I softly say while caressing his cheek. Habitually, his head curls into my hand when we're alone like this, but now he remains taut. "Look at how you've thrived. Did you ever see yourself becoming a psychologist before that madness happened? You're a doctor with your own private practice. Think about what Dad would say to that. It's a huge deal." He cracks a ghost of a smirk. "Maybe you just need to eat." I open the room service menu. "What do you want?"

"Nothing. You get food. I'm going to bed." He shrinks over, elbows to knees, forehead to hands. I tug him to face me and run my hand from the apple of his neck around the back of his head. His head turns into the action that grounds him, leading to a short-lived smile.

"If you're hurting, I'm by your side the whole way. Do you really want me to leave?"

"No, I don't. Sometimes I wish you didn't always know what I need." He lays back and pulls the bedspread over us.

Try as I might to cover the surrender in my eyes, I can't. "And I'll always love you. Always."

"So you prove time and time again." His voice reflects the pain of our reality. He gives me a little grimace before pulling my head into his shoulder. "Good night, Lily."

"Donovan, did I do something to upset you?"

"You are the only one who never lets me down. Good night."

℁

"Wait. Why are we doing this?" I ask Donovan while on the verge of entering our childhood home.

"Because I haven't spent enough time on the funny farm already." Donovan springs a toothy grin and wobbles his eyes. It removes a minuscule amount of the tension that remains from his mood of yesterday. Being on a funny farm with him sounds heavenly. Actually, being locked in an inescapable room filled with fang-bearing, rabid rodents sounds appealing compared to entering this place.

We step inside and Donovan places a small bouquet of Lilies of the Valley, tied with a blue ribbon, and a paper bag on the floor before hanging his keys on a hook inside the closet. I debate fleeing until Donovan turns to help me with my coat. Damn chivalry! Now he's slowed my getaway. It may be only by a few seconds, but with Lana Beckett around, those seconds will seem as long as it takes to lick my way across the Great Wall of China.

Donovan grabs the flowers and the bag before heading up the stairs. I make for the den. "Hey, where do you think you're escaping to?" he asks.

"The liquor cabinet. Want to join me?"

His shoulders drop. "We dumped all the alcohol the last time we were here."

"You're right," I say, heading toward the kitchen. "Hopefully there's some vanilla extract in the cabinet." Donovan grabs me by the shoulders and walks me up the stairs. "Fine, I'll detour by the bathroom. If I OD on cough syrup, it'll be your fault!"

A few steps away from Mom's room Donovan abruptly stops and shoves me inside. "Losers first," he whispers.

Dick!

"Hi, Mom," I chime, sounding way too perky for even the biggest of morons to believe I want to be here. I plant a kiss on her forehead before plopping onto the edge of the bed.

Her grin is a mile wide. "Hi, Lily. I though Donovan was coming. Where's Christopher?"

"Donovan's here." He's just trying to beat me to the medicine cabinet.

Donovan enters faking a cough and snickering. He places the flowers on Mom's nightstand before giving her fading glow of happiness a kiss on the cheek. "Hi, Mom."

Mom's eyes scamper back and forth, just like they did when she exploded years before as she unearthed our secret; only this time there's nothing to hide. "Don't tell me you two are here alone again."

"Christopher's working and Anna just started her new job," I say. It sounds like I'm moaning.

"New job?" she inquires of Donovan. "I thought she loved her old one."

You haven't told her yet?

Donovan scrunches his shoulders and subtly flips his hands up. *I've kind of been avoiding this.* "She loved the job, but neither of us wanted to be in Colorado. We just moved to Venice. Here, this is from her." He hands Mom the bag. "It's more of that herbal tea that helps cleanse your liver."

"Venice?" Mom badgers more than asks. "But you don't speak Italian."

Donovan closes his eyes so she can't see them spiraling into his brain. "Venice, California; near Los Angeles."

Mom looks as blue as three men in a Vegas act. "You two live near each other now?"

"Yep, even with bumper-to-bumper traffic, Lily is never more than an hour away, usually much less. You should see her shop. You'd be proud."

Mom gasps and runs her eyes down me. "Is that really wise, you two living so close? Don't Anna and Christopher know what's going on behind their backs? I can't believe what the two of you go through for a little kinky sex."

Every bit of life that pumps through me funnels out my legs and oozes into the carpet. Incredible. Ever since she started knocking on death's door this woman has turned merciless. It's bad enough to constantly samba with temptation, but with all of her accusations maybe I should whip out a white flag. I'm struggling to be faithful to my husband, who might as well be lost at sea, even though my soulmate tempts me constantly, and I'm called a whore anyway. My eyes float to Donovan as I rise, confessing to him that I'm emotionally destroyed. "Excuse me. I need to visit the rest room," I utter.

Dismayed by how little our mother thinks of us, I head down the stairs without the pretense of my excuse being real. I open the doors of the liquor cabinet and stare in exasperation. At least she's springing for decent stuff now that the Grim Reaper's calling. Donovan's feet hammer down the stairs. Meanwhile, I open a bottle of vodka and take a swig. A scratch on the wood paneling entertains my vision. It's not Donovan I don't want to face, it's the situation. He touches my shoulder with trepidation, and the words I really want to express are swallowed. "Vodka?" I ask.

"No," he firmly replies, taking the bottle.

Donovan looks at me through the laceration in his heart—the one akin to mine. His lips part, and then disappear into his mouth. My lips touch his cheek and force a smile before I yank the vodka back, walk out the front door, and dump the remainder. I head out in the direction of Christopher's old house with no idea why.

ॐ

My emotions kaleidoscope as I sit on the curb across the street from where Christopher once lived. Visions of my past fill my brain; me crawling into his bedroom window, spending lunches here to avoid his fan club, and the fit I pitched when he broke my heart and returned to England.

I'm about to fall from grace, again. One of the reasons I compartmentalize who I am is due to an indiscretion that Lilyanna Eccles cowers from. When I'm her, I see myself as faithful. After all, what defines cheating? Is it a thought? A kiss? Making out? What if you stop right after you start? Is that cheating? It's not when I'm Lilyanna Eccles, because that's how I live with myself in light of a foolish moment. When I'm alone with Donovan, I strive to be Lily Beckett— the girl who believes that kissing is cheating. That keeps my lips to myself—at least now it does. The one time it didn't, we stopped, and I've forced myself to believe that made it okay.

Donovan pulls up in the car, then hesitantly joins me on the curb. "Funny how I can quote your words from twenty years ago but it took me forever to remember where you said Christopher once lived."

My damp eyes remain fixated on the house. "How did you know where to find me?"

"You always go to Christopher." My head snaps to him in anger for his words. "I don't mean that the way it sounds. I know you really love him."

"Then what did you mean?"

"Ask your hypnotherapist." Gently he tucks the hair that shadows my face behind my ear.

I snatch his hand and place it on his lap. My voice whips forward. "Not here."

"I just want to comfort a friend."

"We both know you'll never be just a friend. Donovan, you're right. We need to keep those adjoining doors shut. In fact, we need a lot more distance." My eyes drift back to Christopher's house. "I miss him. Christopher always takes away my pain—at least he does when he's around." My stomach tightens, and I head for the car. "I can't be here anymore. Please take me to the hotel. I'm sorry, but if you want to go back to Mom's, you have to do it without me."

Donovan follows and opens my door. His face is reflective with thought. As soon as he gets behind the wheel he states with resolve, "If you're done, I'm done. Some things we are still in together."

We drive out of town as fast as we can, neither of us looking back.

16

The heat of an Indian summer day holds nothing compared to the fire in Cindy's eyes as she blazes up to Robert like a super nova ignited inside a grease trap. "Damn it, Robert! What the hell is this?" she scorns. She's holding a vat of buttercream in a sickly shade of dying-grass green that is oxidizing into brown.

"Oh, did Hector finally finish it? How'd it turn out?" Robert asks.

"Disgusting!"

"Well, that's what they ordered. You know how weird rich people are."

"Robert! The cake is to be iced in avocado *colored* buttercream, not flavored!"

Oh, Lord, I can't take those two today. I flee into the back of the shop and then gasp when I see a shadow looming near my desk. "Geez, Donovan, you scared the crap out of me. How'd I miss you coming in?"

"I snuck through the back. With our need for distance, I thought I'd put these on your desk and run." He slips his hands into his pants pockets while nodding to a bouquet on my desk. "Happy Liberation Day," he says, in commemoration the day he finally confessed his feelings.

A wave of relief pulses through me. "After all the tension, I wondered if you'd acknowledge it. Come out to my car. I have something for you, too."

Donovan follows me through the kitchen. "Hi, Donovan," Robert says while practically drooling. "How did I miss you coming in?"

Donovan reacts with a demure smile and an effeminate wave. "Bye, Robert."

Robert proceeds to run his eyes down Donovan's backside and exhale a sigh of dreaminess. "Such a waste. What I could do to that—Ouch!" Cindy storms up and smacks him on the arm.

"You're so cruel!" I whisper to Donovan. His reply of a little shrug and an eye flutter are uncharacteristically girlish. "Stop it!" I laugh.

Though the tension has dissipated, awkwardness regarding his gift prevails. Originally it seemed a sweet token. Now I realize it's an improper symbol of undying love given to one married person by another. I hand him a small black box from the glove compartment of my car. "I bought this before we went to Rhode Island. It's probably inappropriate, but Happy Liberation Day." Donovan's smile builds as he uncovers an ornate, antique gold pocket watch. "It was made around the time Jonathan was born. Since we seem to have transcended time I thought it to be appropriate."

His eyes seem hypnotized. "It's perfect, Lil. Absolutely perfect. I really wish it didn't have to be this way."

I divert my eyes to my fidgeting hands. Not only do I need to dodge my view of him, but I also need to avoid my reflection in the car window. I'm unable to face myself for agreeing with him.

Upon opening the watch he observes lost time. "Eleven years ago tonight. I really thought we'd be together forever. I've thought about it endlessly. You're still the only one who sees me as I am. The night before we left for Rhode Island, Anna and I had it out. My own wife doesn't even know me. Either that or she purposely sets off my triggers. It makes me think I'm wasting time being myself." His eyes drift away from the watch before he shuts it. "I need to go. This whole thing with putting distance between us is really going to suck." He stammers, just shy of giving me a hug. After a quick peck on my cheek he gets in his car and drives away.

&

Succumbing to the grumbling arising from my stomach, the lure of freshly baked delights is avoided in lieu of a granola bar from my locker. When I drag out my purse, a scrap of pink paper with a typed message falls to my feet.

I can't believe how much I can still miss you. Life is too short to not have more time together.

The love note brings forth a chuckle. At least Christopher realizes his handwriting leaves a lot to be desired, but I am so grateful that he finally remembers that we exist.

A few steps away, reality firmly places its hand on the back of my skull and slams it onto the floor. Christopher does a lot of sweet things, but he never leaves notes. However, while notes are an emotional trigger for Donovan, they were the hallmark of the relationship we shared, and he snuck in here this morning.

Sweet thoughts of yesteryear swirl up as the abandoned pixie dust that brought about our relationship a decade ago is blown back into my path. Notes followed me everywhere—written on milk cartons, in a bag of flour, on the back of the grocery list—even when putting down the toilet seat. The lump in my throat proves that if he's trying to revive the past, he just found the jumper cables to my heart.

Back at home, I find a dozen sterling roses in the center of an elegantly set dining room table. Christopher races to get Chinese take-out placed with the presentation of this being a holiday. I fear this means he'll dare to wash our china himself. The last time, two plates and a saucer needed replacing.

He dashes up and kisses me sweetly before handing me a cocktail. "You're home early," I say. "To what do I owe all the honors?"

Christopher fusses as he places the silverware one inch from the table's edge, just as his family's butler always does. "Whatever do you mean, luv?"

"Flowers, the cocktail, dinner—reminders of you follow me everywhere."

"Did you see me image in one of your tea biscuits?" he asks while polishing a knife. The utensil drops onto a fragile dinner plate, sending a twinge zipping across the nape of my neck.

"No, but I'm feeling rather spoiled." And very lucky the plate didn't chip. "It's been a rather noteworthy day," I hint, before surveying him over the brim of my Gimlet as I sip. Crap! This is exactly what my mother does when she attempts to be sly.

"Ah, I'm glad things went well. Have a seat. I'll round the children."

Damn. This is not a comforting moment.

Christopher continues to be an angel and draws me a warm bath before putting the children in bed. My body sinks into the inspiriting bath, and the cacophony from the foaming bubbles represses the surrounding world. It leaves me to my thoughts of uncertainty regarding the source of the note.

In the next room, my cell phone sits on the nightstand. My hopes for a call may be foolish, but they fill me nonetheless.

Water trickles across the bathroom and onto the bedroom carpet as I retrieve the device. When I return, the bubbles snuggle my body, but that which can comfort my soul is out of reach. My eyes fixate on the phone, hoping it will chime despite my knowing that Donovan wouldn't dare acknowledge his actions after what happened in Rhode Island.

I grab the phone and my eyes again lock on it in expectation. Clearly my Jedi mind trick needs work or this thing would have succumbed by now. Finally I cave and click the call button.

"Hold on," Donovan whispers. Shuffles rattle in the background before he resurfaces. "Sorry. Everything okay?"

"Yeah, I was just thinking that life is too short not to have more time together. I'm taking advantage of a free moment to enjoy you a little."

Silence hangs in the air before he replies. "I thought we were cooling everything?"

"So did I."

"I really have to go. I'm sorry." His tone gives me no readable emotion.

"It's okay. The guy who oversees getting the kitchen back in order called out sick tonight, so I have to get up stupid early and do dishes. Yay!"

"That's too bad. I'll call you later."

I toss the phone onto the floor and slide my head underwater, only to wuss out on sucking it into my nose.

17

At four in the morning, a knock on the bakery's back door jolts me into dropping a whisk into the bleach tub, nearly causing the chemical-laced water to splash onto my face. My sleepy body drags itself to open the door to find an overly caffeinated Christopher. "Hello, luv!" he exclaims. His arms burst out to greet me. Bags support his bloodshot, baby blues, yet his grin is infectious. Behind him, our children yawn while clutching pillows and sleeping bags. The display removes every trace of my early-morning crankiness.

"Are you crazy? You have to be at your own job in a few hours."

"Certifiably bonkers—but I came to help anyway." He nods to the children. "They came to sleep in the front. Go on," he says, motioning them to the shop. "I promised those ridiculous pancakes with whipped cream and chocolate drops if they behave themselves. I figured you wouldn't mind the junk food, being it's in exchange for a little adoring help."

"Not at all!" I take his hand, and our arms swing as we enter the kitchen. My face reflects happiness. I place his hands into the warm, sudsy water. With a nuzzle and a peck on his cheek, I grab a mixing paddle and return it to its home before my sights resume on Christopher, who notices my peering. His eyes light with a captivating gleam once so long gone it's now almost alien.

"Remind you of something?" he asks.

"Yes, my old boss and mentor, Josette, tricking you into working. She got pretty good at it."

"Especially once she learned to only let me wash unbreakables."

My head tosses back in mirth. "Like that ever made a difference! You once dented a heavy-gage steal pan simply by dropping it onto a rubber mat. Then there was the time you shocked us by setting down a tray of dishes without breaking a single one. However, you placed it smack onto the top tier of a wedding cake Josette had just finished."

Christopher hangs his head at the memory that now brings forth amusement. "How she didn't off me is beyond comprehension."

"I owe much of my success to that moment. Josette stabbed a fork in the center of the cake and laughed while demanding you eat your mess. That's when I learned that no recoverable calamity is worth an uproar."

The memory causes mischief to swirl in my brain. I sneak off to the walk-in, not with the intent of reliving old times, but determined to save my marriage. A chocolate mousse cake begs me to take it captive. One way or another, I'm going to enjoy what I've craved.

On my way to nab forks, I reach into the sink and flick some suds at Christopher. He snickers when they hit his nose. My focus returns to the mousse cake with the intent of feeding him a forkful, then licking more off of his neck, but watery suds, likely meant to find my arm, splatter before me. Seriously? His aim is as good as that of an eyeless creature that lacks appendages.

I grab a handful of lather and nail him in the stomach. He then grabs two more handfuls and swats them at me. I dash away while shrieking and digging my hand into the mousse, ready to let him have it. Christopher swoops me up and swings me, and the cake plops to the floor. The mousse flies off of my hand and smacks into his face. His foot lands on the splattered mess and he slips onto his unpadded bum, plopping me between his legs, just shy of the family jewels.

"Ouuuch!" He winces with a chuckle.

"Oh my God! Are you okay?" My knee hits the mousse and slides out from under, causing me to land on him in a rather wifely position. The resulting kisses spark. I turn into a stick of dynamite whose fuse has been lit too long. The chocolate on his face, merging with our kisses, makes him taste sweeter than ever.

"Hmm…" he moans. "Maybe we should head home for some breakfast."

"Or you can stay and eat this," a voice booms over us.

My body jerks around to find Donovan towering above. At the widening of my eyes he breaks into a smile and flashes a wave. How many flavors of wrong is it that I feel guilty for making out with my own husband? "Ugh, hi." I smile uneasily. "I didn't expect to see you today."

A hasty puff emits from Donovan's nose. He forces a grin and drops the bag onto the counter before boring his hands into his pockets. "I thought I'd help with the dishes you were complaining about last night. Looks like you don't need me after all."

Donovan, I know what that means, and you're wrong.

No, Lily. We both know I'm not. "You two enjoy it. I have stacks of papers piling up at the office."

"Thanks, mate," Christopher states. He helps me to my feet. "You should join us."

"Nah, I'm good. Thanks." Donovan leaves, but my undeserved guilt remains.

"Let's eat. I'm bloody famished," Christopher raves.

So am I. Too bad I'm going to starve.

18

A feeling a sin looms from above when I enter my car to head home from work. It causes me to hunch my head like I do when rain pours and I'm caught without cover. The longer I drive, the more my head descends into my shoulders. When I pull up to a stoplight I examine the interior of the car. A slip of pink paper drops from my visor and causes me to jerk. Fear, hope, and confusion lock in my throat.

My love for you is endless and shall never die.

Suddenly my ten-minute ride home requires a one-hour detour. I enter Donovan's office as he does my bakery, like it's a second home. Donovan sits at his desk, pouring over paperwork. Despite logic and reason, I jump into the boiling cauldron. "This has to stop. I can't live with you being constantly in my head."

He rattles his noggin, still looking to the papers. "Hello to you, too." His face reflects a quandary. He puts down the pen, and his eyes shift upward. "Does this have something to do with the hypnosis?"

My words halt just short of bursting forth. Notes are one of his emotional triggers and anything involving them should carry a hazard label. I force my tone to be calm and stick my hands out in gentle warning. "I need you to stop sending me love notes."

"What love notes?" Donovan looks like a five hundred-piece jigsaw puzzle just smacked him in the face and rained all over him.

"The ones you've been sending since we got back from

Rhode Island."

"Lily, I haven't sent you love notes in ten years. I've written and shredded them, but I've never left one anywhere."

"Who would leave love notes at my work and in my car?"

Donovan's hands scrub through his hair. "Look to your left ring finger. The answer probably resides there."

"They don't sound like they're from Christopher," I utter, toying with my rings.

"You have no idea how much I wish they weren't. Unless you have a new admirer, your husband is the culprit."

In the shelves behind Donovan sit three groups of photos representing what he has described to me as the three aspects of his life: reality, where the photos are of him and his family—hope, where the photos are of him and me—and fantasy, where a lone picture of him and Eric sits, because he sees Eric as the father he wishes he had. Donovan taught me to compartmentalize, just like he has here. Maybe I'm trying so hard to do it that my perception of reality is distorted to where I can't comprehend Christopher being so Donovan like.

Donovan's pen hits the desk. "Lily, I'm not doing so well with this distance thing. When I thought of us before it felt like being haunted by a ghost that's actually alive. Now I feel I'm mourning the loss of a loved one."

Anna enters the office. Her eyes drift away at the sight of me, and I can swear her energy dwindles. Donovan now seems uncomfortable in his own skin. Jealousy erupts within me.

This is bad. Maybe these notes really are from Christopher and I just want them to be from Donovan to the point where I refuse to see the obvious. I excuse myself, fleeing for home and knowing more than ever that serious damage control is required on my marriage.

৪৩

Christopher sits at his desk in the back corner of our partial-basement. "Seriously, Eric, I've no idea what to do," he says to his computer monitor. The pen in his left hand taps wildly on the desk, and he sounds utterly miffed. "We should have had the contract last week. Something is amiss."

"Look," Eric's voice emits through the speakers, "if the headliner has told their agent they want you then prepare the best you can and wait. Headlining bands often don't have much control."

Christopher flings the pen onto the desk. I feel he is tossing in the towel. "I just wish I knew if it's safe to order merchandise. That's the only way we might make money. Even then the venues take a twenty-percent cut. I don't know how we'll eat if not given sales clearance, let alone who will sell for us."

First notes from a questionable source; now unconfirmed tour dates that may lead to stubborn starvation. Something strange is going on. The universe smells like a trashcan outside of a Chinese restaurant during a heat wave.

19

Romantic faux dating, past lives intertwined, heart-soaring notes—they all create a cyclonic threat to my cherished marriage.

Yesterday, Donovan's assurance that he wasn't responsible for the letters of adoration only granted partial relief. My internal civil war goes far beyond that which can be equalized. Christopher has never failed to make me feel cherished in that special way only someone who loves every bit of your being can. Donovan is like that and more. He rocks my world on a spiritual level, enthralling me with his every motion. Once you know how it feels to have your soul satisfied, it's hard to not crave it, let alone resist caving to its temptation.

The problem might be that I've never exposed a certain side of myself to anyone but Donovan. With him it just kind of emerged, and I surrendered all vulnerability. I feel cheated because I can't be that way with my own husband. Am I too embarrassed, or do I really not want that with anyone else?

This must change—for the sake of my head—for the sake of my marriage.

I stand in the bathroom, clad in a black PVC cat suit—tail, ears, insanely tall boots, and little cover on my crotch. Before looking in the mirror, one last stomach-quelling breath is captured. Relief fans my sweaty brow upon seeing I don't look as ridiculous as I feel. My clammy, PVC glove-covered hands toy with a whip. Will the whip freak Christopher out?

Lord, what am I doing, and why am I questioning it? I never did years before. Donovan loved it when I surprised him like this. Then again, Donovan would have found me irresistible in a muumuu and mismatched turban.

Jitters set in as Christopher's Mini pulls into the driveway. I step into the smattering of light that beams from the candles lining the stairwell as he enters the house and closes the front door. "The children are with the nanny until ten." I sound like a phone sex operator. "I hope you are not too disappointed."

His keys and jaw drop in tandem along with my knees. My hand slides up his jeans and stops at the perfect spot to tell me this outfit is appreciated. I kiss my way up his body and slink the whip around his neck. Playfully, I tug. With frigid eyes he follows my lead up the stairs and into the candlelit bedroom. The whip is tugged in gentle suggestion he lie with me. A speck of fear lights his eyes.

I give him a gentle ultimatum. "Put your hands through the bars on the headboard." He swallows with force and obeys. After I use the whip to capture his hands, I yank down his pants and savor the taste of the creamy skin that trails to his groin. His uncharacteristic silence is replaced by gentle moans of pleasure.

With a maniacal grin, I scale him and flick one of the buttons on his shirt with my finger. My eyebrow cocks in self-righteousness before ripping his shirt open with a force that sends the buttons flying across the room and pinging off the walls. I grab a bottle of cinnamon Emotion Lotion from my new arsenal of toys and rub it over his lean muscles while blowing sensual warmth. Mercilessly, I take him higher and higher. My lips eventually suck him deep into the void. My tongue toys him with little flicks that are followed by clamping lips and pulses of suction. My lips pop away and leave him wanting more.

As his tension begins to dissipate I throw myself on him, slide him inside, and roll my hips into his, pressing down so deep that he has me completely filled. My grind is slow, yet unrestrained, and I savor every drop of pleasure it brings. I again take him to the edge, and then pull off before he reaches the point of no return. With a weakened disposition, he turns his beautiful blue gaze to me in a silent beg for mercy. Not only have I been rather unpitying, I'm more than ready for the grand finale myself.

I glide onto him, nuzzling my head into his neck with a purr. "I'll release you, but on one condition." My fingers toy with his baited lips. "You must promise that once released, you won't cower. I've unleashed the panther in me, now it's time to expose the tiger in you."

Christopher loses his face of submission and growls—bearing his teeth like he wants to go for my throat while tugging violently at the whip. The bed bounces with the force of a California tremor. The moment the whip is loosened he springs on me—pinning me to the bed as he goes down for the kill, his teeth ripping at my neck. His touch is perfect—violent enough to thrill, yet soft enough to feel safe. He has me enraptured, and I am utterly vulnerable to his every whim.

He jams himself into me with a guttural sound, and I clamp like heated shrink-wrap. Nothing is held back as he pounds into me. My body responds with a hot, liquid ache. I throw my head back with a muted scream as he shudders into me with a fanatical release, causing me to seize with pleasure in a violent rage.

Christopher draws me next to him in an embrace so gentle it's like the stroke of a feather. It brings me the kind of warmth and love in the afterglow that only he can—my heart and body completely satisfied.

Yet my soul sheds a tear.

20

Smack!

"Shit!" I scream after sliding with the grace of a hippo on ice skates and falling on my bum. "What the crap is on the floor?"

Jenny dashes in from the front of the store. Robert and Cindy bolt through the back door. "Oh my God! Lily, what happened?" Jenny shrieks. "You're bleeding all over the place! I'll call 911."

Splattered everywhere is the contents of a cake pan that was headed for the oven. Since it was Red Velvet, I look a gory mess. "Jenny, I'm fine. It's batter, not blood." I run my fingers across the floor and am reminded of a slippery bowling lane. "Is the floor coated in buttercream?"

Cindy smacks Robert on the arm. "Damn it, Robert! I thought you cleaned that!"

"I did!" he whines. I'm disappointed that he omitted a foot stomp.

Cindy lets him have it. "Obviously not very well. I swear Robert, one of these days your laziness is going to kill someone. That big, red smear could be Lily's blood."

"I'm sorry," Robert says to Cindy. "I wiped it up, but I must have missed some."

"Wiped it up!" Cindy asserts matter-of-factly. "That was six kilos of meringue buttercream! You have to mop it with detergent and extra hot water."

"But that damages my delicate skin. I don't want scaly, man hands like others around here have."

"Damn it, Robert! I swear—"

"Hey! Mr. and Mrs. Bickerson!" I interrupt while waving a hand in the air. "Would one of you please give me a hand?" Apologies are yammered as the three help me to my feet. My right ankle throbs, so I hop on my left foot, forgetting about the buttercream that still covers the floor. My arms turn me into a pinwheel as I start going down again.

"You okay?" Jenny asks after Larry, Curly, and Moan catch me.

"Yeah, I'm fine." Or so I genuinely think until I put weight on my right foot. The bolting pain causes me to jump, and the jump causes me to slide again. The Powerpuff Girls catch me just as I start to go down.

I lean on Cindy while Jenny and Robert dash off for ice and a chair. When Robert returns, he bounds with the attitude of a hero. "Here you go, beautiful boss." My eyes spin to heaven. He then berates a returning Jenny who is dashing in with the phone. "Nice of you to join us. Where's the ice?"

"Lily, you need to take this call," Jenny says, fretfully. "Antonia fell off a swing and hit her head. An ambulance is taking her to UCLA Medical Center."

The beeping of the heart monitor tethered to the person in the bed next to Antonia *thumps* in my head. Where the hell is the damn doctor? Doesn't he know there's a parent totally freaking out?

"Your daughter's in room six," a woman outside states. Thank God. Someone needs to stay strong and assure me Antonia is going to be all right, but at least Christopher will cry with me.

"Why didn't you call?" Donovan accosts. He bolts to the other side of the bed and kisses Antonia on the forehead. "Hey Scrappy," he says with a sympathetic tone. "Sounds like you took a pretty bad fall."

My head shakes to clear it. "Wait. What are you doing here? Did you tell them you're my husband?"

Donovan's stare tells me I should know the answer. "Jenny called to say you hurt your ankle because Robert is a klutz and that he was taking you to the hospital because you couldn't drive, and she couldn't reach Christopher. You had to change first because you were covered in red batter that wasn't blood. Oh, and an ambulance came because Antonia hit her head and blacked out. Geez, Lil, what is it with you and whacky counter girls named Jennifer? What did the doctor say?"

Jennifer? Oh Lord, Jennifer, from when I worked with Josette. How have I missed that similarity? "Nothing yet. By the time I arrived one had already ordered a CT scan, then went home at the end of her shift. We're awaiting test results."

Antonia wraps herself around Donovan's forearm like it's a huge teddy bear that brings forth security. "Uncle Scooby, you'll make sure I'm okay, right?"

"Of course." Donovan's words sound barricaded in his throat. His free hand glides across Antonia's brow, caressing the hair out of her eyes. "With me around, you will always be fine."

The image of a paternal Donovan with his mini-twin brings a gallop into my veins.

Donovan, something may have happened with her.

"Lily, are you okay? You look hazy."

Footsteps thunder in my head. Our tender moment is interrupted by the whip of the privacy curtain. My eyes jerk to the beautiful giant before us in shock. "Julian!"

"Lily!" Julian's eyes jet across the bed. "Donovan?" They then glide to Antonia and grow firm. Suddenly the room appears to be a confessional informing Julian his theories about Donovan's intentions were correct.

"Julian, thank God," I say in relief. "Do you have Antonia's test results?"

With the cock of an eyebrow he twists his head to bring his attention to the chart in his hands. "Um, yeah." His eyes scrutinize the papers. "Eccles, right?"

"Yes. I'm Lilyanna Eccles now." It's not only a statement to Julian, it's a reminder to my compartmentalized self.

"She has a very mild concussion. You'll have to watch her for the next twenty-four hours."

I exhale in relief. My eyes drift back to the still lovely, albeit disrupted, sight of Donovan and his twin. "See, you're going to be just fine." Donovan assures Antonia. His focus on her remains beautiful and, unlike his mind, unfazed by the presence of Julian.

Relief veils me when Christopher runs in and heads straight to Antonia's side. "I got here as fast as I could. I've been out of my mind with worry."

"Everyone's fine," I assure. "Julian—I mean, Dr. Sandowski just gave us the news."

Disappointment clouds Donovan's face at the arrival of Antonia's father. After releasing her hand with a little squeeze and a kiss, Donovan departs. He cups Julian's arm as he goes. "Thanks, Julian. By the way, Lily messed up her ankle at work today. Will you please take a look at it?" A quick smirk aimed at me is his only goodbye.

"Julian?" Christopher asks. "You all know one another?"

For the first time, the music from the two-years-apart dance calls. "Christopher, this is Dr. Julian Sandowski. Dr. Sandowski, my husband, Christopher."

Christopher staggers with a hint of uncertainty to greet Julian. "A pleasure."

Antonia calls out to her daddy, and Christopher goes to her side. A ton of bricks falls from the sky. Julian's head dips back, spouting a gusher of words. "Oh! This is the guy from Manchester!"

"All right. I'm up a gum tree. Someone want to fill me in?" Christopher asks rather impatiently.

"Julian and I dated when I was at the Culinary Institute. He was a lifesaver when my father took ill. Donovan and I owe him big time for that."

"You owe me nothing," Julian says. He rolls over a stool and motions for me to put my ankle in his lap. "The crazy tension gave me good training in bedside manner. How is your mom?"

"Not well. She's suffering from advanced Cirrhosis."

"I'm sorry to hear that. How's Donovan doing?" he measuredly asks while removing my sneaker.

"He's good—really good. He's a psychologist, married to a"—gorgeous, totally unfair looking—"nurse. Ouch!" I flinch at Julian's touch to my ankle.

"Psychologist? Really? Wow! That's disturb—that's great. How did you do this?" Julian asks, examining my ankle.

"Fleeing the bank. I never should have gone back for my Tommy Gun." Dr. Dreamy chuckles at my jest. "I slid on some buttercream at work."

"Slid, huh? Did you hear any kind of pop when it happened?"

"No, but I'm going to pop Robert for being a klutz and then not cleaning his mess."

"Can you walk on it?"

"Yeah, no problem."

"Okay, let's watch." Smugly, Julian crosses his arms.

My shoulders sag. "Fine! You win."

"Not even going to try to humor me, huh? Must be pretty bad," he concludes while rising. "We'll get it x-rayed. Can you take a few days off?"

Christopher chimes in so fast he almost interrupts. "She certainly can. Owning your own shop has to be good for something."

"You did it?" Julian asks with hopeful eyes.

"Yep! Pâtisserie de l'Amour in Westwood."

"Westwood! That's impressive." He crouches over Antonia and gives her hand a squeeze. "We'll get you home soon. Be nice to your mom. She's going to have a hard time walking for a few days." Julian then shakes Christopher's hand. He towers over him so much it is almost comical. "Nice to meet you."

"You as well," Christopher says, still looking bewildered. After Julian departs Christopher's jaw starts to flap, then quickly halts. Conversations regarding our two years apart are still off limits.

"Go ahead," I say, welcoming his questions with a gesture of openness. "You have carte blanche, but only for this one thing."

Christopher looks gobsmacked—like God came down and thwaped him one on the face. His eyes search the room as his head bounces like a marionette seeking thought. "Bloody hell! Is that what you did when we were apart?"

I nearly choke on his phrasing. A nurse comes in to wheel me off to x-ray, and the temptation to leave Christopher with a parting zinger is too great. "No, Christopher, that is what I did for seven months while we were apart. The rest is an even bigger secret."

Christopher's coloring switches from pasty to green as I ride out of the room. I'm totally going to pay for this.

21

Being stuck on a sofa on Halloween sucks, especially after already suffering two days of imprisonment. Once Christopher leaves, I'm defying the law and doing something he deems crazy—cleaning the house.

"There. Now you look the perfect lout," Christopher proclaims upon placing an eye patch on Graham. "Bugger, I left your sword in the boot of the people mover."

"When were you in Disneyland?" I wonder aloud. "I thought that died along with Mr. Toad's Wild Ride." Christopher's bloodshot eyes look at me like I've lost all touch with reality before his meaning sinks in. "Ah, the trunk of the mini-van." Dear God, where does he get this stuff? If nothing else, my husband is unique.

Christopher returns from the garage, and Graham claims his weapon with enthusiasm. Antonia hops in wearing a Bugs Bunny suit. Could it be any clearer how she spends her time with her uncle?

Christopher bends to kiss me before leaving. His droopy features show he's sleep-deprived. My lips surrender a long, luscious kiss in appreciation before I murmur into his ear. "You've been amazing while working your butt off at your job and with the band. How about I make it up to you with another special night?" He salivates so much drool may soon slide down his chin.

"Daddy, come on!" Antonia tugs at Christopher's shirt with impatience. Graham is already at the door, shifting back and forth on his legs in an effort to contain his excitement.

Christopher takes my hand. Ever since the cat suit incident his voice has been laced with adoration. "We won't go too far. I love you."

"I love you too. Enjoy every moment."

They head off into the dusk, and my eyes scan the facts of my existence. If I can't at least straighten this room, I'm either taking Christopher up on the offer of a maid or renting a bulldozer.

Twisting myself off of the sofa, I grab the mail that has piled up and hobble to the recycling can in the kitchen. A letter addressed to me is the only thing that doesn't find the bottom of the bin. A twinge of disturbance hits my brain when I discover it contains a slip of pink stationary. Its top dons a single bouquet of daisies.

Every breath I take, every bump in the road, every twist and turn in life reminds me how much I need you in my arms.

The computer-printed envelope lacks a return address, and has a postmark from last week in Santa Monica, which is after Donovan denied his involvement. Unlike the others, this one sounds exactly like his notes—the kind he romanced me with once upon a time. Enchantment twirled around me every time I uncovered a new treasure, fueling my desires to compose my own.

A twisted moment of hope breezes past, wrapping me in the comfort of days gone by. Suddenly the warmth turns cold, and I quiver, questioning if he is aware of his actions. The nefarious frost that slithers around my spine brings forth concern that Donovan is regressing and needs to be put back on the funny farm, yet my heart longs to surrender in harmony with his madness. Without him, I will never be complete.

I hobble into our home library and retrieve a list of Donovan's trigger points. While it has diminished over the years, five remain. New Year's Eve brings about depression. Purple dresses remind him of the New Year's Eve he shattered my emotions. He won't eat cereal, because it reminds him of Bob's harassment that fateful night in the supermarket that lead to our demise. Handwritten jottings of any kind often bring a sense of loss. Lastly, not being seen for who he is makes him wish he were someone else. Just before the notes started, he said Anna doesn't understand him and he felt he was wasting time being himself.

The letter is slid into a book along with the notes. When he comes over at lunch tomorrow I'll get to the bottom of this madness.

❧

Donovan's visit is likely to be a huge pain in the ass. Not only do I need to talk to him about the letter I got yesterday, today we need to finish discussing the affairs of Count Draculana. Apprehension shrouds me as I greet Donovan at the door. Without even a peck on the cheek he gaits into the kitchen, places a bag of food onto the table, and heads for the refrigerator. "What do you want to drink?" he asks.

"Nothing. I have a Margarita in the family room."

Donovan follows me as I head off to grab my glass. "So you're drinking while on pain pills. Yeah, that sounds exactly like something you would do." His eyes flip to heaven. "What gives?"

"I have a bum ankle, I'm trapped at home, and we need to deal with the drama of Lana John Silver. It's making me a tad crazy."

"Liar." He smirks, nabs my cocktail, and dumps it in the kitchen sink.

"Fine," I huff. "Let's eat and review this stuff. I need it over with."

"Now let's see if I can figure this one out." Smugly he leans against the breakfast bar. "The last time I saw you was at the hospital. You were in massive pain and wouldn't admit it. We saw Julian ... Ah! Setting your sights on the good doctor must have put your hormones in a spin."

"Stop. Let's eat before my blood sugar crashes."

"So your scrawny dreamboat doesn't measure up to ... How was it you described Julian in the past? The Greek god whose incredible body is mouthwateringly handsome and perfect in every way?"

I turn back and grump at him. "Stop it, Donovan. Christopher may be trim, but he isn't built like a kid anymore. Besides, those are cruel words coming from the man who married a tropical Playmate." Suddenly the air reminds me of viscous pea soup. My vision hides from the truth my mind scarcely braves to face. "When it comes to intimacy, you are the only one who can satisfy my soul. I'll always love you, Donovan. Always."

"Hey," he steps forward and raises my chin. His breath cools my pooling tear. "I'm sorry. What's bringing this on?"

"I got another note. They bring back so many memories of how fantastic we were."

"Lily, I would love to send you letters again, but I don't dare for so many reasons." His voice is melancholy yet strained and holds its resolve.

"Are you sure? When I see you, you push me away, but in those notes you pull me closer. It's like you're two people and you don't know it."

"Lily, that's crazy."

"Is it? Which way is more like the real you?"

He catches a breath, then stutters it out. "You'd better show me those letters."

Wordlessly I lead him to the library. His hands subtly quiver as he takes each slip of paper. "Are you all right?" I ask.

"I still don't do well with notes, especially right now," he says, rolling his neck and shoulders. He sets the notes on the desk, then rearranges them while glaring and tapping his knuckle on his lip. "Someone laid them out on a computer, printed a single page, and cut it. So while it could initially have been compulsive, the rest are premeditated."

"Donovan, whoever did this knows where I work and live, along with how to get into my car. Could you possibly be doing it without knowing?"

Donovan becomes expressionless. A disturbance seems

to brew within. He leans over the desk, and his hands press down in symbolic support of his cognitive weight. "Motivated forgetting," he mutters. It causes the hair on the nape of my neck to lift. "Not only is it highly unlikely, these don't sound like they are from me."

His fingers press harder onto the desk, the tips going white. The notion of Donovan sending these and not knowing once seemed disturbing yet romantic; now the possibility is terrifying. "But Donovan, one of your triggers is that if people don't see you as yourself, you wish you were someone else. Just after we got back, you said that Anna—"

Donovan cuts me off with a snap of his head, making my worry all the greater. "That's it!" His hands shove down on the desk, and the leverage propels him back. "I don't need to put up with you making phony notes just to get my attention." He storms out of the library. His feet *thump* down the hall, and the slam of the front door leaves me more stymied than ever.

My hands fly to the sky as I speak to the universe. "Ladies and gentlemen, please put your hands together and welcome back, Dr. Jekyll and Mr. Hiding!"

22

My feet dance me down the stairs. I'm being sprung from jail and am thrilled to return to work after nearly a week of incarceration. I head into the garage. A *thunk* comes from outside when someone drops something into my mail slot. Sneakered footsteps scamper down the driveway before a running car speeds off. It's before dawn. Who could be leaving me mail at this hour? Nervously, I open the mailbox, wondering if I've just been left anthrax. Inside, is an envelope sporting a computer-printed label addressing it to Christopher. The return address is that of his job in Hollywood, yet it lacks the record company's logo.

My suspicion kicks into overdrive, and I violate my husband's privacy. Inside the envelope resides a simple note on lavender stationary adorned with hydrangeas.

A wise man treasures his wife, or someone else will.

Okay, seriously. What the crap?

A black smudge hides under the label. Underneath it, the previous address is perfectly eradicated, making the San Diego postmark irrelevant. Someone is certainly going through a lot of trouble to get a message across.

ॐ

"Donovan, please," I groan into my cell phone as I cower in the back of my shop. Hearing that I got another note sent his inner lion roaring. "I'm really scared these are coming from you."

"You mean you hope they're from me."

Why did I bite the bullet and call him? I should have stuck it in a gun and shot myself instead. "No, the possibility freaks me out. Last I saw you, you muttered something about motivated forgetting. You're just as concerned, aren't you?"

"Fine, Lily. I'll swing by in a few hours."

Donovan's image on my cell phone is slammed onto the desk in similar fashion as to how you used to be able to slam down an old phone. I wince before yanking the phone back; thankful I didn't crack its face in lieu of Donovan's.

"Hey, Lily." Jenny dashes forth with a twinkle in her eye. "Do you have more than one brother?"

"Nope. Thank God. I have enough problems with one."

"Then you'd better put your ring back on before you walk out front."

"Who's out there?" Jenny is far too excited for it to be someone famous.

"Last week some Adonis came in and was oddly glad you weren't here. Now he's back hoping you are. Seriously, Lily, this guy massively rivals Donovan. In fact, he's so tall he could take Donovan down in a heartbeat."

I snort at Jenny and head for the front, now knowing exactly who's here. "Hi, Julian," my voice sings.

"You look a lot better," he says. "How's the ankle?"

"Good, but I can no longer play a didgeridoo."

With a snicker he rattles his head. Jenny's fussing behind the counter and her faux coyness reek of begging for an introduction. "Jenny, I'd like you to meet my jailer. Julian, this is Jenny."

"Nice to meet you," he says. His smile flashes with a dazzle that may make her pass out. "Your jailer?" he asks me.

"It's your fault I went stir crazy last week. I gave myself a lecture on the social value of cream cheese. Then I made, and took, bets against myself while playing solitaire. I can't decide if I'm in the hole or ahead seven hundred, sixty dollars and twenty-three cents because of you."

Jenny steps up to be helpful. How did she manage to hold back this long? "Is there anything I can get for the doctor?"

My God, girl! Put your tongue back in your mouth.

"Yeah, I'll grab some stuff for the ER crew," Julian replies.

He goes for his wallet, and I stop his arm. "Load him up, Jenny. It's on me. Do you have time for a cup of coffee?"

Julian shoots me a sideways glance. My shoulders drop in surrender. "I've cut back. It will only be my second caffeine shot."

"Yeah, and how many have half-cafs have you had already?"

"Shh!" I scold before bringing our cups to a table. Immediately my inquisition begins, because Jenny is going to be all over me the second Julian leaves. "So, how did you wind up in Los Angeles?"

"Lily, why does any man do what he does?"

"You? Mr. Career Path? Mr. I Have To Be Out of School In—"

His cheeks flush. "You made your point. After we split, I was pretty lonely until I met Doreen in Med School. Fate brought our internships to almost the same county. It was great until we got to actually spend time together. Man, I was wishing I was back in Med School!"

I chuckle. "That sounds bad."

"So, uh, Donovan's a psychologist? Didn't see that one coming. I've always been a little worried about you being around him." Suddenly he stiffens. "No, actually, for years I've thought of tracking you down, because I've been so concerned about his temperament."

Lord, is he really going to dig up last decade's testosterone battle? "Julian, there was never anything to worry about."

Jenny bounces up with a pink box that she wasted our best ribbon tying. "Here you go."

"Thank you," he says while beaming at her. "I also need to order a dessert for Thanksgiving."

"I highly recommend a pumpkin mousse cake," Jenny says coyly. "It'll knock your stethoscope off." Lord, she's even twirling her hair.

"Sounds perfect," Julian replies. The corners of his lips practically glide to his eyes.

The appearance of Cupid's Arrow makes me feel like a third wheel. While heading for the kitchen, I muse at how Donovan has again lost a girl to Julian.

&

Donovan enters through the back door of the bakery and grabs my arm. "Come on." He drags me to my desk.

"Why are you being such a dick? You're scaring the crap out of me."

"Why? Because the last time I acted this way I was being abused and on the verge of losing my mind? Because now you're getting notes that you claim are from me, knowing perfectly well I'm praying they aren't?"

"You forget there's also the possibility that my family is in danger. I don't know what's freaking me out more, the fear of what may be happening or how you're handling it."

He steps back and the anger clears from his face. "I'm sorry. I'm worried no matter where they're coming from. Just let me see them." Donovan looks to my desk where a bouquet of vibrant fall colors bloom. "Where did those come from?" He's doing a poor job of suppressing animosity.

"Christopher. Where did that come from?" I ask just as cantankerously, snapping my finger onto his wedding ring.

His eyes drop in regret of his tone. "Sorry. I thought that maybe they came with the note."

"No, you just don't want anyone else giving me flowers." I smack the stack into his palm.

Closing his eyes he mutters, "You're right. I don't."

I push back the lump that lodges in my throat and retrieve the latest note from my purse. "This is the one that came for Christopher. Take a good look at the envelope. Who would send letters trying to keep us together?"

Donovan's eyes flicker back and forth. Suddenly they halt. "The husband of the woman he's having an affair with. That slimy prick. I'm gonna rip his scrawny little arms off!"

"That's impossible. Christopher would never cheat. He isn't capable."

"Everyone is capable. It's just a matter of opportunity and if they choose to take it. You should know that."

He's right. I know it all too well.

He rotates through the notes, scrutinizing each one in search of a clue that reveals that he is not a party to this madness. He then braves opening the one that arrived this morning. Donovan's tension deepens at the sight of the paper. Like a shot he heads for the door. "I have to go."

"You know who did this, don't you?"

Donovan halts. "Client-therapist confidential information," he firmly states. My concerns about Donovan's sanity and Christopher's fidelity are addressed not only with words, but also from eyes that emit so much heat my cheeks feel like hell's flames surround me. "Rest assured that you have nothing to worry about. This will stop today!" He continues to storm out.

"Oh, no you don't! You are not allowed to run out of here without telling me who it is," I insist while in hot pursuit.

Donovan's stride doesn't falter as he enters the back lot. "You have to trust me, Lily. It's better that way, and start locking the back door!"

I slip in the way of his driver's door. "Someone is threatening my husband and you want me to ignore it? Anyone that foolish should be in a Tarot deck with a big zero over her head."

He practically spits his words at me. "If you're so keen on not ignoring it, then why haven't you called the police?"

"Because I thought it might be you!"

"And you're still concerned that it is and I've snapped. Great, now even you don't trust me."

"Trust has nothing to do with it, but protecting my family does. How would you feel if this happened to you?"

"I would trust you, just like I always have. Call the police. We both know there's nothing they can do. Meanwhile, I will actually fix the problem. Now will you please get out of my way?"

"Here we go again!" I storm back into the bakery in disgust of our situation.

&

I feel like a stalker—sitting in my minivan, parked next to Donovan in the lot of his office complex. Once his key is almost in his car door, I press the button for my passenger window, rolling it down behind him. "Can we talk? Please."

His shoulders drop. "Yeah, I've been waiting for this. I thought we were past the sneak attack phase though."

After this morning's display I've no patience for his bellyaching. "The need to protect my family has nothing to do with my ability to trust you." I unlock the passenger door.

His eyes meander to where the click of the lock emanated before he leans back, glances around, and gets in the car. "I'm sorry," he says, his voice is remorseful as he puts his elbow on the car door, and leans his head into his hand. "I really overreacted about this whole situation."

"Why won't you tell me who it is? I don't know who I'm more concerned about, you or my children."

"I filed for a Civil Harassment Order on Mike today. The police know everything I do. Trust me, the guy is freaked and wants to stay off of the police department's radar. You won't get another note."

"Mike who?" I ask.

"Palance. He's been harassing me since Christopher fired

him."

"How do you know—He's a patient! That creepy bastard is a patient!"

"They're called clients, Lil, and I can't—"

"Oh, yes, you'd better! He's a patient of yours. How else would you know—" Suddenly, the obvious kicks my butt with a wallop. If I didn't have my seatbelt on, I'd be booted into the next county. "He sent those notes trying to scare Christopher into backing out of the tour! That's it, isn't it?"

Donovan's eyes roll so hard they may spiral down his throat. "You know I can't talk about these things."

"Really? Come on!" I gesture like I want to upside him one on his head. "Ugh! It makes so much sense. They started right after Christopher fired him and the tour came through."

"Okay, fine. I know a little too much about him, and I asked Christopher to keep him away from you. He wanted to fire Mike immediately, but I persuaded him to wait so it wouldn't be so obvious. Are you happy now?"

"You do know this has nothing to do with my faith in you, right?"

"Yeah. I can't blame you for how you acted," he says. That may be so, but he look so hurt. "It's just that you're all I've ever really had, and now even that is nearly gone. This distance thing sucks." He bails out the door and drives off, taking half of my soul with him.

23

The sensation of my unearthly foot hitting the ground after coming off of the last step again brings forth apprehension. Heading down a long, dark corridor, several doors reside before me, each with a white glow seeping around the edges. Sadness burns my throat as I pass the door entered on my previous sojourn down this hall. Daring a few steps further, I opt for a portal across the way. The moment it opens, happiness floods me.

"What do you see?" Susan asks.

The image is soul soothing. "An open field. Flowers. Lots and lots of wild flowers." I feel a familiar presence, and giggle with no idea why.

"Do you know your name?"

"Clara," I say without question.

"Is it day or night?"

The words roll out effortlessly. "Dusk. We've been here all day assembling tents. We are war refugees. New Bedford. Seventeen seventy-eight."

"Why are you laughing?"

"I'm with someone who makes me happy. Christopher— I mean, Charles. It's getting dark, and I'm tired. He's brought me into a tent, and I'm drifting off in his arms." My mind begins to fade when I jerk and gasp.

"What is happening?" Susan inquires. Her tone attempts to bring forth composure.

"Someone has bolted into our tent, hissing the word traitor. He's has Charles by the collar, and is trying to kill him."

"Do you know who it is?"

"My brother, Daniel. He doesn't trust this man."

"Why?" Susan asks.

"Daniel discovered he is British. Charles was sent to destroy our village by setting fire to our tents while we sleep, but he would never do that. Daniel keeps screaming at him to stay away from me."

Noise builds outside, sending my pulse racing. My breath turns rapid, knowing the villagers want to kill Charles. A woman runs in, pointing to Daniel in accusation of him being the traitor. She is a Tory and is protecting Charles, thinking he will still turn on us. As Clara refuses her command to flee, my current self identifies the accuser as Lana Beckett.

I am overpowered from behind by a woman who cups my mouth and drags me off. Charles follows after us, fleeing as the villagers take Daniel away.

"No! You can't take him from me!" I scream on Clara's behalf, defying Anna, the woman who drags her away from Daniel. Clara continues to be stifled while vowing never to be silenced again. "I told Daniel months ago that we should go elsewhere, before I ever met Charles. That we should find shelter alone and be free, but he never listens to me! How do I get him to listen to me?"

Susan speaks rapidly. "Lily, we need to stop. When I count to three, start floating away. One. Two. Three. Pull away, Lily. Pull away. Return to me."

24

On today's episode of "Lilyanna Eccles Must Be Totally Insane," I again attempt to become friends with my sister-in-law. For years I have known my guest star to be a sweet lady who is dedicated to her husband and daughter. However, the last time I tried to get to know her, she lied about martial arts lessons and made me feel like I had the personality of a wet noodle. Today I hope to walk away feeling a step closer toward friendship by making the small gesture of meeting Anna at her work for a fifteen-minute coffee break. Even with our tiny amount of time, we struggle for conversation. Maybe her job is getting the best of her.

"I can't imagine working around all these patients," I say, toying with the rim of my paper cup as we sit in the hospital's cafeteria. How trim Anna looks compared to her oversized uniform is distracting. Lately it seems she is going for the comfy look. "You must be a strong person to help people while they're suffering."

"It can be a challenge," she responds, sounding bored, "but if you have the ability to turn into someone else, even just for a moment, you can walk away from pretty much anything and be unfazed."

So Donovan and I aren't the only ones who compartmentalize. I wish I could be as unaffected by life as she appears to be.

Anna's eyes drift off into space while I struggle to find a topic she deems conversation-worthy. "I'm sure Christopher would be mortified if he knew my cluelessness as to how his soccer team is doing. Mind bringing me up to speed?"

She flashes a smile, but can't be bothered to look at me.

"I'm sure Christopher would never be disappointed in you."

"He's an amazing man. So is Donovan. We are both very lucky."

Anna brightens. "Donovan is incredible. I am lucky to have him, and I will do all I can to make him happy." Her voice is sprinkled with idolatry. Whenever Donovan isn't around she sounds like a different person, but as soon as his name comes up she changes back.

"You have always seemed very dedicated to him."

"He's very dedicated to me, too. I'll make sure he is never alone, just like my daughter will never see me as anything less than perfect. That's pretty much all that matters around here, right?" Anna rises, then looks directly into my eyes with a seemingly genuine smile. It's something she rarely does, and it freaks me out. "It was really nice of you to come by. This little visit perked up my day. We should do it more often. Call me again, okay?"

The enigma marches on.

25

With a single motion, Christopher sends my heart racing. Sparks fly with a *crack* when he plugs in a light. "Aw, blow me!" he exclaims. His colorful slang causes me to choke on my cocktail.

I've reclined on the patio for three hours while watching hilarity ensue. It started when Christopher bought a playhouse for the girls. Anna, now known as Mrs. My Husband Bought A Fixer-Upper And I Have To Deal With It, offered to help with the assembly—her husband offered to watch. This would be long over if Donovan hadn't said, "Hey, this thing needs overhead lighting," and escaped to the hardware store. Two hours later, Donovan has completed his useless contribution and reclines next to me; both of us partaking in spiritus frumenti while I fear my house will burn down.

"Hey, watch the effing and blinding," I mind Christopher. "There are children and ladies present."

Anna examines Donovan's handiwork. "Honey, I think you may have crossed your wires."

"Color me shocked," I say. "Donovan's had his wires crossed ever since I can remember."

"Nope! Only since Thanksgiving fifteen years ago," he teases. "All right, I'll get off my butt and help again."

"Yeah, I'll join you," I offer out of guilt. Concurrently, we sip our cocktails and sink deeper into our chairs.

Christopher's head bounces as he rants. "Now why would we want to ruin your good time? I'm sure you'd rather lounge around and watch me go off."

"Well, actually, yes. That would be far more entertaining," I say.

"Yeah, we'd rather sit here and give you Omar Sharif," Donovan adds.

"Omar Sharif?" I ask.

Christopher looks at me agape while Donovan lets me have it. "Man, Christopher is right. Your Cockney is so bad even your rhyming slang sucks."

"Bloody 'ell! Is that any way to talk to yur skin an blister?" I say to Donovan. In the corner of my eye, Christopher cringes.

Donovan is all too quick to reply. "Boy, that one sure fits. If anyone is a blister to me—"

Christopher turns indignant. "Oh, why don't you two pissed-up cheeky yobs put a cork in it and bomb off somewhere."

"What did he say?" Donovan asks with a snicker.

"He told us to go to hell."

"Ah."

Our antics are interrupted by the buzz of my cell phone. Sadly it was set to silent, else I would have recognized the custom ringtone of galloping horses representing the four horsemen of the Apocalypse and stayed in my chair. It's either get this over with now or Buckaroo Pestilence will call the store. God only knows what Mom would say to the staff.

Slipping into the library for a moment of privacy, I hope for a rock to appear, not for me to hide under but to bang my head on. "Hi, Mom," I answer brightly, certain that she can hear my eyes roll and my body cave.

"Hi, Lily. Has Christopher left for his tour yet?"

Lord! Already? "No, Mom. It doesn't start for several months."

"Tell me more about who he is touring with. Is Eric coming with him? Will they come to Rhode Island?"

"No, Mom. Definitely neither one of those things. He's only hitting major stadiums in big cities."

"I was thinking if they played at Larry's Tavern they could come by, and I could fix them dinner. Are you sure they won't be in the area?"

Donovan enters in search of a book. Finding one on cocktails, he pulls it down and flips through it. "Pretty sure, Mom," I say. I slip my hand over the phone and whisper to Donovan, "You are not going to believe this conversation! It's a whole new level of crazy."

Donovan smothers his face with his hand and groans. "Dear God, what now?"

"Is Christopher there?" Mom asks. "I was hoping to congratulate him in person."

Oh, no way is that happening. How stupid does she think I am? "No, Mom. Christopher and Anna are setting up a playhouse for Antonia and Sunshine."

"*Shh*. Now she'll know I'm here!" Donovan whispers.

"Oh, is Donovan there?" Mom asks. "Let me talk to him."

"No, Mom. Donovan is helping."

"Oh, I'll just try his cell in a few minutes then."

"Turn off your phone so it goes to voicemail," I whisper to Donovan. "She's going to call you."

He throws his hands in the air. "Thanks for nothing!" He then motions for my phone. "Let me get it over with while I'm half-crocked."

I hand the crazy man the phone while concerned that he may need a new shrink. "Hi, Mom!" Donovan says a little too brightly. He then contorts his face as if gagging. It causes me to chuckle. "Yeah, Mom. Everyone is fine. We were going to call you a little later."

"Liar!" I whisper, swatting his arm and giggling.

"I don't know. I think we are having ham because Lily always says you are what you eat, and you know what she's like."

"Hey!" I say. He reaches out and grabs my arm, pulling me close and stealing a nibble off of my ear before putting his hand on my head and shoving me away, causing us both to snicker. It might be time for us to stop drinking those Pumpkin Pie Martinis.

"No, Mom, Lily and I are horsing around. She's not only

an amazing cook, she's become quite the bartender."

"Don't mention alcohol to a cranky lush with Cirrhosis!" I whisper fervently. Donovan's face contorts again, but this time its in confusion. "What?" I ask.

He puts his hand over the receiver. "She's laughing and calling me James again."

I baulk and leave. "I'm out of here. I've had enough crazy for the day." Seriously, why on earth does that man try so hard?

Inside the kitchen, I find Anna searching a cabinet. "Can I help you find something?" She jerks at my voice.

"Oh, sorry," she says timidly. "I just thought I'd try to lend a hand. Is there anything I can help with?"

Yeah, like I want *her* touching my food. "No, thanks. I think we are all set." Donovan emerges from the library with his head hung low. "Hey," I say to him. "You okay?"

He digests thought before he speaks. His flaring nostrils and grimace of irony tell me he's a kaleidoscope of anger and confusion. "I'm fine. It's just hard knowing Mom's suffering. I also hate that a part of me feels she's getting what she deserves."

"Donovan, remember how she always told us you have to lie in the bed you make?"

"Yeah, but ..." Donovan darts to Anna who has her hand over a pot of simmering stew. He yanks it back just as she releases, sending a handful of salt flying over her shoulder. "Seeking luck?" he asks with a broad smile.

"I was only trying to help. It tasted a little bland."

Donovan's grip on her wrist tightens. "Anna, we've talked about this. I don't know what it is with your taste buds, but you need to lay off the salt." His eyes land on me. *Could I have possibly screwed up more? I never should have let you go.* "I'll be back in ten minutes. Have another one of those drinks ready." I follow him to the door and he stops me. "Actually, cut me off indefinitely. People like me shouldn't drink." He begins his journey, and I can't help but feel that his path is paved in regret.

26

Gastric ulcers grow like fertilized bamboo as the phone rings. My task of verifying that Mom's will is up to date feels like I'm burying a body before God has taken the spirit. Hopefully she won't answer and will neglect calling me back. If I'm really lucky, Godzilla will attack California, making it impossible for all calls to get through and planes to take off for the next decade.

"Hello?" a weak voice answers.

Damn. "Hi, Mom. It's Lily."

"Lily, dear! How is Christopher?"

Some things never change. "Everyone's great, Mom. Look, I really don't want to have this conversation, and it's unfair to beat around the bush. I've been put in charge of making sure your final wishes are upheld. Would you please verify that the latest copy of your will is in your safe deposit box? We don't want any question when we retrieve it."

"You haven't gone to my safe deposit box yet?" She sounds freaked. "You didn't misplace the key, did you?"

"No, Mom. We will retrieve your will when the proper, respectful time comes."

I sense her hand brushing me off. "If you had bothered to get it, you would know that it is current. Everything goes to Graham and Sunshine."

Two out of three, huh? Dementia is an evil beast. What a horrible thing to forget a grandchild exists. "That's a great idea to leave everything to the grandchildren. Since trust funds for Graham and Antonia are already established, why don't you leave everything to Sunshine?"

"I wouldn't want Graham to think his grandmother does not love him. He should be included."

"Okay, so everything goes to Graham, Antonia, and Sunshine."

"Oh, no." Her voice is riddled with warning. "Nothing goes to Antonia. I will have no association with that demon spawn."

"What?" I say, nearly choking. That comment was so far over the line it jumped past the equator and landed at the South Pole.

"Then again, I suppose it is not her fault," Mom continues. "I don't blame you for not telling her, but have you at least told Christopher?"

"Told Christopher what?" My mortification makes it sound more like a demand than a question.

"Oh, Lily, please! You gave birth to her eight and a half months after you were here for Christmas. You and Donovan claimed that you had visited friends that morning. Christopher and Anna were off with Graham so you could have done anything you wanted and did. Don't tell me you haven't figured this one out yourself."

My emotions take over, causing my diplomacy filter to fail. "Are you fucking kidding me? I've tolerated a lot of your bullshit, but this has gone too far!"

"Lilyanna Beckett, watch your language!"

"Eccles! It's Eccles, Mom. It's been Eccles, faithfully, for ten years."

"Faithfully!" she mocks. "Then explain why Antonia looks just like Donovan. Christopher must be blind if he can't see the truth. I thought more of him than that."

Sadly, both sides of me know that her suspicions are not unfounded, because when there is no protection, it doesn't take a male moment of pleasure for the little swimmers to release.

Damn it! We stopped! How much longer will I feel this guilt? Or is the question, when will I accept my error?

My voice booms like dynamite. "Antonia looks like Donovan because they are related through me, or have you forgotten that Donovan is your child too?"

"Sharing genes never mattered to either of you before."

My brain is about to boil out of my skull. After over a decade of keeping my emotions in check and being a dutiful daughter, despite my better judgment, I finally let her have it.

"The hell it didn't! Why do you think Donovan and I split? It had nothing to do with your twisted plan to keep us apart. We both wanted families and weren't willing to involve a child in a web of lies. The only thing you have ever had a hand in with us is brutally destroying and nearly killing your son!" I manage to stop just short of calling her an evil, manipulating cunt. God, I don't want my family to be this way.

Mom responds by plunging the jagged knife in even deeper, dragging it across my chest, then heading for the salt. "If that is how you choose to see it, then obviously you are a terrible parent! I hope that someday karma will bite you in the ass and you will have to lock up your uncontrollable brats. Maybe if you had been beaten like Donovan, your tone would be more respectful."

God, please bring my nineteen fifties subservient mother back. Who is this delusional woman filling her body?

"You don't deserve Christopher!" she berates. "I don't want to see you again unless you spare him of who you are. They would have a better life without you. In fact, don't come home for Christmas, any of you! Just let me die the shamed woman I am. Hopefully someday you'll find the same fate!" Her phone flies across the room with a blood-curdling *slam*.

⅛

Smack!

My vegetable cleaver lands on a clove of garlic, smashing it to a pulp before I drag the knife over it, smearing its smelly goodness over the wood cutting board. This is much like how I kill spiders, not giving them a chance at mercy. If the creepy bastards cross into my territory, they asked for it.

Smack!

Again the cleaver mutilates a clove. The splat is then minced with heavy thuds that slam grooves into my cutting board and dulls my knife. *That woman's* words haunted me all night. I've strived to find virtue in her only to be rudely insulted time and time again.

Smack! Smack! Smack!

Christopher flops onto a stool across from me at the kitchen bar, interrupting my slaughter. Dreamily he rests his chin in his hand, his head tilted to the side with his long, soft-brown hair shadowing his hooded gaze. His presence brings me back to the best part of my reality.

"Coffee," he mutters.

"What? You hate coffee."

"Coffee," he repeats, barely conscious.

His natural glow brings out my smile and causes my anger to dissipate. "Seriously, who are you? Since when do you drink coffee?"

"I don't. The stuff is bloody awful, but I'm at the end of me rope. The one night I had time to sleep *someone* kept me awake with her tumbling and sighing. Then she finally gave me some peace at four by getting up, only to come down here and make a ruckus. After an hour, I'm surrendering to the enemy."

"I'm sorry, darling." I say with a pouty lip. "How about some strong black tea instead?"

Suddenly his eyes pop open, and the blue orbs in front of me dazzle. "I've a better idea. There are still items in that nightstand of yours we have yet to use." He reaches out and halts my chopping before guiding me to the stairs. A few steps up the collage-lined stairwell, I tug back on his hand.

"Come here," I say, motioning with my finger. "Look." Inside a collage from our first year together, I point to a picture of him jousting with a drumstick on his first Thanksgiving. "You know what I remember most about that day?"

"How I almost cut off me finger when I tried to carve

the turkey?"

I chuckle. "No, though looking back that was rather entertaining. What I remember most is what happened after you left. You called to wish me good night and said words that changed my life forever." He steps down behind me and enrobes my waist. Our eyes blur over the collage as the memories flow. "You said Grace wanted me to be the daughter she never had. It scared the breath right out of me. I had never thought much about us in the long term, but when you said that everything changed. It was one of the biggest moments in my life, and it ultimately led to our marriage. I love you, and I love my life with you. You bring so much light into my world."

Christopher kisses my head and tightens his hold. "I didn't think it was possible to love you any more than I did then, but now I know love was only beginning to grow. I love you more now than ever, and I know that tomorrow I will love you more still."

With a little nudge, he takes me up the stairs, reminding me of the beauty of our marriage.

ℬ

Thanks to my amazing husband, and two of his Martinis, when Donovan and crew arrive relaxation is no longer alien to my universe. However, about an hour after their arrival, I concede that no matter how enjoyable the day is, a sense of incompleteness will follow me. An eraser rests in my hands, but can I dare the risk of smearing the shadow, thus extending its depth?

I cower in the library. If I make this call, the phone in my hand may turn out to be my own voodoo doll. Just shy of pressing the call button, every muscle in my face clenches, and tears begin their descent. I miss my Mom. I miss my real Mom—the one who loved her children. The one with whom I played with dolls. The one who played old records and danced around the house like a teenybopper. That beautiful woman who tried to be both a nineteen fifties housewife and my teenage best friend. I love her, and I miss her.

Can I possibly take it if this call goes the way of the last one? I don't want that to be my last memory of her, but I can't take another betrayal. The whole situation is so incredibly wrong.

I set down the device, yet my hand remains on it in hopes that my touch will transmit my message. "Happy Thanksgiving, Mom. I love you." With a deep swallow I remove my hand and walk away. It's time to hold my children.

27

"Good morning, boss!" Jenny cheerfully sings. I'm not buying it for the price of a poppy seed.

My eyes refocus on my notes for the Anthem Records anniversary party we are co-catering in three months. "Good morning, Jenny. Did you have a nice Thanksgiving?"

"Umm, it was all right, but a little disappointing," she claims with a faint pout.

I am so playing into her hand and know it. "And why was that? Too much studying? Still can't decide between Art History and Marine Biology?"

"Today I'm leaning toward Geology." Her fingers toy along the antique display case that holds the day's goods. "Thanksgiving was a little uneventful, and it got me wondering. Are you having your annual New Year's Eve party this year?"

I view my sketch of a cake shaped like a record with a critical eye. This is a terrible idea in light of my generous budget. "It wouldn't be an annual party if I didn't." I set down my pencil and fake pondering. "Then again, maybe I shouldn't. With everything going on here, and—"

"Lily, that's not funny!"

"What? Do I need to work on my bedside manner?" My lips purse to suppress laughter at the poor girl who slumps in disgust with herself.

"Is it that obvious?" Jenny asks.

"Oh, yes. Obvious is indeed the word. So is discernible, transparent, palpable … Yes, we are having a party. Yes, I will invite Julian. I thought you were sneak attacking him when he came in for his Thanksgiving mousse cake and boldly slipping him your number tucked into a cream puff?"

Jenny turns sulky, making it harder not to laugh. "We were so busy I didn't get the chance. Robert helped him."

I groan at the thought of Robert's feminine flamboyance versus Julian's masculine charm. "I'm sure Robert loved that way more than Julian did. Jenny, why is it you fall apart over guys like Julian, yet when celebrities like Johnny Depp come in you are totally calm and collected?"

"Because Julian is real and Johnny isn't." Her tone makes her odd statement sound like a common fact that shouldn't faze me.

"Oh, I'm sure Mr. Depp would love to hear this."

Jenny shakes her head at my obliviousness. "The personalities of movie stars are often best left in my mind where I don't feel I have to be a perfect ten to get their attention. So, if you'd invite Julian to your party ..."

"I'll try to sway Julian to come. If he has to work, you can pretend I insisted you pack a plate and bring him food."

She gets all touchy-feely while grabbing my arm, jostling me as she bounces. "Have I ever told you you're the best boss ever?" she asks, skipping off without waiting for an answer.

"Only seven times in the last two weeks. I must be slipping."

❧

"What the hell do you mean?" Christopher screams from the basement. "Two weeks? Are you bloody kidding me?"

Christopher yelling is something that happens about as often as a fish guts itself. Quickly his fire is extinguished. "No, I'm very sorry," he continues. "Two weeks is perfectly fine. We appreciate the opportunity. Kindly send over the contract, and I'll sign it immediately."

This sounds bad. Is he now leaving in two weeks?

"That deceitful yob!" Christopher bellows as he storms up the stairs. "Mike came in and did a buy-on with his new band! They are paying to play our spot on the tour. We just lost all of the non-West Coast dates!"

28

The Croissant Karma Police are after my staff and me with a vengeance. The pins on our dough sheeter won't stay in place. Half of the time I run it, the top roller smashes onto the bottom one, thus ripping hard butter through the delicate layers of dough. Since today is Friday, I can't get a guy out to fix the machine until next week, killing a large part of our weekend sales.

Trying to dissect the maladies of the laminator myself, I'm now covered in grease thanks to the stripped gear that is the cause of misery. Hysterics tempt me to dive into it as I take a call from Cindy, who sounds like Kathleen Turner impersonating Fozzy Bear. She's just the latest flu victim, along with Jenny and Robert. I'm about to call a temp agency, or drive to Hollywood and grab a crack head off of the street, when Donovan calls. I beg into the phone without even a hello, "Please, please say you're calling because your afternoon just freed and you would love nothing more than to bail out a helpless damsel and sell cookies!"

"Right, Lil. You don't even know the meaning of the word helpless." Despite the sarcasm, his shaky voice prepares me for the pool of emotions he is about to hurl me into.

"How bad is she?" I ask in enquiry of our mother.

"Remember the time I called you in school about Dad? It's that kind of bad."

My chin meets my grease-covered apron in memory of the call I got while in a Confectionary Arts class informing me of our father's imminent passing, only then I was covered in chocolate. It seems fitting that I am now doused

140

in a slippery mess. "How long?" I ask, hating myself for hoping there won't be enough time to get to her.

"They don't know. The Doxorubicin is causing heart problems. I'm canceling everything and heading out now. I really need a few answers as to why she lost it with me."

"Is Anna going with you?"

"No, she has to take care of Sunshine. I can't allow that poor little girl to see this kind of suffering or how I react to it. I'm pretty freaked out."

"Donovan, there is no way in hell you're going through this alone. Take Sunshine with you. I'll call Mom's neighbor who used to watch us. Hopefully Mrs. Callahan is free this weekend. When I get there, we'll either leave the kids with her or Christopher will take them all to Mom's."

I hang up the phone while feeling the urge to plug my nose, knowing I'm about to jump into a bucket of my own blood.

৪৩

On Saturday afternoon, Antonia's head is crammed into my shoulder as I pray for dear life. It's fitting that the final flight to see my mother is the most turbulent and stomach churning I've ever experienced. A lightning storm resides outside our window. The plane's dips are so heavy they put my stomach into my throat and almost out the top of my head—like Mom is making one final attempt to throw evil into the world.

The captain again comes over the loud speaker, assuring us that all will be fine in this rather sudden and unexpected, freak occurrence. However, the only freaky thing about it is what, or rather who, in my mind is causing it.

Once on terra firma, the terror and stress send my stomach to doomsday. Twenty minutes later I emerge from the bathroom. Christopher and the children wait concernedly, looking just as bad and still clutching airsick bags. Finally, we are composed enough to get our luggage and drop the kids with Mrs. Callahan. The horror of the flight was so head clogging that it blocked the obvious until Christopher and I exit the hospital's elevator. The world speeds around while my head perceives my motions as languid. This is the same corridor where I stood with Donovan the last time we saw our father. It was here that Donovan referred to me as his love—a signal that the tide was about to turn.

Frozen bile seems to chill its way up my throat when I walk past the room where my father died—the same room where he asked for forgiveness. Donovan's silent denial was so out of character that I knew my world was about to fall apart, though I had no idea of the enormity.

Christopher places his hands on my arms with the deepest of love in his eyes. "Shall I enter first?" he asks. The existence of my heart becomes increasingly obvious. Each pump sends a ripple of tremors through me. Letting Christopher come was a huge mistake.

Donovan bolts out of Mom's room, shutting the door behind him. He steeples his hands over his mouth while deeply inhaling. My heart rate continues to excel as he approaches. He looks back toward the door and shakes his hands to flick off the tension. His face is ashen.

"Thank God you're here," he says. He yanks me toward him with a tight grip that punctuates the underlying meaning of his speech. "It's about to get ugly in there. It's probably best if you and Christopher left."

I jerk back and search his eyes while wondering if he really wants us both to leave or just Christopher. There's no way I'm abandoning Donovan. "You two stay here," I say. I smack both of my hands on the door to Mom's room, shoving it, and myself, forward. Just a few steps inside, I stop and wonder what the hell I'm doing.

Mom's bed faces so she can't see me. Anna stands to Mom's right, being the dutiful nurse and holding a plastic cup of apple juice while Mom sips the last of it through a straw. Anna's lips awkwardly upturn at me. Is she concerned that her being a good person to my nemesis will put her in trouble with me? Silently I mouth, "Thank you." My words bring about her relief.

She dabs Mom's chin with a napkin, then adds water to the flowers that I can safely assume are from Donovan and draws them into Mom's view. Anna pulls away the tray table, and I motion for her to join me outside. She takes a deep look into Mom's eyes then closes her own. Anna's ability to compartmentalize may be failing her, as she seemingly has a hard time divorcing her compassion for a patient from the hatred of the woman who caused so much damage to her husband. Finally I understand what Donovan sees in her.

With a final squeeze of Mom's hand, Anna leaves to join me in the hall. My arms open to her. She hesitates before complying with the embrace. "Thank you, Anna. Thank you for doing what I should, and thank you for looking out for Donovan. I'm so glad he has you."

Her hold tightens and she caves to tears, bring about mine. She gives me a bright, yet apprehensive smile, followed by a subtle nod. "You're very welcome. I'm very happy to have done that."

Anna's eyes stay locked into mine. It concerns me that she will see through my lie. "Would you take Christopher for a walk? I don't know if Mom will talk to Donovan openly with him here."

"Of course," she says. "I want answers too."

As we enter the room, Donovan and I remind ourselves to stay sturdy and accept that whatever comes forth may be the last thing we want to hear. My vision avoids Mom until we both reach the end of the bed and turn to face her. I take Donovan's hand in mine. There's no way in hell I'm letting go—no matter what.

Mom's weathered head hangs with her eyes closed. Her body sways with queasiness. Is the display before her the cause, or is it attributable to how she has spent her final years filled with hatred? Her eyes peer up, and then drop back down with a groan of anguish. "Where are Christopher and Anna?"

Donovan and I remain strong and silent, suppressing a natural inclination to yell which is likely counterproductive to the goal. Maybe a rational approach will pave the way to the answers as to why she was so cruel to her son. Without raising her head, she halts my thoughts by screaming the loudest she can, "Where are Christopher and Anna?"

"We're right here." Christopher bursts in. He looks ready to foam at the mouth. Donovan releases his grip on my hand, but my grip on his remains firm. Christopher stands next to me in solidarity. My breathing ceases as he folds his arms and defiantly faces my mother, displaying a side of him I have never seen. Anna remains by the door. Her dark hair conceals her face like a veil of mourning. When she peers up, Donovan motions her over, puts an arm around her shoulders, and kisses her head.

"All right," Christopher continues to storm. "You want us all, you've got us all. It's none of my business, but if this is what it takes to give Donovan his answers, then so be it."

Mom's eyes scrunch. One hand sits on her stomach, tensing. Getting that for which she has strived seems to be bringing her the hell she has earned. A visage of evil formulates on Mom's face, and my brain scuttles in search of a way to get Christopher out of here. There's nothing to stop her from blurting her words while we run for the door, so if I'm going down, it will happen while standing strong, not while fleeing like a coward.

She knows she has me in checkmate and looks to me like it's my turn to take the beating. Donovan's arm leaves Anna. He straightens and steps behind me, placing his arms around my waist and showing he has my back no matter what she spits out. Donovan's words are gentle yet stern. "It's okay, Christopher. Mom's not going to budge. I've accepted that. Whatever is behind this, at least it was between her and me. She never directly hurt Lily." His words sound like a threat to our captor, defying that we are at her mercy.

Mom's breath shallows and pearls of sweat form on her

brow. Anna's training gets the best of her and she heads toward Mom. "Lana, why don't you have some more cool juice? I'll get you a damp rag."

"You are just like that man," Mom accuses Donovan, gasping through her words. "You brainwashed her, then took her down for your own satisfaction."

Donovan's grip on me becomes flaccid. "What man?" he asks.

With a grab to her stomach Mom hurls bile all over herself, turning the bed into a field the color of dying grass. Anna heads for a bedpan. "You all might want to leave now. The DNR is still in effect, right?"

"Yeah," I utter. Christopher drags me out of the room, but my hazy vision is unable to pull away from the misery before me.

Donovan joins Anna in crouching by Mom's side. As Mom collapses, she mutters, "Innocent little girl."

Outside of Mom's room, I huddle in Christopher's arms, wishing that Donovan would spare himself from that which is unfolding. Anna storms out of the room and down the hallway, furiously hollering, "That damn bitch! Another fucking problem!"

Donovan emerges with streaming tears. "Lily, Mom's …" His sentence is completed with sobs.

My hand absorbs his tears, and I give a nod of understanding. "Did she give any indication at all what she was referring to?"

Shaking his head, Donovan turns away, not wanting to face another mystery. Christopher gently kisses my cheek before checking on Anna, grievously knowing that he can never understand the new layer of hell Donovan and I now face together.

Moment upon moment passes as we crumble, the touch of our foreheads forming a heart of desolation that is drenched in conflicting emotions. We are flooded with memories of holiday cheer, laughter-filled snowball fights, vacations at the beach, Mom's spirited dancing in the kitchen, our father's jabs at Donovan's masculinity, my nights of crying over watching Donovan turn from loving to hateful, Mom disowning us, and now a new mystery—it's all a blurring kaleidoscope of pain.

Finally my lips mutter the words neither of us wants to admit needing. "We're free."

29

A stale stench crawls up my nose when I enter my parent's room. It, along with the nightstand, hold reminders of suffering—a spit tray, an empty glass with a straw, and numerous bottles of medication. A jab hits my heart as I discard the items. The blue ribbon tied around dead Lilies of the Valley sells out that they are the ones Donovan brought when we last visited three months ago. In light of the new mystery Mom brought forth yesterday, I'm unsure if seeing them would help Donovan feel love or bring about a greater disturbance in his soul. With a snap, the vase and its contents are thrown into the trash.

Bags and boxes of clothing donations are gathered before I move on to clean the vanity where my grandmother's antique brush set calls for salvation. Suddenly the dreary house turns lively with a jangle of music that transports me to my childhood. Tossing the brush into the box of things to send home, dreariness is abandoned as I rush downstairs, following the perky melodies of some of my favorite Brits with an indelible smile.

Christopher sits on the floor while admiring Mom's scrap book. I plop down next to him. "I thought we could use a little cheer. I found your mum's old cuttings. She really had a thing for Peter Noone."

"I warned you!" Before us sits an album cover whose photo has been forever etched into my heart. "Is this what we're listening to?"

Christopher nods as the cover commands my attention. During my meltdown before Christopher returned to England, this was one of the albums that absorbed my anguish. One particular face calmed me, assuring that all would be fine. How have I never connected the dots? "Christopher, this man here. Is that Eric?"

"Yes, he certainly looks different with longer hair. Nobody cut it back then."

My eyes lock into Eric's. Suddenly I know him from more than the present. In this life he was a silent guardian during my meltdown, but nearly one hundred years before, he was a different kind of guardian—one who slipped William's family money when he was in jail.

Donovan enters the room with heavy-footed steps, returning from retrieving Mom's will from the bank. His puffy, red eyes are locked on the liquor cabinet, which she again restocked after he again dumped. He glares at the whisky long enough for his sight to blur before abandoning it, using Christopher and I as a diversion. "Glad to see that you two aren't sitting on your fannies and doing nothing," he says, teasing.

Christopher goes aghast. "I beg your pardon. I'll put up with you still referring to me as scrawny, but emasculating me is a little much."

Donovan gives him a snicker. "What? I was just making a bad joke about you two being lazy. Now that you mention it, you are looking a little rosy in the cheeks. Seriously, what the hell are you talking about?"

"I don't exactly have a fanny to sit on."

"I thought you didn't want me to call you scrawny?" Donovan quips.

"Um, Donovan." I point to my crotch. "This is a fanny in England."

"Sorry, man," he says to Christopher. "I was referring to your boney ass."

The look of gloom returns to Donovan's face. He plops on the floor to join us. He picks up the empty album cover and languidly flips it over, pretending to read the track list. "It's been too long since I've seen these guys," he utters softly. "I need more fishing trips with Eric before it's too late. I still feel bad about missing Derek's funeral. That guy was hysterical. Hard as hell to understand though."

Mom's scrapbook continues to hold Christopher's vision as he talks to Donovan. "He certainly had a rough start in life. He came from war-torn East London. People there were considered working class tradesmen and that was all they were ever expected to amount to. His parents worked hard to get the family out of there."

Donovan tosses the album cover aside and turns his sights to the pages Christopher flips, forcing him into the moment. "Grandma sure had a lot of stories about the war. It must have been hell over there. She hated growing up among the smog from the factories."

"You know, luv," Christopher says to me. "You never told me much about your Dad's mum other than she was English. Where was she from?"

Donovan perks up at the opportunity to kill my marriage, sending a cringe through my gut. "Yeah, Lil, where was she from?" he asks with a raised brow.

"Um, from somewhere in the middle I believe."

"You believe? We know all too well where Grandma was from. I swear that Mom married Dad because of it. Try going east a bit."

Crap, Donovan. Shut up!

"Well, the middle would be about Sheffield and east of that is Manchester. Was your gran a Manc?"

Donovan turns his head, totally afraid to look at me. "Um, not exactly. Our family is from a little more east." He snickers.

Damn it, Donovan! Shut! Up!

"The next area over would be—No! Bloody hell, no! Do not say it, Lilyanna! Do not say what I fear you are thinking. You'd better not be toying with me!"

Donovan leans back onto his elbows. His smug grin shows he's mighty pleased with himself. "I can't believe you never told him!"

"He wouldn't have married me if I did." My head cowers. "He may divorce me now."

"No! Lilyanna, this is not at all funny! You Scousers are all alike!"

"Hey! I resent that," I proclaim. "And I'm not exactly a Scouser. Me gran was from Islington."

"Bloody close enough!"

Donovan continues his quest to destroy my happiness. "Christopher, I would like to take the opportunity to remind you that three-quarters of your household has Scouser in their blood."

I swat Donovan, hard. "Stop not helping!"

"Three-quarters?" Suddenly reality kicks Christopher in the bonce with a soccer ball. "Oh no! Not me own children! Really, Lilyanna, how could you do this to me?"

"Well, I figured if I could deal with the trauma of being married to a Manc, then you could do the same for me." Christopher almost chokes on his gasp. "Besides, it's very romantic—kind of like a Capulet marring a Montegue."

"Yes, but they offed themselves, which is sort of what I'm thinking now."

"You mean you wouldn't have married me anyway?"

Christopher *huffs* and crosses his arms in protest of his life. "Well, I suppose I would have," he caves. "At least this way I sort of saved you from your family shame. I wonder if Anna knows about this!" Christopher drops his arms and storms out of the den while calling for Anna. Donovan and I barely contain our laughter. When I can catch my breath, I'm gonna slaughter that git.

30

The children's shrieks cause me to race down the stairs. The trash bag in my hands bounces against the wall, hitting my legs as I go and nearly causing me to trip. Anna crouches on the kitchen floor, pulling a sheet of cardboard off of a large plastic bucket as she and the children peer inside. "See," she says with her nurturing voice, "she's perfectly fine." Antonia takes a step back and squirms. "Don't worry," Anna assures. "Mice can't crawl up the smooth plastic." She hands the bucket to Graham. "Can you take this outside and release it far from the house without touching it? Don't forget your coats."

Graham takes the bucket outside with Antonia and Sunshine following behind. I exit with them. They go to the far edge of the yard while I take the trash to the garbage can just outside the door. Graham dumps the mouse. The girls squeal and run away while he watches it scamper around his feet. The girls then head back toward the mouse, only to again shriek and run, thus brightening my mood as I dump the last of the trash from Mom's room. I head inside, more concerned for the poor mouse than for the shrieking kids.

A *stomp* booms as I open the door. "Got ya!" Anna exclaims. As my view hits the kitchen, she lifts her foot off of a flattened mouse. It's ghost sends shivers up my spine. She picks it up by the tail, heads for the garbage can, and flings it in. "Eh, at least your friend made it out alive. Now you can meet up with Lana. Maybe she'll share her secrets with you."

Once Anna resumes her cleaning, I brave entering the kitchen. "Did they manage to dump the mouse out okay?" she asks, nonchalantly.

"Yes, with the help of a little squealing."

Anna chuckles. "Good. I feared for the poor thing. Graham was so scared he actually tried to stomp on it. I wasn't thinking clearly when I handed him that bucket. I'm glad it worked out."

Suddenly I'm more creeped out by her lie than by her annihilation of the poor mouse. Actually, it's not the lie, it's how well she told it. If I didn't witness the display outside I would have believed her. I still almost do. She should get a talent agent.

"Well, looks like were done here," she says with a breath of relief. "Shall we head out to lunch? Dealing with all this has made me hungry."

Funny, dealing with all this has made me sick.

31

A cardboard box, a worm infested hole in the ground, or a meat grinder?

It turns out that my bailing on helping with Mom's burial arrangements is quite the opposite of disrespectful, since part of me wants to skip the luxury of a pine box, throw Mom in the mud, and be done. Anna and Christopher are less than thrilled that they were shoved off to handle the funeral arrangements. Clearly the compassion of Nurse Anna has dissipated since her husband got a new mystery instead of his answers—hence Christopher's involvement. He is the voice of reason, though he's rather disgruntled about it.

The surviving Becketts have spent the morning rummaging through the garage. It is mostly bare and unchanged since Donovan helped Dad clean it the week of his final Christmas. If we are going to find happy reminders of our childhood, it's here.

Donovan grabs a box of ancient playthings and sits on the cold, cement floor while looking at treasures in wonder. My mind flashes to Christmases past and his excitement over new gems. "Looks like there are some things you might like to keep."

"Nah. Almost everything in this house is best long gone," he states while gliding a model airplane.

"No way. Your face has the same glow as when you unwrapped those. We should keep the mementos of when we had a fantastic family."

"You have no idea how much I want to remember. I'm just trying to let go a little." He dumps the plane back into the box, and his eyes scan the garage, resigned to the end of

153

a part of his life.

"There are some things you should never let go of. You know that."

"You're right." He looks down at the box with a semi-smile of resignation, yet his eyes sparkle with a glimmer of hope. "Some things I wish I could hold on to a little tighter. Life slips away too quickly not to cherish that which is worth loving, but sometimes you need to weed through the buildup that you should have discarded long ago before you find the treasure chest that reminds you of who you are. Then you just need to keep it close."

"I found something matching that description." From under the tool bench I unearth a true treasure. "Think fast," I burst while tossing him a football. Not just any football— *the* football. His throat swells as he marvels at it, like that little ball is the source of great power. "Careful," I warn while sitting next to him. The shiver sent up my spine from the chill of the concrete floor is muted by his presence. "That thing is capable of magic. It can make you fall in love."

"Boy, can it ever. You know how on all those supernatural TV shows there are cursed objects that should be locked away forever? This is one of those objects."

"I prefer to think of it as charmed." I snuggle into his shoulder. Memories float over us like sweet perfume. His breath melts into mine, and I become jealous of the marriage of our molecules. Forcing my heart away from our growing sense of longing, my lips rise with the intent of giving him a kiss on the cheek—sweet, innocent, sisterly. He has the same intension with a kiss to my forehead, but the ability to calculate distance is elusive, and our lips touch in the corners. A thrilling jolt of terror freezes us when the miscalculations are realized. After baited hesitation, Donovan veers to the left and softly finishes what nature started—what it wanted fourteen years before. Regaining our beauty, even if only for a moment, makes me whole again.

Magnetically our foreheads meet. Donovan looks as consumed as he did the last time this football shared our touch, causing my voice to stammer. "I uh, I think we had better put that in the box—quickly."

"No way. This comes on the plane with me." Cupping my jaw like a fragile possession, his breath touches me like silk. "I'm never letting this treasure go."

His words lock in my throat, making my need to flee all the harder to vocalize. "We'd better go tackle our rooms." Popping up, I shove aside vulnerability so we can face the task we dread most. "We get in, grab what's important, throw the rest in boxes for charity, then run and never look back. Easy."

"Yeah," he sighs. "About as easy as it is for some people to throw a football."

Oh, his snicker is so wicked I really want to let him have it. "Hey, I seem to recall the last time I threw a pass at you, I nailed it."

He clears his throat so as to imply something dirty. "I think you got pretty lucky with that pass. Actually, luck had nothing to do with it. It was all in the ball."

"Stop looking so smug! Besides, some would say it was you who got lucky!"

"Touché!"

☙

Filled with the relief of surviving a battle, my mind sees only a faded photograph as I take a final look at my former bedroom. With the exception of a few mementos, nearly everything was discarded. My eyes hood before I turn away, not wanting to see the door close. Though I am no longer that girl, a part of her hurt still resides.

Entering Donovan's room is just as painful. His eyes are fixated on the corner where his nightstand once sat. Resignation rings in his words. "The last time I stood here, I thought we would be together forever. Until today this room contained us as we should have been. Now it knows what happened. The last bit of everything is now dead."

My fear that any consoling in this empty house, where so many battles were fought, may cause me to again try to fight our war keeps me at bay. "We should have had Christopher and Anna help us," I say. "It would have been easier."

"No," he states with resolve, suddenly coming alert. "Then I wouldn't be able to give you this." Crouching down where his nightstand formerly resided, he peels back the carpet, removing the pad with it. "This is yours." Donovan reveals a colorful canvas of devotion and sorrow. The section of floor is covered with dated drawings, poems, and the words, "I'm sorry," inscribed over and over again. "All those nights I hid in here, this is how I spent my time."

My knees meet the floor so I can examine the depiction of love. He points to one of the many apologies after another. "This is from the day Lisa left my room half undressed. This is when I yelled at you for giving me a note that dinner was ready. This ornate one is from the night of the school dance when I first realized how badly I was hurting you. I spent every moment of your hangover working on it."

I touch his hand, halting it from progressing to the next offering of remorse. "Donovan, it was never your fault. If anyone owes apologies, it's me. I should have handled myself differently."

"Lily, we've been through this before."

"I should have left you alone, but I knew you were hurting. I wanted to help you so badly and couldn't find a way."

My jaw cradles in the comfort of his touch. My heart breaks all over again at the memories his words bring back. "I didn't exactly make it easy on you. I should have told you the truth."

"You were only trying to protect me."

"And you were only trying to get me to open up," he gently insist. "We were teenagers thrown into adult problems. Your aggressiveness was the only reminder of who I really was. Without it, I would have faded away. No one knows how to love me like you."

"No matter what I did I felt I couldn't get a handle on what you needed," I confess.

"That's because your old soul was speaking to your new body that was being driven into a frenzy by teenage hormones. When I fought you, it made you crazy because you knew me so well that it was a signal to your old soul that something was desperately wrong. Remember the time your English teacher called Mom and hinted that you may not have written your creative writing project because your voice was so mature? That's why. When I wrote Alex's letters I couldn't figure out where the hell my words came from, then I found Jonathan and it became clear. Add that in with teenage confusion and we did the best we could."

The intensity of his words make me want to flee, both into his arms and out the door. How do I turn my back on the sorrow he has just uncovered before me? "This floor has given me back a piece of the past. Now I have to walk away again."

His eyes search mine. "Do you really still want to hold on?"

"Of course I do."

With a firm look of resolve, he grabs a screwdriver and hammer off of his desk. He then drops to his knees, hunching over the floor and whittling the blade into the wood. "We are eternal," he declares, chiseling one length of an infinity symbol into a board. "I promised to ensure you got everything you wanted in life. You said you wanted us to be together in the end, and we will be. We are still in this life together."

He hands me the tools to complete the pattern. "You bet we are," I declare, carving in my own length. After engraving the last bit of wood, I abandon the tools, feeling like I've taken a stand against the world.

Donovan nuzzles his chin on my shoulder, enrobing me

from behind and locking on like shackles. "I swear Lily, give us another chance and I will never let you go."

My heart flatlines. I've become accustomed to remorse, but this assertion sounds like he's actually asking. Is being in this house bringing about his sudden aggressiveness? Panic brings my words spurting forth. "Donovan, we need to get out of here."

"Not before I grab a saw out of the garage." Abruptly he rises and heads for the door. "Once we each have a loop of that symbol, then we can walk away."

My eyes return to Donovan's testament. Words of apprehension should come forth, yet as my fingers follow the curves of our reaffirmed devotion, my lips mutter, "We'll never walk away."

32

Our stance is strong, our hearts weak while looking down into a cave of despair and relief. This is where the body of my mother will reside. To my left, I finally lay eyes upon my father's tombstone, and my stomach churns. I was banned from this spot over a decade ago, as was Donovan. He stands to my left with one arm around me, his other hand holding that of his wife, just as my other hand is interlaced with Christopher's. All of the tensions in our bodies pour into each other, clinging to the cornerstone that only our bond can provide.

As the snow wisps down from above, my father's glare imposes from below. He never knew about Donovan and I; now I feel he has somehow learned. Though Donovan and I stand strong before their remains, we feel less than victorious.

The straps that suspend the coffin send it on its downward descent. I expect the feeling of a chapter ending, but the realization that I have never grieved for my father makes the final sentence a fish too elusive to catch. A few moments after learning of his death the remainder of my family crumbled when Mom's years of betrayal surfaced from the abyss. There was little time to heal from the shock before I learned how deeply the knife she wielded repeatedly plunged into Donovan, and he needed me to tend to his wounds.

Trekking through the snow, we start to leave Mom behind when Anna puts her hand out to stop me. "Lily," she says softly, nodding back in the direction from which we came. Donovan has collapsed onto his knees into the mattress of snow that covers the earth. Mutely he sobs into his hands. Anna stops Christopher from following as I head to Donovan. "We can't help them," she accepts. "Only they can help each other now."

Joining him on my knees I take Donovan into my arms. A moment ago my heart was as frigid as the ice below that shivers my spine, but now I need to help this poor soul who has already suffered so much. The closure of all those years of abuse are slicing through him.

"Irrational thinking," he says, consoling himself. "Irrational thinking tells me it's my fault she's dead. She started smoking again and drinking because I put her through hell. I will not succumb to it."

Though he is a different man now, the damage inflicted by his pain years before still shadows our lives. My concern compels me to face Anna and Christopher, still standing by the car, looking so helpless. "It's okay," I call to them. "Pick up the children, and we'll meet you at the hotel." My darling Christopher starts to protest before Anna motions him to her rental car. A rip shoots through my heart as they drive off, wishing Christopher could be by my side at this moment when I so desperately need him holding on to me, unknowing if I can keep it together, even for Donovan's sake.

My eyes beg for Donovan's heart to liberate all it has sealed inside. "You can say anything, irrational or not. We need to both let go."

With tightened eyes he draws in calming oxygen, centering himself. "There has to have been something I could have done differently," he anguishes. "Maybe if I didn't fight her every step of the way, we all could have come out of this less damaged. Maybe then she never would have started drinking herself to death. Maybe—"

"Maybe she would have died a bitter old fool anyway," I snip. Donovan's reserved pain has just punched my snapping point. I've already let go of my real mother, now it's time to say goodbye to the monster in the dirt.

"Mom treated you worse than a prisoner of war." I back

away from Donovan so my arms can flail out my anger and accent my words. "Hell, the Geneva Convention was created to ban what happened to you. Why can't you just hate her? She deserves that. I hate that bitch! I absolutely fucking hate her! How can you give her even a drop of your compassion? She forced you to hurt me while using me in an attempt to gain information to support her delusional theories about you. Theories that were driven by hatred of a stereotype that you wanted nothing to do with. Look at both of you right now. Who's the victim? There's a vast difference between the Mom we loved and the devil she became. I'm not the least bit sorry for that bitch and neither should you be!"

Softly I cup his red, tear streaked cheek in my hand. "Donovan, why have you struggled for so long to find forgiveness?"

Semi-hooded eyes reflect his quest for inner peace that calms his breath like a stream on level ground. "Because I had a crazy dream," he confesses. "Remember how dedicated Mom's parents were? They enjoyed nearly sixty years of marriage and died never having kissed another, surrounded to the end with love from their family. I wanted that. I wanted to find one woman and have everything with her. It's one of the reasons why I couldn't bring myself to act on us early on, but I couldn't fight it anymore. My feelings for you were too strong—so strong that I knew the one person I truly wanted was already in front of me. The cruel reality of it was unimaginable."

He takes a moment to gather himself by inhaling another cleansing breath of frigid winter air. "It killed me inside when you lost your virginity to Christopher—like my dream died. God knows I wasn't perfect, but when that happened, it was like I had already lost and all my waiting was in vain. When I met Marcia I thought I could move forward. Then I screwed that up, and I kept losing more and more of what I wanted. The last bit I could cling to was all of us getting together for Christmas every year. For all the nightmares it brought, for as awkward and scary as it always was, I don't regret a moment of it. Mom was the last of her generation. At least we passed on a taste of that to our children."

His eyes turn deep into the dirt-lined cavern before him, his tears splattering like the pain in my soul. Donovan's voice strengthens, morphing from hurt to intensely serious. "We could have had it, Lily. It was in our hands, and I don't understand why we were robbed."

Snow falls upon us like tears from heaven, as if the angels mourn fate's cruel joke. Stolen moments like these are all that remain of Donovan's dream.

33

Christmas Eve finds my home all aglitter and sparkle with the charm of an enchanted wonderland. Twinkling lights and boughs of pine and holly enliven my home, but it's the nine-foot tree in the family room that captivates me. The Balsam Fir, enshrouded in colored lights and ornaments dating back to Christopher's great-grandparents and mine brings forth sweet memories. Tucked up toward its top is the Teddy bear Donovan gave me. It's still adorned with the silver football necklace, and Donovan's note has been sewn inside the hat.

This Christmas brings forth the dawn of new traditions. In what may be my worst idea ever, after Christmas Eve dinner we all rough it out for the night on the family room floor next to a roaring fire. After singing carols over video chat with Christopher's family as they welcome Christmas morning, we all fall asleep, only to soon be awakened by the jingling of bells.

A jolly "Ho, Ho, Ho!" emits from the kitchen as Donovan strolls to us in a full Santa suit and carrying a huge sack, reminding me of how Dad loved to dress as Santa Claus when we were kids. The children bolt out of their sleeping bags and go in for the attack, gathering at Santa's feet as his butt hits the sofa. Anna grabs her camera to preserve every bit of the sight. Where the heck is Christopher?

"Ladies first," Santa says.

Anna nudges Sunshine to sit on Santa's lap. Sunshine looks up to Santa in awe, completely speechless at the man in the funny suit—her eyes wide, her mouth silent and agape, her brown hair a mess of loose curls. She holds the silent pose as Santa asks what is on her list and continues to maintain it as he reaches into his bag and hands her a stash of gifts. When Anna takes Sunshine away, her little gaze stays locked on the man with the bag.

"Okay, Antonia. Your turn," Santa encourages.

"Christopher," I call out, still wondering where he is.

Antonia shoots me an incredulous look that practically tells us she knows we are putting her on. She plops into Santa's lap, looks up at him, then back at me. "Please, this isn't—" In a near panic, Anna and I *shh* her. Antonia returns her sights to Santa, giving him a half-hearted snicker. He replies with a blinking eye roll and adds a wink before forking over her stash.

Damn it, Christopher, where are you? You're missing Christmas.

Next is Graham's turn, but he defaults to Anna and I. "Santa said ladies first." I don't think I could be any more proud of the kid. Seriously though, where is his father?

Santa then calls Anna over. He clears his throat and claims to have presents for the big girls, too. The contrast between Santa's big puffy suit and Anna's small frame is comical. When my turn arrives, Santa whispers words that turn my veins into a network of gleeful tingles. "Tomorrow night, check the book in the library where you kept the phony notes. The one in there now really is from me." He follows it with a quick peck on the cheek and a brotherly shove off of his lap.

Graham takes his turn, but Santa's sack has gone empty. Santa asks his elves to find where the present could have gone. Anna and I look behind the sofa where a new guitar was to reside but is now missing. As if the perfect timing had been pre-orchestrated, the guitar appears in the hands of Christopher who is dressed as Father Christmas. He looks ridiculous in his coat, that is almost a long dress, and pontiff style hat with curved walking stick yelling, "Happy Christmas!" His eyes survey his family who is at a collective loss for words. He is too, until Donovan dashes to him.

The hinge on Christopher's mouth sways before Martin

and Lewis start their act. "Oh, bugger! I thought I was taking care of this," he whispers to Donovan.

Donovan clones the hushed tone. "Seriously? This is what you meant when you said you were going to put on a bit of a fancy dress to do? I was kind of worried. Actually, you do look a little like Uncle Miltie."

"Uncle who?" Christopher asks.

"Come on, Christopher. How long have you lived here? Wait, are you even wearing pants?"

"Bloody well right I'm wearing trousers. It's brass monkeys out there!"

Donovan looks astounded. "Seriously, Christopher, no one else in the world sounds like you. Where do you get this stuff?"

I bring the guitar to Graham and wish him a Merry Christmas while the Santas continue their unarmed battle of wits. When it comes to men, I really know how to pick them.

೮౧

On Christmas afternoon, the children drag Christopher and Anna out to the yard to break in their new soccer ball. Donovan joins me in the family room with the intent of finding a Christmas movie on TV that we haven't already seen fifty thousand times. Instead of dominating the adjoining sofa as per usual, Donovan plops down so close his leg grazes mine. We exchange little grins before he lands the channel selection on *A Christmas Story*.

"I thought we were going to find something new?" I ask.

"Nah, I feel like reliving old times." He tosses the remote onto the coffee table before surveying the room. His words are muted. "Remember the last time we watched this together on that amazing Christmas weekend we had? The only one we spent alone?"

"How could I ever forget? You spent all of Christmas Eve day distracting me with temptation while I fixed a feast for two. Then we had an undesirable visitor—"

"Yeah, thanks a lot for inviting Cruelana DeScrooge to drop by."

I come to my own defense. "If I hadn't called her—"

"Then I never would have called her to pay for Harley, and I wouldn't be here right now." His lips gently grace my ear, and the touch makes me feel I have slid onto a bed of satin and clouds. My gaze casts downward in fear that if I look up, someone will be watching. "After I got past my brain hemorrhage we had a wonderful, romantic night curled up by the tree that took up half of the apartment."

He pulls back, and my eyes lock onto his. My words bloom forth in awe. "The next day you played Santa Claus while I sweated it out cooking at a shelter."

"That's not how I remember it," he corrects as his finger traces my jaw, his lips nearly fluttering on mine. My God, what is he doing? "I seem to recall the 'real' Santa supposedly got sick and you volunteered me as a replacement."

"And you fought me every step of the way," I say. The ocean in his eyes enrobes my soul in waves that pull me under, begging me to drown with him.

"Only because those alleged therapists told me if I ever looked at children they would practically burst into flames from God's wrath. I was shaking when that first kid hit my lap, but eventually I saw how wrong those people were. If it hadn't been for the hope I got then ..." My hand touches his cheek, absorbing a drop of the sorrow that seeps from his eyes as he continues. "A week later we had the most amazing New Year's Eve. I got to spend the night holding you and telling you I love you."

My being enlivens at the memory. "You said it constantly and each time in a different language."

"Twenty-two of them, one for each month I spent hurting you. I've never said it to anyone else in anything but English. That was one of the best days of my life," he asserts in delicate reverie. "Every day with you was one of the best of my life. I miss you." From the tree he pulls off the Teddy bear, removes the necklace that adorns it, and fastens it around my neck before touching his lips to my cheek. "I've never recovered from that fall."

My eyes draw into his with a devotion that has not been seen since the days of chivalry. "Donovan, what's bringing this on? You're usually not so open about this stuff when people are near."

" 'This stuff' is us, Lily. Just because we've been denied being us doesn't mean we don't still exist. Others need to live with who we are, just like we do. I don't know how much longer I can pretend we're something different."

Dear God, I don't know either.

From outside, a soccer ball hits the family room window, jerking me back into reality. Taking advantage of the intrusion I jump up. "We shouldn't be missing out on the reason we split." Without haste I head outside, into the cloudy winter day, and join the game.

☙

The light of the alarm clock covers my face in a soft glow while its progressing numbers remind me that life is passing by. Finally, Christopher's breath deepens into a low snore. Like a paranoid ninja I slip out of bed and head down the stairs.

Is the frigidity of the knob on the library door brought about by the weather outside, or the betrayal I feel stepping through this portal, knowing a letter from a former lover awaits?

Excitement and apprehension course through my nervous system when I grab the designated book off of the shelf. Hidden in the section on making gum paste lilies is a sheet of stationary that bares an uncanny resemblance to the stationary on which I once wrote letters to Donovan, sharing in the madness of an alternate reality.

To My Lovely Lady,

You are, and will always be, the force that drives and inspires me. On my brightest days, you are the warmth that shines upon me. In the darkest nights, you provide the voice that soothes me. Because of you, I face each day knowing who I am and the good I bring into the world. Because of you, I am whole.
Until the end of forever,
Donovan

After placing the book back on the shelf, I head for the family room, unable to bring myself to return to Christopher. I curl up on the sofa and turn on the TV. The *A Christmas Story* marathon continues. Quickly I change the channel, only to return to it, and then flee again. Finally I settle on an infomercial and stare blankly while striving to force myself into a panic over the details of the New Year's Eve party to come. The diversion proves to be a terrible idea. This will be the first New Year's Eve Donovan and I have spent together since we split. How do I move past the impending pain of the night while finding a way to heal?

"Cannoli," I softly mutter aloud. "I'll switch from cream puffs to cannoli. Maybe I should stuff the cream puffs with cannoli filling …"

෪

Within the darkness, a ray of light emits from the hotel room's lamp. Donovan and I sit on a bed, fighting to keep our hands off of each other. This would be so much easier, and far less dangerous, if I were allowed to touch him.

I must be dreaming.

"It's absolutely ridiculous that we have to lie and sneak off just to get a few decent hours alone together each year," Donovan says—his fingers threading my hair, his voice tender, seductive. "Why does it seem that whenever we think we have a moment of peace, someone interrupts us?"

"We have to find a better way," I say, my heart racing. His proximity and the need to hold him draw me nearer. "This little bit of

time isn't enough. I need you too much and in too many ways."

Oh no. Not this. I'm in a hotel room in Rhode Island, six years ago.

His lips call to me, and I try to resist. Mentally I retreat, yet somehow find his chest touching my breast. Our breath unites as our bodies freeze, yearning to propel forward. I want the assurance I once felt when we were pressed together, and I know that comfort is but two thin sheets of fabric away.

I have to wake up. I can't let this memory continue, even in dream form.

He draws closer, then gently pulls back, his lips never quite having met mine. He stares, awaiting a sign to proceed. Finally, I dare touch his hand to his cheek and his lips join mine. How I love the taste of his skin, luscious and rich like fine chocolate, accented by kisses that flow like cream.

Tenderly we drop onto the bed, our legs entwining as we press together, each fueling the desire of the other with our own. His hand slides up my back, and I drop mine to his ass thus making way for him to grab my breast. It's all I can do not to rip my blouse off for him.

Finally, his hand finds its way to my chest, his thumb stroking my nipple through the fabric that I wish would melt away. Gently I pull him toward me, encouraging his crotch to meet mine. He's already in motion, growing at my touch. I ooze and tighten as my breath shudders.

He unbuttons my blouse while kissing his way down—his warm breath causing me to further tighten. My hand forgoes its grip on his ass, in search of something even firmer. It slides into his pants, and my wish is fulfilled as his erection finishes building in my clutches.

His mouth latches on to my nipple, gently suckling the silky skin that has puckered in excitement. Reluctantly I stop stroking him, but it's the only way I can remove his pants. The resulting sight brings about a tremor of excitement. Donovan's grin turns broad and wicked as his eyes capture mine. They stay held until the ransom is paid in the form of my jeans and underwear.

With gentle kisses, he brings himself on to me. Our naked bodies make me lose what little sense of reason that remains. His skin electrically charges mine, and the little pulses it brings intensify when our crotches meet. God, how I have missed this perfect touch that makes my hormones take over all sense of reason. I need more. I need him inside where he belongs—his body an extension of mine, just like our souls.

His tip brushes against me, and my legs part further to welcome him. He slides inside, then pauses as I whimper in pleasure. The heat generated by our union fuses us together, and I tighten around him. Slowly he begins rolling into me at delicious pace. Immediately my body begins to teeter on the edge of the ultimate pleasure, and I long to feel him burning inside me. We've been denied each other for too long. How it is this man has so much power over me? Only he can make me so helpless, so willingly vulnerable. It's more than his ample size or his open heart. Others possess those qualities, but no one other than Donovan can ...

"Donovan, stop!" I screech, wrapping my arms tighter around him, clinging and unwilling to face anyone. "I can't do this!"

His eyes rise to mine, filled with love and understanding as he caresses my cheek. "You'll never stop, Lily. You'll always love me. You know in your heart we belong like this."

He never said that. We stopped! Dear God, we stopped, and we both felt remorse. Lord, how every last grain of my existence wanted more, and it's making me ache for him all over again. He's inside me, both in my head and in my body. I can feel him pressing against me. I'm so fired up that I need to finish what we started. For years I've despised myself for allowing it to start, but in my dream there is no reason to hate myself for finishing.

I grab his ass and slam him in, his dick piercing me as I exhale a groan so deep it vibrates in my ears. As his lips claim mine, the heat of his passion radiates through me, causing me to clamp down so tightly my entire body tenses. "Deeper!" I beg, wanting him to take me higher—back under his magical spell that makes my soul melt into a puddle of honey so he can lick me up, and I can ooze deep inside the very depths of his being, coating him with my desire.

I grip harder, appreciating the tightness of his ass. My hands cannot be tethered any longer as they slide up, pushing in as I run them upward until the delight brought on by his thrusts makes me dig my nails in, causing him to moan.

His hands hit the bed, and his head tosses back—my signal that he is close to the point of no return and trying to restrain himself without disturbing the pace of my excitement. Suddenly he pulls out, then kneels and twists my hips, straddling one of my legs while holding on to the other. He brings himself back, deeper than ever while slowing his roll, hitting me perfectly.

The ocean in his eyes floods over me, reminding me that I am with my soulmate, the man who loves me endlessly for all that I am. How he colors my soul with happiness is more erotic than the tightness of his chest, the curve of his ass, or any move in the Kama Sutra. My body responds to my soul's yearning, and I wrap my legs around him, grab his face, and draw him down. With our eyes locked together, we ride the avalanche, embraced for the crest of the thrilling climax that sends our souls colliding. At the end of the ride, our souls fuse, reunited for all of time.

34

Less than an hour after the designated start time of our annual New Year's Eve bash, the house is full and swinging. With each wave of arrivals, electrical outlets grow increasingly scarce as the impromptu band adds musicians.

Each year, between Christmas and New Year's, it takes all Donovan and I can muster to avoid depression. Donovan combats the "cognitive reasoning that tells him he's a screw up" by overloading on volunteer work. I throw myself into making cookies for homeless shelters and futz over this party. We also avoid talking to each other; thus, we haven't spoken since before I read his letter.

Finally feeling that my hostess duties are complete, I plop myself midway up the stairs to gaze at the crowd. The place is so densely packed that it's hard to find anyone, that is, anyone who doesn't tower over everyone else. In the far corner of the living room, Julian talks to Donovan. Why can I feel Donovan's discomfort from across the room? Are those two going at it already? It might explain why Anna is suddenly cowering behind Donovan and scratching at her arm.

Donovan senses my spying. His heart tears at mine as our eyes meet. He points me out to Julian who then sways his way through the sea of people. "There you are," Julian says as he sits next to me. "This is quite the shindig."

"And it will only get crazier once the alcohol kicks in."

Julian clears his throat. "I saw Cindy and, um—Robert out there. Is anyone else from the bakery coming?"

Geez! He's as transparent as air. "Yeah, Jenny should be here soon," I shoot him a wink and a smile.

Julian chuckles. "That obvious, huh?" He stares at the

glass in his hand while shifting the weight on his hips. "Donovan pulled me aside and apologized for his attitude years ago. He then genuinely thanked me for my help when your dad was ill. It's amazing how much he's changed."

"You sound skeptical." He also won't stop fidgeting or face me.

"I've always been concerned about you," he confesses. Finally I get spotty eye contact. "Anna seems pretty timid. She's really an Acute Care Certified NP?"

"Don't you mean she missed her calling as a model?" I try to hide being disgruntled while eyeing her in a slinky black dress and clinging to Donovan, who is obviously discomforted.

Julian's eyes shift around the room. His finger taps the lip of his glass. As I begin to leave to check on Donovan, Julian interrupts my concern. "Actually, Lily ..." Julian grabs my arm and leads me into the library, shutting the door behind him. "Have you ... Has Donovan ever hurt you— physically?"

I'm so taken aback my face exaggerates its movements. "What? He's never done anything of the sort. Julian, Donovan has really changed, but even before he never touched me in any way that wasn't welcome." Julian's brows ascend at my choice of words, confessing his real issue is morbid curiosity over something that is none of his damn business. It leaves his mouth stuttering to catch up with his brain.

"What the hell is going on with Donovan and Anna?" he demands more than asks.

"What?"

"Jesus, Lily. There's makeup covering grab marks on her wrists, and she won't make eye contact, like she'll be in trouble if she does. She's also clinging to him like she fears being around anyone else. Every time someone comes into sudden contact with her, she flinches. I've never trusted that man. If he's—"

Christopher slips into the room to grab a pen out of the

desk while my words are already in motion. "Julian, don't you dare accuse Donovan of hurting anyone. He has never been that kind of person." I turn to address Christopher, but Julian lets his words fly.

"Really? Because I remember him differently."

I snap back at him. "And I recall you being the instigator in the only argument that came to blows." Again I turn to Christopher. "Hi, hon—"

Julian steps on my words. "And I recall the way he treated you. He sounded like an abusive bastard while looking at you like a lost—"

"Everything all right?" Christopher imposes.

"It's fine sweetie. Julian and Donovan have never seen eye to eye. I'll be out in a moment." Christopher still looks concerned. "Really, honey. We're fine." Christopher's eyes shift to Julian's in stern concern. "It's okay," I assure.

Julian resumes his tirade the second Christopher leaves. "So again you cover for Donovan. What the hell is it with you two?"

My hands toss up in surrender before my words berate the crap out of Julian. "He's my best friend who has been through hell largely because people misjudged him, much like you're doing now. If you knew the cause of his former actions, you would be completely ashamed of yourself. Why can't you just take two seconds and see what he has become instead of judging him on what he was, which was never his fault!"

Julian's hand purses his lips to halt his words. His other hand dives into the pocket of his slacks, making the big, strong man look like a bullied schoolboy. "I'm sorry. I just— I've always worried for you. You're right. I think there is a lot I don't understand."

It's lucky for Julian that he's backing down. I'm damn tired of Donovan not getting due respect. Suddenly the room goes dark, the music stops, and groans of disappointment fill the air. From outside, Donovan shouts, "I've got it."

"Oh, no!" I fret. "The last time he did something electrical I almost called the fire department. We may need your medical skills soon." I fumble for the door, only to smack into it. "Crap!"

"You, okay?"

"Yeah," I moan. "Where are the damn lights?"

The lights pop back on as I reach the kitchen. The brightness brings forth a new revelation. With the rest of the house so dimly lit, I thought Anna's dress was black, but it's actually deep purple. What the hell is she thinking? This is one of Donovan's biggest triggers, and on New Year's Eve of all nights.

Anna stands in the kitchen while cleaning the counter. She lets out a self-conscious slip of a smile. "Sorry, I know the kitchen is your domain, but I thought you could use a hand."

If I didn't know better, I'd swear she was clueless. Donovan said she intentionally steps on his triggers, but this is beyond cruel. Suddenly Anna and I are in a contest for a Best Leading Lady award. "Wow. Thanks. That's really nice of you. Did you see I hid your favorite sparkling water in the fridge?" I ask while opening it. "I know you don't drink champagne or apple cider," or anything else with calories, "so I wanted you to be provided for."

"I did. Thank you."

The perfect weapon sits in the fridge, nearly smiling at me. With calculated placement, I set an open container of spaghetti sauce on the edge of the counter, teetering on the corner to Anna's right, then slip away. As she turns to continue cleaning, she bumps into the bucket, splattering her chest with sauce. Her shriek makes my soul do a happy dance. "Oh no! Your poor dress!" *Take that, you skanky bitch!*

Anna's eyes and mouth widen. Frantically I go for the paper towels, surprised that she has yet to utter a word. Try as we might, there is no way that sauce is coming off. "Oh, this is terrible!" I say. My performance is so good that I almost believe the event wasn't pre-meditated. "I have a sweater that would go great with that dress. Would you like to try it?"

Rapidly she nods before following me upstairs. Inside the bedroom, Anna squirms in avoidance of the mirror as I search my closet. I hand her a black, V-neck Angora sweater with rhinestone buttons and a rabbit collar. She snatches it, and a hint of a bruise peers from under her wide rhinestone bracelet. My teeth clamp in concern. I refuse to believe that Donovan has hurt her, but retaliation for something would explain her pulling the trigger.

"There you two are." Donovan's gaze bounces between Anna and I as he enters the bedroom. His eyes are locked on the dress as Anna whips on the sweater. The dress now evokes a new emotion, and he fights to suppress laughter. "I heard there was some kind of problem in the kitchen. You two okay?" Donovan's eyes lock on me. *Thank you, Lily. This is exactly why I love you.*

"Clumsy me had a little accident. Do I look okay?" Anna asks, sheepishly.

"You always look perfect," he says, before turning to me. "As do you, except—hold on a moment." He heads to my jewelry box, then fastens the infinity necklace he gave me around my neck. "Much better. You know, you really should lock this door. Sometimes people get the crazies at big parties. You always have to think two steps ahead of nut jobs." Anna shoots Donovan an evil glare as he slips his arm around her. "Come on ladies. Let me escort down the two most beautiful women here."

ॐ

As the countdown on the television begins, Christopher zigzags his way through the labyrinth of guests, reaching me just in time to take me in his arms. "Three, two, one, Happy New Year!" the crowd yells. Cheers are bellowed and noisemakers rattle as streamers propel through the air accompanied by little pops upon their release from party favors. All of these make for a vivacious backdrop that accentuates the hope we all grasp by putting faith in the turn of a calendar's page.

Christopher lays a stationary kiss on me with a mad passion that he has not possessed in years. The power causes my legs to buckle. I feel my bum will soon hit the floor. His lips leave with a *pop*, bringing forth bold grins. "This year is going to be fantastic, Lilyanna! Something tells me big changes lay ahead—big, scary changes that will culminate into something we can't possibly foresee. I'm so lucky that I get to experience them with you."

Again he blesses me with an adoring kiss, but this time I don't let him pull away so easily. Grabbing the back of his head, I press him closer while loosening my jaw, drawing his tongue to join mine in a tender tango. When I release him, he nuzzles his cheek into my hair, making my body warm.

"Hey, Christopher! Come on!" Fred yells from across the room, eager to resume playing. With a quick kiss on my cheek Christopher dashes off. Ah, the glamorous life of a musician's wife!

His hair cascades across his cheek as he picks up his guitar. With a twist of his neck it flies from his face, revealing eyes that penetrate me and upturned lips that silently say, "I love you." I return the sentiment, and the band plays on. Christopher illuminates in the way that he only can while playing, and I fade into the crowd.

After a song, I embark on a quest for champagne. I'm about to fill a glass when Donovan appears before me, holding my coat. We share a smile as he nods to the patio door. He knows I have a task for which I need prodding. I've spent the last week seeking the proper way to heal our wounds, and I have finally found an innocuous way to do it while being true to who we are.

We shuffle over extension cords that cross the yard before heading down the block for an uninterrupted moment. Our journey ends at a small park where we sit at a picnic bench. My voice stammers while making my mission known. "It's been far too long since we've spent a New Year's Eve together. In fact, in the last fifteen of them we've only had one good one. That makes fourteen times I've wished I could make the pain go away. Next year we need to start new traditions, but tonight I want to bandage the past."

I gather our hands between us; exactly as he did the one New Year's Eve we spent in our own version of heaven. "Feliz Año Nuevo," I say as his eyes search me in question. "Bonne Année, Felice Anno Nuovo," I barely utter, my vision fogging as my actions bring forth more emotions than I ever expected. "Frohes Neues Jahr, Onnellista Uutta Vuotta." Donovan remains transfixed; supporting my quest, knowing how hard it is not only to get the words out, but also the pain. "Un An Nou Fericit, Godt Nyttår, Bon An, Issena T-tajba, Sretna Nova Godina." A trickle streams from his eyes as I continue. It lands on my hand, drowning in a tear of my own. "Felix Sit Annus Novus, Hauoli Makahiki Hou." Gasping for breath, I force one final push through the laceration in my heart. "Sun Lin Fi Lok, Sana Saiida—Happy New Year."

Unbridled hope shines in his eyes. "Ah, what the hell." Grabbing the back of my head he pulls my lips into his, bringing about the completeness to my soul that I only feel when we are this way. Together we are perfect, and nothing changes that.

Slowly I retract, and then quickly yank myself away with the indiscretion smacking me in the face. I begin my journey home alone. I only wanted to move forward so we could be like everyone else on New Year's Eve. I should have known better. Donovan and I will never be like everyone else.

Donovan runs up behind me. "Lily, wait. I'm sorry."

"Married!" I scream at him, holding up my left hand. I then pick up his left hand, forcing his ring into his view. "Married! We may not be able to control our feelings, but we certainly can control our actions. What happened to the man who wanted to stay faithful to his wife?"

"He died along with Lana Beckett," Donovan mutters.

"Look, I'm sorry. This distance thing with us is killing me. Let's go back to the party and forget about this for a few days. When I get my head together, you can, and should, let me have it. Please?"

Seriously? He knows I won't let him pull the wool over my eyes. "No, something is up. 'Forget about it for a few days' is the new equivalent to 'I can't tell you.' We are not going down this road again, and I am certainly not going to ruin my marriage over your inability to talk to me."

Donovan turns snippy. "Dare I forget how lucky you are! Maybe I don't have the perfect marriage. You not only lucked out in finding Christopher, but you obviously made the right decision with choosing him over me."

My nails dig into their palms. "What do you mean *choosing* him over you?"

"The second Christopher entered your life you forgot about me." Donovan pushes a finger toward my face. "You saw how much I was hurting the first New Year's Eve after you met him. Sure, you were there for me then, but after I was forgotten until Christopher moved back to England. When I checked into Harley you bailed on me all over again."

Oh, I am so ready for this. This fight has been a long time coming. "You constantly made it clear that I shouldn't contact you and every time it broke my heart. As for checking into Harley, you, in no uncertain terms, left me." My finger slams into my chest so hard it stabs. "I may have had a choice between being with Christopher versus starting my life completely over, but I never had the option between the two of you. You're the one who left a note behind telling me to be with Christopher. Have you forgotten that little tidbit of information?"

"Don't give me this crap!" he hollers indignantly as his face hovers in mine. "You could have waited for me to recover and then told me you wanted me. You knew damn well there was no way I would have refused, but no! Instead you went running off with Christopher. Damn it, Lil, the engine on my car hadn't even cooled."

The screaming ends as my words sag from the heaviness in my heart. "I only did what you insisted was best. I was willing to give up every dream I had for you." My face shies in embarrassment, knowing somehow we are both right.

"I'm sorry." Donovan puts his arms around me, touching my heart like only he can. "The stupidity of my actions made me defensive. Truce?"

"Yeah," I utter.

Donovan walks me out to the curb where a streetlight burns. He then dabs under my eyes, removing the last bit of sorrow from my face. "Never, ever will we fight again. I promise you that, and I always, always keep my word to you. Come on, let's get you back."

His words of anger echo in my brain. A few doors away from my house I touch his arm, stopping his steps. "What do you mean you don't have the perfect marriage?"

The question breaks my heart. His fading eyes whimper that it breaks his too. "Truce, remember?"

"Sorry."

Inside the backyard, Christopher sits on the bench, talking to Jenny and Julian. Upon seeing me, Christopher dashes up and gives me an adoring kiss on the cheek. "There you are. I was wondering where you two went." Donovan continues on as Christopher pulls me aside. "Are you all right, luv?"

"I'm fine. Donovan and I were just off patching old battle wounds."

"I can tell. You seem tense all over. Can I warm my wife with a dance?" he asks, offering his arms. When he's actually around, Christopher never fails to bring me joy.

Despite the smiles we share as we dance in the walkway, one thing stands out clearly among all of the muck in my brain: I hate New Year's Eve.

35

"All right, confess!" I playfully demand of Christopher while coming home from our last opportunity for a night out before he goes on tour.

"Whatever do you mean, luv?"

I scrutinize him with a smirk. "Your constant fidgeting tells me you're up to something."

"I've just too much on me mind with the tour and all." Christopher scratches his neck with the force of discomfort.

"Liar. Confess!"

"My cousin called," he says. "She's having a boy and wants to name him after me."

"That's fantastic. Why didn't you tell me?"

"Honestly, it just doesn't feel right, so she agreed to let us name him like we did our own children."

"Oh, no," I groan at the memory. "The kid may get his doctorate first."

"Come on. Let's give it ago. We'll start with Paul."

"Hmm," I muse. "Since our children each have three names, shouldn't we name him Paul John George?"

"Leave it to the Scouser to come up with that one," he groans. "What about Ringo?"

"I see no reason not to follow our three name convention, thus one of the Fab Four is exiled. Since Ringo always gets the least respect, he's the natural choice."

"Poor Ringo." Christopher touches his hand to his heart in mock sympathy. "I knew we shouldn't have emasculated the Hollies with Antonia Roberta Allena."

"Our daughter is worthy of her namesakes. Besides, you often remind me that there are Hollies we left out. Hey, here's an idea. How about we don't name him after a British band?"

Christopher shoots me a look like he's responding to a request to assassinate the Queen, causing the car to swerve before he lets me have it. "I recall this started with your idea of using the name Graham, referring back to the wobbly you threw when I left America for England."

"Okay, okay. What about a modern band? Like someone our age is supposed to know."

"Not on your Nelly!" Christopher straightens and becomes insistent. "You have to stick with the classics where you know the catalogue will remain strong. I'm trying to do right by this child, not curse it."

"Right, because in the defense of Graham Peter David, Herman's Hermits and The Monkees never did anything less than stellar."

Christopher fidgets in his driver's seat. "Well, you may have something there. I'm glad you left Mr. Nash out of that little comparison."

"Bloody well right!" I chime. "Mr. Nash is perfect. Besides, he was a Hollie before joining Crosby, Stills, and Nash, and I was raised to believe that puts him next to God. Mom at least got one thing right."

"Speaking of your mum—"

"Oh, please don't."

"Well, I know of no other way to segue this," he says, pulling his Mini into our driveway.

"Do not say you want to name him after my father, nor anyone else in my family."

"No, luv. I'm trying to bring up a rather cracking idea, but I'm not too sure you're going to like it."

"If it has to do with the memory of my mother—"

"No, luv, forget about her." Christopher shuts off the engine in frustration with himself. "I don't feel like a very good husband leaving you alone for two weeks. Now that Donovan's here, I see how I miss my own family and—"

He must have invited Grace to visit. I could live with her around, but only if she brings the maid, the butler, and a driver and they stay at a hotel.

"Eric's coming," Christopher says. To him it seems to be the greatest idea ever. "He'll arrive the day before I leave and will help with cooking and the kids. All those years of being a bachelor have taught him a lot. Since he rarely got to spend time with his own daughter when she was a child, this will be good for you both."

"Wait, he's coming tomorrow? Our house has barely recovered from the party two nights ago. How long is he staying?"

"I want to spend time with him when I return, so overall it will be eight weeks."

Is he serious? A childless, bachelor musician, in his mid-seventies, cooking and helping me watch the kids? What the crap is he thinking?

"Come on," Christopher says, bounding out of the car. "I can't wait to tell the children."

I need a nap. Hopefully my blood will congeal in my sleep.

ଓ

After barely setting foot in the foyer, Eric is at the ready with a hug that screams gratitude. You would think he is supposed to be the one to benefit from his visit. "Lilyanna, luv, you look fantastic as always. Are you well?"

Let's see, my husband dropped an anvil on my head in the shape of a houseguest while my ex has my heart in a tailspin to the point where if I talk to him, I'll either scream or bawl. Oh, and I'm pretty sure that I knew you in a past life. "I'm as great as my crazy life allows."

"Well, I'm here to help," he says, rubbing his hands together. "Say the word, and I will perform magic."

Now that would be something. Eric turning out to be Mary Poppins? Well, he is English, but he failed to bring an umbrella.

Graham tugs at Eric's shirt. "Which room are you staying

in? Can you stay with me?"

Eric's eyes warm at the request. "Actually, I've talked your father into letting me stay in the guest house. I'm here to help, not get underfoot."

Yeah, we'll see how that goes.

ॐ

On the evening after Christopher's crack-of-dawn departure, I'm smacked by blaring classic rock from the family room and a wonderful aroma emanating from the kitchen as I open the front door. My foyer and living room are immaculate—almost sparkling. However, the sight of Eric dancing as he cooks is downright enchanting. He yells as he rushes to lower the volume of the music. "Cracking. You've just enough time to wash for dinner. It is dinner time, right?"

I'm dumbstruck. "It's exactly what should be dinner time but rarely is around here. Something smells amazing. Did you cook?"

"Oh, it's nothing special, really—just roast chicken with potatoes, carrots, and a salad. I hope you don't mind me taking liberties with your kitchen. I tried to keep it tidy."

Is he kidding? It's practically spotless. Unable to resist the urge, I taste the gravy. My mouth sings as fresh tarragon and parsley enliven my tongue. Is England redeeming itself? "Eric, this is incredible, but you didn't have to do this. You should enjoy your vacation."

"Honestly, being with family is all I want. Everyone back home is old, sick, or dead," he says, tossing down a dishtowel. "I don't have much purpose there. I know eight weeks is a long time for a house guest, but I'm the happiest I've been in donkey's years."

"Donovan and I had so many problems with our parents that it's almost a relief to have only each other, but I did feel absolutely lost without him. Then again, Donovan and I seem to be of a different breed from the rest of the world."

"Speaking of which, where is the devil?" Eric asks while pulling dinner out of the oven. "We haven't spoken since before Christmas. Christopher led me to believe he's here all the time—even joked about giving him a room."

"Actually, Donovan called yesterday wanting to discuss something with me over dinner tomorrow night. Would you mind watching the kids alone?"

"Not at all. Remember, I came to help." He heads upstairs. "I'll round the children while you change."

Apparently Mary Poppins has a brother as youthful as Peter Pan.

ॐ

"Hello, luv!" Christopher beams at me over video chat. Drawn curtains and a nightstand whose lamp illuminates the motel room frame his image.

"Wow!" I glow at his sight. "We haven't done this in ages. I can't say that I've missed it. Life's much better when you are here."

"And I would much rather be there. I've been gone less than a day, and I already can't wait to escape mayhem." Christopher laughs as Dennis runs behind him, jumping and waving. "You're looking exceptionally lovely. How are things?"

I giggle at Dennis while replying to Christopher. "I would say as expected, but that's hardly true in light of a sparkling house and a singing chef who makes a mean roast chicken. I could get used to having Peter Poppins here."

"Who's Peter Poppins?" Fred asks, popping his head in, crossing his eyes, and sticking out his tongue, then disappearing.

"It's my new nickname for Eric, though I don't plan to ever tell him. He's like a boy version of Mary Poppins."

"Well, I'm glad you're provided for," Christopher says. "I sure miss ya, luv." A chorus of ooohs and kissy noises taunt in the background. Kissing his fingertips, Christopher reaches them out to the screen. I'm all too happy to reciprocate the gesture that again tugs at my heartstrings.

"I miss you, too," I confess. "Call me again tomorrow. No matter how late, okay?"

"Promise."

36

From the bottom step of the metaphorical staircase that is now so familiar, I run for the farthest door. This time I'm going to see how it all began. Donovan's recent actions are a full-on assault on my heart that draw back the feelings I've spent years pushing away. Has my time with the man I am destined to love forever always been a mess?

Without hesitation, I throw the door open and step into the light. My mind wants to be ready for whatever hits me, but the truth is, my earthly body is scared rigid. As the light dissipates, dryness surrounds me. I sense sun and wind filled with sand, yet my hands feel cool. "What do you see?" Susan guides.

My soul is in harmony with this life, and the answers to Susan's impending questions are clear. "Clay walls. A dirt floor. Dust. Sand. A few stools. Pottery. This is Egypt. I'm wearing tattered sandals and linen."

"You are a very old soul. It explains much about who you have become. Are you happy?" Susan asks.

"Immensely. My two girls make me smile. They dance around me as I knead bread. Near the oven, a jar is fermenting old bread into beer." How is it I can smell these things?

"Where is your husband?"

My heart races in happiness. "Bathing in the river. He's been hunting and brought us a fox. I can't wait for him to return. I've missed him so much."

"What is his name?" Susan asks.

"Bes. It means protector. The name is perfect for him. My name is Tadinanefer. My husband—he's home."

"Tell me about him."

"He's perfect—strong, loving—so very gentle with me and the children. I could love him forever." And I do. It's Donovan. There's not a doubt in my mind. "He's sitting on a stool so I can rub oil perfumed with wood and flowers on his back. I'm anxious to touch him, but I also want this finished. His aroma is always best after the oils blend with his own musk."

"Okay, Tadinanefer," Susan interrupts. "Let's see what else we can find. Try stepping outside."

"No. I want to cherish this moment forever. Just let me stay in his warmth until I die old in his arms."

"Is that what happens?"

"Yes."

"Then let's keep you there for awhile. Enjoy the love."

37

Why the hell am I in front of a motel? Seriously, what the crap is up with Donovan lately?

As per his earlier instructions, a text is sent announcing my arrival. When Donovan meets me in the lot, he grabs me as if I've returned from the dead—nuzzling his face deep into my hair, clutching my body.

"Donovan, why are we at a motel?"

He nods a request to follow him. "I have something to show you. Mom kept her will in Pandora's Box."

A single lamp illuminates his room where stacks of paperwork reside all over the table and on the encompassing floor. The markings on a collection of paper coffee cups reveal he's been guzzling mint mochas. "I'm sorry," is written on each of the dated cups that go back to before New Year's Eve.

He sits on the bed and clutches a stack of papers. His half-hooded eyes look to the sheaves. "Do you remember when we had all those Martinis and I went for a walk because talking to Mom really got to me? She said James is my real name. I figured it was the dementia, but after she died, I retrieved these from her safe deposit box."

My heart stutters as I sit on the bed and shuffle through the stack. Before me glitters the key to that magical chance at the acceptance we have always desired. They are papers showing the adoption of James William by Lana and Edward Beckett from Audrey Beckett and an unknown father. Additional papers reveal a name change to Donovan James. My words fall without clarity in my mind. "You're—you're my cousin. Why would she hide this? Do you think this unknown father is what she meant when she said you are just like *that man*? Why would she change your name?"

"There's more. I sent for Aunt Audrey's Death Certificate."

The second the paper hits my hand, the word "suicide" jumps off of the page and smacks into my gut. "I thought she died of heart problems."

"Yeah, apparently a broken one. Whomever *that man* refers to, Mom's anger towards Aunt Audrey's death was transferred to me. She then deepened the cut by robbing us. First cousin marriages are legal in most places. We could have taken this paperwork to a courthouse and been married years ago. Now all that holds us back is ourselves."

My face freezes. Finally my mind pries open my mouth, bringing words forward with hesitation. "So this is why you've been acting so differently since Mom died."

Donovan takes my hands. "Come with me and start over."

"What about Christopher and Anna?"

His scratching at the back of his head is forceful as he paces to vent frustration. "The complexities of my relationship with her seem endless," he says contritely.

"Donovan? What aren't—"

"Yes, there is something—some things I'm not telling you. They're personal and are some of the many things about Anna that make my life hell. I'm in this crappy motel because she kicked me out—again. She actually did it before New Year's Eve, so we put on yet another show. It happens all the time, and it happens for the same reasons I've stuck by her." His eyes plead up at me and seek understanding. "This is one of those rare cases where wrong is also right. We're right. We've always been right. We could have all we've ever wanted. Look at me," he says, cupping my face— drawing me in and making resistance futile. "Really look into my eyes a moment."

I cave, releasing my guard as we open our hearts for a speck of eternity. Everything we have locked away for so long rushes back—the amazing things we make each other feel, our hopes and dreams, all that we have been denied, the truth from which we can never escape. With eyes that beg me to love only him his soul wraps me in a cloak of adoration. The angels whisper their blessings as our lips meet—locked to each other, conveying eternal love in their dance. When we pull back, our eyes reflect a desire to entwine our souls for all of time.

"I've never stopped loving you, Lily."

My whimper is scarcely suppressed as we give silent commitment before our lips meet again, bringing our bodies down onto the bed below us, sinking us into heaven.

The taste of his skin and the warmth of our beings turn me into an instrument of yearning. Slowly his hands slide under my shirt, glide it over my head, and toss it aside like a forgotten flower. In the next heartbeat my bra and his shirt join it on the floor. It feels like an eternity since we've been like this—skin-to-skin, soul-to-soul. Charges flow through me at his touch, and I pray this magical feeling never ends.

His cool hand slides down my bare breast followed by his tongue. Gently he suckles my nipples and the ecstasy it sends through my body cannot be compared to the euphoria in my soul. No one should have the power to keep us apart and infringe upon God's beauty. Never have I loved another like this. No other man has ever—

"Oh, shit! Donovan, stop!" Halting at my words, our eyes freeze into each other's. "What the hell are we doing?"

Donovan takes a deep breath and hides his vision to the site of our indiscretion. "Stopping," he burst out firmly. "We're stopping." Pulling the bedspread over us, he enrobes my body in his. "No more," he assures. "No more until we agree what to do next, no matter how long it takes."

"I have to go!" I dart off the bed and scramble to put on my bra. My fingers have lost all agility.

"Lily, I'm sorry," he says, advancing.

"Stop! Stop right there. You said to give you time and then I could yell at you. Consider yourself yelled at, twice. I'm taking these papers with me." My feet flee so expeditiously, that I'm still pulling my shirt over my bra as the door slams behind me. While racing for my car, I pray that once inside, I'll wake to learn this nightmare was merely a hallucination.

ॐ

I'm barely aware of the road before me. Drops of guilt trickle down my cheeks as I force words that my heart needs to face.

"I cheated on my husband."

The last time I blinked away the tears of indiscretion and foolishly lied to myself. Now I need to face my actions.

"I've hurt that sweet, beautiful man," I cry.

No. No, I didn't. We stopped. Both times we've stopped. It's not cheating if you freak out and stop.

My stomach lurches, and I swallow hard and fast. Burn creeps up my throat as guilt turns my tears into smoldering embers. Racing to quell the burn I smear them onto my sleeve. If I could rip my face off, I would.

A block away from my house I pull my car to the curb. Profound sorrow screams forth, knowing I soon need to face my children. "No. I'm Lilyanna Eccles, and without sex it wasn't cheating. I won't wallow, because I didn't cheat," I shriek over and over again, trying to convince myself of innocence. Finally I force myself forward, wishing there were a way to yank out my deceitful heart and feed it to vultures, just as it deserves.

ॐ

With a painted smile, I go through the motions of putting the children to bed, and then cower in my room with the documents. Aunt Audrey's cause of death might as well be written in neon. Mom always said Audrey was much like Donovan—loving to the core. Was she trying to tell us the truth?

The power the adoption papers hold scares me. Now more than ever I know my life could have been different. This one, stupid piece of paper could change so much. Actually, I could just as easily hurt my family without it. This document may make it legal, but legal is not always right.

Deep sadness floods me when I curl into Christopher's pillow. He has only been gone two days, and his scent has already faded; yet somehow Donovan's shirt that he gave me nearly a year ago still carries his essence. It's like a metaphor for my recent learning; Christopher is always here for the now while Donovan is with me for eternity.

My video chat rings. I click the answer button, sucking back guilt and pushing forth cheer. "Hello, luv!" I burst with an exaggerated gleam at Christopher. "You're looking rather lovely." Instantly my eyes feel like rafts on the ocean.

"Hey! That's *my* line. You can't go stealing my lines!" He laughs.

"Maybe I just miss you so much I feel the need. How are you darling?"

"Sweet as nuts. We had a cracking time tonight, but as much as I am enjoying this, I certainly miss you." Christopher kisses his fingertips and touches them to the screen, yet I feel them claw into my heart.

I reciprocate, wishing our fingers could interlace. "And I miss you!"

"I had an idea for a name for the baby. How about—"

"Darling, can we please talk about something else tonight?"

"Can't stand up the master of musician names, eh?" He fakes straightening a necktie, bringing about my laughter, yet also deepening my guilt. "How's my lovely lady?" he asks. The question turns my pooling water into a tsunami. Never has Christopher used Donovan's words. "Darling, what's wrong?" Christopher asks. He looks like he wants to jump through the monitor and console me. To conceal my guilt, I reveal the contents of Pandora's Box.

Christopher looks sickened by the news. "With your mum, none of us ever did know which way was up. It's unfortunate she didn't get the same help Donovan did. He's doing incredibly well for someone who nearly went off the deep end."

Suddenly I'm kicked in the head. Did the universe send me a puzzle piece?

"Hey, Christopher," Dennis calls in the background. "A reporter wants you."

Christopher starts to reject the opportunity, but ironically I now need him to put his job first. "Sweetie, I insist you enjoy the chance at exposure. Call me after for a brighter conversation. I love you," I say with heartfelt enthusiasm, then disconnect the call before he can protest.

My attention returns to the adoption papers. Something about the signatures rattles my core. Why do I suddenly see that Donovan never showed me the paperwork for Mike's restraining order? Maybe my love for Donovan makes me blind to the truth—just like how Julian pointed out the marks on Anna's arm over which I so easily lost concern.

I hop online and order rushed copies of both my parent's marriage certificate and my aunt's death certificate. In a few days, I'll at least know what matches.

38

Repulsion runs through me. My veins feel filled with my own sickness. Last night guilt plagued. Today frustration rules. The contrast makes me despise myself.

Snatching my purse from my locker, I head out, hoping fresh air will reform me, but nothing on this earth can make me comfortable with myself. Fighting the urge to race my stress away, I meander through the streets of Westwood and land on Sunset Boulevard. Twenty, snot-sob filled minutes later, I've traveled a whole four miles and find myself in front of Donovan's office. I should have headed for the La Brea Tar Pits. Diving into muck sounds appropriate. Then again, I'm already neck deep.

Bolting into his private chambers, I neglect the formality of a salutation before sniffling out my words, certain that my face is unrecognizable from the streaks and smears of eyeliner and mascara. "You leaving was the hardest thing I ever experienced. If you hadn't shoved me away, I would have stood by your side without fail. I kept asking if you were sure. You said it had to happen." I halt Donovan as he heads toward me. "No, stay where it's safe. You're not allowed to do anything but talk to me."

"I had to do everything I could." He gulps back a sob. "You were sick—so, so sick. It was like watching you die."

"What would you be like today if we had pressed on? Couldn't we have recovered?" Tears pour down my cheeks so heavily my sinuses drain. Against my better judgment, I let Donovan dab my eyes with a tissue.

"Remember how we used to go for long walks? I kept changing our route because we lived near both a school and a park. Kids were everywhere, and you always looked so sad.

One day a little boy couldn't get started on a swing. You ran over to help him, and looked so happy. I wanted you to always be that happy."

"I was happy," I implore, sniffling with a snort. "I was happy with you."

The sadness in Donovan's eyes deepens. He kisses his tissue that holds the product of my sorrow and begs for my understanding. "But that was a glow I could never give you. It killed me to know it was my fault you would never have it."

I push on, feeling we are in a tug-of-war as to who hurts the most. "What about the glow I had with you? It was my decision too."

"A decision that was making you ill," he tenderly asserts. "I loved you too much for that."

"I would have gotten past it, but what about you, Donovan? If I had let you recover and come back for you, or if I had rebelled and told you I wasn't going down without a fight, what would have happened?"

Donovan squeezes his eyes, releasing more sorrow. I grab a tissue then crumple it. I want it to be useless. I itch to touch him without the barrier a tissue would provide. My hand surges forth, absorbing his tears into my skin. "I made a huge mistake," he confesses. "I fell prey to dichotomous thinking. After I shoved you away, Dr. Coe got through to me. It wasn't an all or nothing situation."

My hand that has been dampened with his sorrow touches my own cheek, bringing his tears to mine. Everything about us should be together.

"I sabotaged us." Donovan's voice rings with contrition and self-hatred as our foreheads meet. "I would never make that mistake again. Now I can face anything. What about you, Lily?" He turns brave, his words sounding like a challenge. "With the life you have, can you come back to my side and face anything?"

"I've no idea," I hesitantly whisper.

"I'll always love you, Lily."

"And I'll always love you," I burst with devout insistence.

Pulling my head to his chest he utters with fragility, "I cheated on my wife yesterday."

The stab felt from the knife of his words renews my sobs. "The fact that we again stopped doesn't change it, does it?"

"What the hell were we thinking?"

I wish my confession were not true. "Both times I was thinking the same thing I am now. No one makes me feel the way you do. While there's a big difference between sex and making love, the difference between making love and sharing your soul is vaster. So many people never know how that feels."

"You make what we did sound almost forgivable."

"I wish it were."

39

Four days of melodrama have put me completely on edge. While awaiting the arrival of an expressed package that may imply my soulmate is crazy, I duck into my office and embark on a quest to cyber stalk the man staying in my guesthouse. Eric's fan base sends my head spinning with several websites and forums filled with devoted women. Quickly I learn more about the man than I have in all of the years I've known him.

Eric Christopher Taylor, from Salford, started in a skiffle band when he was twelve, then joined The Chestermen at sixteen. He was an apprentice in a bread shop and kept his job until the band already had several hits, feeling at best their success would last only a year.

I know he enjoys baking, but how was that always left out of our conversations?

Eventually I uncover a post by a fan that acquired true treasure—two pictures from Eric's aunt. The photos make me lose all sense of reason. Unable to believe what lies before me, I race to open the photo album on my computer and find my fingers have turned to sticks from anxiety. Comparing a picture of Christopher as a small boy to one of Eric, it's uncanny how they could be the same person. The second picture is one of Eric in a recording studio. I'm shocked by the man sitting next to him who holds a striking resemblance to Christopher. He is simply listed as being Eric's brother.

Oh, Christopher, you do look like someone in your family; you've just been looking to the wrong man. Grace has kept one hell of a secret.

After a day of anticipation that nearly sends me to the bar, the documents finally arrive. Slipping out the back door to cower from prying eyes, I compare them to the other paperwork. My heart suffocates at the sight of the death certificate that is an exact match. Aunt Audrey killed herself, and I can only speculate that is what Mom meant before she died when she referred to an innocent little girl.

My parent's marriage certificate brings forth limited comfort. The signatures are close enough to believe they are from the same people that signed the adoption papers. Questions again swarm my brain, but mostly I'm filled with disgust for myself and for my soap opera of a life.

"Screw this!"

I stash the papers in my desk before grabbing a small chocolate mousse cake and a fork. I head out the back door, eating as I go and wondering how long it will take me to walk to the beach so I can throw myself into the ocean.

ॐ

After the kids are in bed, I stop Eric as he heads out to the guesthouse. A tray containing a steeping pot sits in my hands. "Feel up to sharing some tea?"

"I'm English. By law I must always accept an offer of tea, especially with such pretty company." Eric takes a seat at the table with me. "I had lunch with your brother today. He took me to see his office. He's done impressively well for himself."

"He'd be glad to hear you say that. He thinks very highly of you. I know he wishes he knew you better. We both do. In fact, I have a confession. I was afraid you and I would have little to talk about, so I cyber stalked you. Have you ever snooped on any of your fan forums?"

Eric goes flush. "I try not to. Some of those ladies know far too much about my life."

My tongue stings when I bite it at the recollection of a story about Eric, a groupie, and a can of Golden Syrup. Eric gives the back of his head a scratch. "I don't know which is scarier, when the information is right or when it's dead wrong. Frighteningly, they are mostly right."

Maybe he's read that story himself.

"Have you seen some of the photos they post?" I ask. "Not only are the captions clever, those ladies have quite the collections."

"I really should have kept picture books. My sister did. Just before she died we had a blast going through them."

"Then you might enjoy a site I found." Conveniently, my laptop sits on the table. Trying not to look eager, I surf for the proper forum. "Here it is. There's a section dedicated to each member of The Chestermen. Yours, by far, has the most activity."

Eric becomes aglow at the mention of his staying power. Each picture brings a smile to his face and a story to his lips. Finally I reach the one of Eric and his brother. "Wow. Who is that man?" I ask.

Eric's brow tenses at the image. "My brother, Christopher Michael. We called him Mick. He passed on a few years ago. "

"Mick could be Christopher's doppelgänger. Are you related to Paul?"

"Umm ... no. Not that I'm aware."

"If I had never seen pictures of Paul, I would guess it was him."

"Yes." Eric's voice becomes distant, like it has wandered to another planet. "Wonder how I could have missed that ... Oh! I should show you a wonderful site about bread making. Let me see if I can find it."

Eric whips a URL into the browser. Kneading techniques dominate our conversation until it's time to say goodnight, and I'm left with a new question: Who is the man that fathered my husband, Eric Christopher or his brother Christopher Michael?

40

Susan grants me guidance as I head down an all too familiar stairwell. "Remember, Lily, this is about past choices and future consequences. Any actions you take as a result could cause a domino effect. Go to the door where you found Rose. Touch your hand to the knob, but do not turn it. Think about your soulmate, and accept what is inside your heart."

The glow that illuminates through the cracks is obscured by an image of Jonathan, making me long for the warmth of his skin. Sadness, pain, and loss claw inside me.

"Now, go to your first life," Susan guides.

My presence at the portal brings a glow from within, as happiness, joy, and endless love radiate into my current shell.

"Now, work your way back. Stop when you no longer feel the joy you seek."

Five doors from my first life the pain of a heavy loss shoots through my being. The insides of my earthly body jitter as my discarnate hand guides the knob. Here may lay the key to ending our suffering—or it all may be a bunch of hooey.

White light floods as I step into an open field. "Homes of wood and stone are erected all around. People gather for a celebration, but I feel queasy."

"Is it a funeral?" Susan pries.

"No, it supposed to be a happy occasion. It's—Oh, that pig!"

"Lily, relax." Susan maintains her cool demeanor despite my anger that snaps me back into the present.

"That pig! That ginormous pig! I'm going to kill him!"

"Hey! What the?" Donovan enquires as I storm into his office while he stands behind his desk, thumbing through a book.

The power in my voice conveys my annoyance. "You started this whole mess!"

His head flinches back. "I thought we put the whole Harley thing to bed."

"Everything was fine until you married my sister, you little prick!"

"What?" he asks, before muttering, "Oh, no," and returning his attention to the tome in hand.

"Do you know how seriously the Egyptians took our promise to be together for eternity? You did fine for the next few lives, then you took my sister as a second wife and cursed us, you huge pig!" Suddenly I wake to his demeanor. "Wait. You just muttered 'Oh, no.' You knew! You incredibly vile, disgusting, playboy! This is all your fault, you colossal jerk! I can't believe you didn't tell me! What else are you holding back?" I grab a thick stack of papers off of his desk. He throws his arms up and chuckles while I sissy-swat him.

"You couldn't have kids, and I needed an heir. It was all perfectly legal."

"Legal? You broke my heart, making me vow to never let us be together again because it was legal? You douchebag!"

His arms drop, taunting me. "Lily, listen to yourself. Isn't this partially your fault?"

"Stop trying to get out of this, you big smelly ass! You're the one who banged half the village."

"Taking a second wife is hardly—" My eyes flair at him, causing him to backpedal. "I'll never do it again. I will never, ever marry anyone but you ever again."

I slam the papers on the desk before looking up at the big dumb jock who again cowers in the corner, chuckling. "What's so funny?"

"You do realize you are dying to beat the crap out of me over something people could argue we're crazy to even consider being real." Donovan sits next to me as I throw myself onto the sofa. Suddenly he looks apologetic. "I think the reason I felt so strongly that you needed to marry Christopher and have a family is directly related to that life. You had every right to be angry. I let myself get talked into something that should have been a mutual decision. I regret it now more than ever."

"Who talked you into it?"

"Elanabeth Bathory, the same pain in the ass woman who has conquered us every time since. I just don't know why she does it."

"Do you think ending this cycle could be as easy as me forgiving you?"

"I've no idea, but it can't hurt to try. Forgive me?" he pleads. His face contorts like a puppy dog.

"Yeah, I forgive you," I say while half groaning and half laughing.

Taking my hands, he inches closer and becomes overtly serious. "Once we move on, whether it's now or in the next go round, it's you and me forever—no matter what the stakes." He tugs at my hand, guiding me to his desk. "Come here a sec. The hospital called. They can't find the copy of Mom's DNR, which is because she never signed it. I need you to sign as a witness." Donovan signs Mom's name to the papers, then hands them to me along with a pen.

"You're forging Mom's papers?"

"It's not like we didn't know what her wishes were."

My eyes jerk to the paper in fear. Has he forged anything else of hers, like adoption papers? Relief hits quickly. "This looks nothing like Mom's signature."

"If I had forgery skills, I could have gotten our college funds signed over without kissing up to Dad. Besides, the hospital just wants to cover their asses."

I sign the paper, not believing the things I do for this man. "Donovan, doesn't all this seem weird to you? If Mom was so ashamed of us, why didn't she bust out with the truth?"

"How that haunts me is the reason why it took me so long to tell you. Then again, Mom did confess in her own warped way. Why?"

"I refuse to fall into a rat trap. We won't turn everyone's world upside down because a piece of paper says it's okay." My frustrations with the world show as I begin pacing. "This is ridiculous. We are told that an adopted child is family to the parents just as much as if they are genetically related. Yet society is more accepting of a romantic relationship between adopted siblings because the two are not related. How conflicting is that? All you need to do is take adoption paperwork to a courthouse and suddenly all is right, but not every state allows it. You need some twisted form of algebra to figure out who can marry where."

My hands fly up in surrender, yet I am far from done. "If genes don't matter, then none of this should be an issue. Yet if two people actually share those genes, all of mankind flips out. Why? Oh, well, it's because of um … birth defects! Really? People can't come up with a better excuse than that? Since when do you need to be married to reproduce? The whole situation is a bunch of malarkey enforced by sheaves made from trees."

Donovan proudly snickers. "You've been working on that little diatribe for a while."

"Fourteen years, five months, and twenty-seven days."

"I thought I was the one who hit my head the day you tackled me."

The charm of his blinky eye roll is currently lost on me. "I want to prove those papers false."

Donovan nearly flips into a tizzy. "Have you totally lost your mind? Then again, maybe you're adopted too and really the product of Billy Bibbit."

I take his cheeks in my hands and address him rationally. "Because the whole thing smells like a skinned chicken that's been rotting in the sun for two days. I didn't believe a word Nurse Ratched said once I started seeing through her lies. Truthfully, the closer our bonds are in all ways, the better in my book. Come over tomorrow after dinner. It's time to settle this crap. Do me a favor though. Whatever I say, just play along."

⊗

Eric and I are just finishing a pot of tea when my video chat finally rings. "Too late!" I say with a smile as Christopher's face appears on my screen.

"Blimey, it's only midnight. We had loads of packing to do since we're about to leave."

"That's not our complaint," I chime. "You didn't let us know what you want for dinner tomorrow. We planned a feast without your input."

"I've been pegged out in a van for two weeks with a bunch of nutter blokes and want nothing other than me wife to pull a sickie so she is there when I arrive. I plan to enjoy seeing you, then sleep the day away with you in my arms. Since I feel I've been gone so long that the moppets have flipped the nest, I'm certain we won't be interrupted."

"Already on it!" Eric yells in the background.

"Cracking!" Christopher exclaims. "How is Donovan doing after learning of your mother's little stunt?"

"New subject!" I chime. "I actually had a name idea. Since we already honored Davy Jones, how about the rest of The Monkees?"

"Not that I would support it, but that would be Mickey, Peter, and Mike. Michael Peter Michael would be barmy."

"No, one Michael and a George," I correct. Finally I came prepared into one of these conversations. I must really love this guy. Seriously, why would I care about music so far before my time, classic or not?

"George?"

Fred steps in behind Christopher. "Are you two at it again?" he asks.

"Yes!" Eric yells back.

I ignore them and continue. It's not easy to come up with

this stuff. "Mickey's real name is George Michael Dolenz. So George Michael Peter totally works."

Christopher leans back in his chair, crossing his arms. "Do you really think we should name the poor child George Michael?"

My lips purse. "Oooh ... Good point." Dennis runs up to Christopher and shakes him. "What are you doing?" I say, laughing.

Dennis throws his arms out in anticipation of applause. "I'm waking him up before we go-go. Come on, let's get out of here!"

"I'm ghost, luv. See you in the morning!"

41

"How about Raymond David Michael?" Christopher asks while pacing through the kitchen.

"Heavens, not again," Eric says with a groan. He stops doing dishes and turns to watch the sideshow.

I'm with him. Besides, I'm tired of always sounding like a twonk when it comes to music. Christopher already has me stumped. "Who would that be from?"

Eric's brows cross in bewilderment before Christopher turns into a puppet version of himself with his bobbing head and display of hand gestures. "Really, Lilyanna! I'm embarrassed for you."

"Not helping," I say.

Christopher thwarts his hands onto his hips and huffs, "The Kinks!"

"Oh." Yeah, because those names are not at all common.

"What do you mean, *oh*?"

"Not doing it for me."

He strolls around the kitchen as if the answer is on the floor. "Okay, how about Peter Roger Keith? Never mind. That's terrible."

Lord! At least that one I got. Eric's been blasting The Who for two days. It is an excellent lead-in for me though. "Oh! How about Paul Mark Keith?"

Christopher's eyes flick back and forth. He's totally lost; meaning his impending wobbly is going to be awesome! He fusses with the pepper grinder on the counter. After weeks of searching for the perfect taunt, I'm going to smash salt into his paper cut.

I milk his torture as I pretend to ponder. "Hmm ... Actually, that doesn't really work. How about Paul Mark Phil or Drake Michael Paul? Oh, that last one isn't bad!"

Christopher attempts a detour. "Speaking of Pauls—"

"Oh, no you don't! No changing the subject because you're lost," I nag.

Eric bites a nail, searching for the answer as well. At least I know he'll get the joke, since he was once in a tug-of-war on the charts with these guys.

"No. Not exactly." Christopher draws out his words, stalling. "Paul is a very common name."

"Yeah, but Drake isn't."

Christopher throws his hands into the air, disheveling his mane. "All right. I give. Who is it?"

With the thump of my foot my hands thrust onto my hips, mocking his earlier gesture. His squirming is delightful! "Paul Revere and the Raiders."

Christopher's mouth drops as he stammers. "You mean those American blokes in the Revolutionary War costumes? No bloody way!"

Eric breaks into applause and catcalls at my trump card. I bow to him before my focus returns to taunting Christopher. "In 1967 alone they had three gold albums. Not even the Beatles can top that. The Raiders were America's answer to the British Invasion."

"Exactly. They're Yanks who represented a revolt against my kind."

"What's wrong with Yanks? May I remind you that you are married to one, both of your children are Yanks by birth, and you have a dual-citizenship, making you half Yank, just like your children are half Scouser."

His mouth goes agape at the killing blow of the S word. "There's no need to get nasty!"

The chime of the doorbell signals the end of this round and allows me to quit while ahead. Answering the door to Donovan, I whisper, "Remember, play along."

"Hello to you, too," he says as I drag him into the kitchen. He waves at Eric and Christopher, and I nudge him into a chair.

"Sit, please," I request. Suddenly I feel discomfort over having him and Christopher in the same room.

"What's going on?" Christopher asks.

Donovan rolls his eyes in the endearing, yet cocky, way that only he, and my daughter, can. "Welcome home," he grumbles. "I'm assuming you mouthed off and we're about to go through another round of palate training."

Christopher's eyes widen in panic that he's blown it. I give him a stress-relieving shake of my head as I hand Donovan a plastic tube with the letter B on it. "What's this for?" he asks.

"DNA test. Swab your mouth."

He dangles it in front of him like he's examining a dead insect. "Lily, are you sure about this? We might open a new can of worms."

"Please humor me."

As Donovan complies, I tilt Christopher's head back, and swipe inside. "Blimey, what's that for?"

"Control test. You should show as not related to us." Labeling it C, I toss it back into the paper bag.

"Got another of those?" Eric asks. Either this is his confessional or he's checking up on baby brother.

"Why you?" Christopher asks.

"Control point. If it shows me as related to Lilyanna, we know the test is flawed."

"Excellent idea, Eric! Here you go." I hand him a kit labeled D.

Donovan's eyes jet to me, as he now gets the reason for my grandstanding. *Seriously?* His eyes float between the two of them. *Oh, it makes so much sense. Damn it, how is it Christopher always gets what I wish I had?*

Donovan's attention returns to the tube he just capped. "It's too bad we don't have Mom's DNA. Who's to say there isn't paperwork I didn't find."

"Ah, but we do!" From the bag of DNA kits I remove my grandmother's old brush—the one that Mom kept on her dresser and often used. Holding it up, I make a spokesmodel-worthy gesture around it. "I packed this without removing Mom's hair. There's a major lab in Los Angeles. I'll drop everything off tomorrow, and we'll have the results in a few days."

Now I just need to swab Antonia tonight while she sleeps.

42

This is one of those days—the ones where, unexplainably, nothing feels right no matter how well things are going. Though it's not uncommon for people to have enigmatic twangs of discomfort, the fluttering that resounds in me is nothing short of ominous.

Donovan has been at the forefront of my mind all day. While that may not be new by any means, the fact that it is coupled with the feeling a hissing cobra is about to strike through my stomach invokes dread.

My heart hums in my throat as I arrive unannounced and open the door to Donovan's vacant lobby. While his colleagues have long left, he remains in his office, which is all but quiet. "Stop sitting on your hands and face me like a man!" Anna's voice barks from inside. In my slit of a view through his ajar office door, Donovan rests his head on his desk, his hands covering it. "Anna, please stop hitting me. You know I won't fight you."

"You don't love me enough to fight. You want me mutilated so I'll hide in shame and leave you alone. Fine! I'll give you what you want."

Anna grabs something off of the desk and darts across the room. *Thumps* and *pops* resound as sharp grunts of pain release from Anna's mouth.

"Anna, stop!" Donovan yells with panic. He runs around the desk as the noises continue. "What the hell are you doing?"

"Giving you what you want!"

"Jesus Christ, Anna, give me that stapler!" Now out of my view, the scampering continues, until someone is shoved against the wall.

"Ouch!" Donovan utters, just before a *smack* resounds. "Ow! Crap!" He then runs past, and his chair is slid aside. More rustling is heard.

"Give me back that stapler!" Anna screams while coming after him. "Get out from under that desk you coward! Handle this like a man!"

"Stop kicking me!" Donovan yells. His voice is covered by Anna's grunts of force. How he can remain calm is bewildering.

"I'm not kicking you. You're kicking yourself," she screams as the kicks continue. They are followed by Donovan's occasional wince of pain.

"I will not succumb to what you are doing. You were supposed to be past this a long time ago."

"Past this? How past it are you, Dr. Big Shot? Why am I now always the victim?"

"Anna, I'm calling the police. You can either stop this nonsense now or keep it going for them to settle. The 911 operator will record the call, and you won't have a prayer in court of keeping Sunshine. So you either stop and keep your therapy appointment tonight, or you forfeit everything. *Choose now.*"

"Fine! You win, as always," she concedes, heading for the door as I scamper under the secretary's desk. "You always get what you want!" she screams through sobs. Exiting his office, she slams both it then the lobby door so she can get in the last word.

After a brief moment of silence, I brave emerging. "Donovan? Are you okay?"

A brief moan comes as he staggers out, wondering why he now needs to face me. Blood drips from a small gash over his right eye. Why does this poor, innocent victim look shamed and filled with guilt? And why is Donovan always the one to suffer?

I grab a tissue and dab away the falling blood. "Why the hell do you put up with that? Why don't you just pick up your daughter and leave?"

He grabs a deep breath to keep himself centered. "Because I was once her. I hurt myself out of desperation."

"So you married her because you felt sorry for her?"

"That is not why I married her. Besides, these are recent occurrences."

"How recent?"

His lips tighten. His head cocks to the side before he twists it back with a deep wince. "I made a promise, okay? She has her own story, and I'm not going to cover for her, but I am also not going to betray her trust—especially when she shouldn't trust me in other areas."

"You're also afraid that if I know, I won't let you leave her."

"Truthfully, yes, but I have to keep my promise."

Finally the deeper meaning sinks in. "If you were once her then ... You didn't meet in school, did you?"

His head oscillates with little jerks.

"Victims support?" Fearing the response, I sit on the sofa to brace myself.

His little jerks morph into nods. "Her father and brother are my polar opposite. Mom would have had every right to make them suffer, and then some."

"They actually raped her?" I choke out.

Donovan sits by my side. "Repeatedly. She would have been lucky only to have been raped."

A burn creeps into my esophagus. "But that's not what's causing the outbursts now."

"No, but abusive situations lead to mind and body overload. Similar overloads trigger irrational behavior. Sometimes she sees pain as compassion. She wouldn't know real compassion if it bit her in the ass, but she can put on a hell of a show. She became a nurse to help her distinguish those two things, but it's been pretty unsuccessful. When she gets out of control she brings me secondary wounding, which is why I'm going to leave. She starts swinging, and I hear Dad saying I'm not manly enough to stand up to her. I won't reward her bad behavior by regressing." Donovan juts a hand out. "Before you ask, yes, she is getting help—lots of it—and no, I'm not her doctor. Neither of us is that stupid."

God, it all makes so much sense; self-defense classes, how she can often be so meek and intimidated, yet also so cruel. "Her body issues are a result, too?"

Again Donovan's lips disappear into his mouth. "Just know that she struggled for years to become the person I married. As much as I want to stand by her and help that person return, I can't take any more risks with my daughter or myself." Donovan stammers up. "Let me walk you to your car. She may still come back."

A million questions fly through my mind as we head outside, all of them an invasion of privacy. Before driving off, I brave one he can't fault me for asking. "Aren't you concerned about Sunshine?"

"Of course I am, which is why I need to leave in a way where I'm assured full custody. I've hidden cameras in the house. As soon as I know I can secure Sunshine, I'm gone." In a rare moment due to the direness of his words, nothing feels magical when his eyes stare into mine. "No matter what happens, please promise that if I ever show up on your doorstep with my daughter, you will take care of her."

The chime of irony resounds to the bone. "I would treat her as my own."

Donovan swallows back the hurt, and waves me off as I drive away. I wish I could rescue him.

43

The barbecued chicken Eric brings in from the patio smells divine. Thank God Eric was in charge. The last time Christopher barbecued the only aroma was that of lighter fluid and burnt fish. So much smoke was created that it set off the detector, causing the kids to flee in a screaming panic that had the neighbors calling the fire department.

"Ack!" An accidental taste from the wrong pot of beans makes my taste buds cringe. "England, you never disappoint." Grabbing two bowls of baked beans, I head into the dining room where everyone has gathered. Imported beans, straight from the can, are placed near Christopher. The homemade ones are placed near me.

"Two bowls?" Eric asks.

"That one is for your fellow Lobsterback," I say, pointing to the bowl near Christopher. "Frankly, I gag just over the thought of them. The other is for those with taste buds."

Christopher looks at me like I've lost all touch with reality. "I thought you didn't like them?"

What? Oh, geez! Christopher's inability to translate the difference between American English and British slang drives me a little nuts. "Gagging for something in England is far different from gagging over something in America."

Eric scratches his head in confusion. "Don't you like your wife's cooking?" he asks Christopher.

"I love me wife's cooking, but she doesn't know beans about beans. Try those Yank ones and see for yourself."

"May I?" Eric asks.

"Fill your boots," I say, handing him the bowl. He takes small spoons of each. The children stare at the act they find too bizarre for comprehension. They've learned to always follow my lead whenever two of the same thing is served.

"You're wasting your time," Christopher sings a little indignantly. "You want the ones like me mum always made."

"You mean like the cook always dumped out of a can," I state. "I love Grace, but I can't see her using a can opener for fear of splattering juice on her hand."

"Too true," Christopher agrees. "Still, I don't understand the kerfuffle over your beans."

I pretend to keep my focus on Christopher's ranting, as Eric tastes the imported beans and shakes his head in memory. "Yep, those are British."

His wording forces my snicker, which prompts Christopher to wave his fork at me and warn, "No comments from the Yank Scouser."

Eric tastes my beans before making a face of disgust. "These are the ones Christopher doesn't like?"

"Yep," I say with a sigh.

Christopher crosses his arms with a smug look, which Eric quickly wipes off of his face. "Seriously, Christopher, you're off your head. I'm calling Grace and giving her a serious verbal lashing regarding your taste buds."

Christopher's mouth goes agape in horror of the betrayal right as the doorbell chimes. "I was raised on these," he claims aghast, as I flee to answer the front door.

Eric continues his chastising. "As was I, but I grew up poor. I'm going to ask Grace what her excuse is."

My smile drops when my hand touches the doorknob. Donovan stands before me holding Sunshine, whose head is nestled into her daddy's neck. "Hey, what brings you two by?" I ask. My hand caresses Sunshine's curls as I attempt to sound cheerful.

Donovan pulls his head back to smile at his daughter. "I thought Sunshine could use a night out. Mind if she plays with the kids?"

"Not at all. Hungry? There's quite the comedy act going on inside."

Donovan sets the girl down and points to the dining

room. "Go on, sweetie. Go enjoy some of Auntie Lily's amazing cooking."

We watch the girl run off with a big smile. When I turn back to Donovan, all pretense is gone and he embraces me. "She didn't see anything bad, did she?" I ask, gripping tightly and fearing the worst. My only consolation is that I don't see any new marks on him.

"No, but Anna's in the car, and I'm taking her to rehab for the next thirty days. Can Sunshine stay here tonight?"

"Of course," I tell Donovan. "Why isn't she staying with you?"

"It's bad enough her mom is freaking out. The last thing she needs is a mental case dad who is struggling to hold it together. My nightmares tonight should be epic."

Lord, how I wish his life wasn't this way. I'd give anything to change it.

Wait. Did I mean that?

"Okay, but can you come back for breakfast? Eric's test results will be back and things could get interesting. We made need a shrink, albeit a broken one."

"Sure, Lil. Thanks."

As Donovan heads down the walkway, I call out, "Hey, call if you need me." With a little nod he continues on and drives Anna into the night.

44

Drinking coffee on a stress-filled day is only wise if you use Valium instead of sugar. Sadly, I didn't have this thought two cups ago.

Donovan and I sit on the porch steps, sipping coffee as the courier van arrives. Inside, Christopher sleeps, completely in the dark regarding the battles going on under his nose. Only one set of answers arrives today. The delay of the hair strand test leaves Donovan and I stressed for another week.

Eric is already on a quest to prepare breakfast when we approach. Tapping his shoulder, I raise the envelope to him. "What's this?" Eric asks.

"Your test results," I say, gently. "Ours will take a few more days."

Eric's eyes drop to the envelope—reminding me of a frightened house cat who's trying to stare down a pit bull. "I suppose you figured it out then."

"Truthfully, I don't know if you're his father or his uncle."

With a shrug and shake of his head, he resigns himself to whatever lies inside. "Will you both be there with us? I've a feeling we're going to need all of the family we can get."

The adults gather in the library, behind closed doors, sitting in reading chairs with a table pushed in the center. Eric sits before me, repeatedly clearing his throat and looking heavenward. Christopher eyes the envelope on the table; concerned that it holds my answers. With swift movements Eric opens it, then hands the contents to Christopher. "I wanted to tell you yonks ago, but I had to respect Grace's wishes. Please forgive me for not telling you sooner."

"What is this?" Christopher asks.

"Our part of the DNA results."

"Our part?" Christopher scans the document, his face going slack. He looks to Eric whose eyes plead for acceptance. "You're—you're my father?" Christopher lays a hand over his mouth as he drops back in his chair. My heart tightens for him.

Eric presses his arm onto that of the chair. It seems that he is fighting jitters. "When your parents had their first huge fight, all looked bleak. Grace escaped by coming to see us lads on tour. My wife and I had an agreement that I could have company while on the road, but there were rules. I broke them by getting involved with someone I had attachment to—and I did it without protection. Not only did Grace get pregnant, it opened me up to all kinds of health issues, thus endangering my wife as well. She saw it as the ultimate betrayal and left me even though she too was pregnant. My daughter was eighteen before I got to spend any real time with her. By then she was so jaded against me that—"

"Oh my God, Ellen." Christopher gulps his breath as if it's a boulder. "You were just getting to know her when I returned home and ruined everything."

Eric looks to the ground. His breath is weighty. "I suppose that's a whole other can of worms. Grace never wanted anyone to know out of respect for Paul, who eventually learned anyway. Constantly I've asked Grace if I could tell you; when you moved, when you returned, after Paul died, when you married, and countless other times. A few days ago I informed her I was doing it whether she approved or not."

"Dad—Paul knew?"

"Yes. Paul knew my family well. When you were little you looked just like me, and the older you got, the more you looked like Mick. It was too obvious."

Christopher wanders to the window. His eyes lack focus. "This explains so much. I always wondered not only why I looked so different, but also why I was treated differently. It's because I wasn't his son."

I go to him in support. Sadly, I am of as much comfort as Eric's words. "Christopher, Paul did the best he could, given the circumstances. Most men would have left. Paul at least tried."

Futilely, my eyes try to grab Christopher's. His pain radiates, making my body ache for him. "He treated me so differently," Christopher says to the grass outside. "Now I know why he set me up to fail in school."

"No, Christopher," Eric corrects. "He wanted you to grow in ways he couldn't. He never meant for you to have such a hard time."

"Funny, I don't see it that way." Christopher storms from the room, leaving the rest of us to stare at each other.

Eric turns to Donovan and me. "I should have told him when Paul died, but I didn't feel I had the right."

Donovan places a reassuring hand on Eric's arm. "You did the right thing. You tried to be a good father and put your son's needs first. That's more than I ever experienced with my own."

Christopher returns with his open laptop in hand, screaming at Grace over video chat like a rabid dog. "You shameless whore! You let Dad set me up to fail just so you had an excuse to come home! You knew I never should have been accepted to that school. I left someone I loved because I thought I was helping to put my family back together, but actually I was the excuse for Dad—Paul—whoever the hell he was—to march you back! And you didn't even have the decency to tell me he wasn't me dad nor that I was returning home to the man who was."

"Christopher," Grace pleads. "That's not what happened."

Christopher storms the room, twitchy and ranting. His face is contorted into a growl as he berates Grace. "It sure as hell is in my eyes! You saw how brokenhearted I was when we left, but what mattered to you was returning home. The least you could have done was tell me what I was returning home to. It would have given me perspective and hope. Instead I got into a world of trouble. All the drugs I did, all the girls I used—all because there was nothing in my life worth caring about! I became worse than you when we were in America! Sure, bringing you home saved you, but it was at my expense, not to mention April and Clara. Clara never spoke to me again after you paid her off to have an abortion. Not a night goes by when I don't pray for forgiveness for your actions. I would have done the honorable thing, but you stuck your nose in and went against my beliefs!"

My throat constricts around the gasp I try to withhold for Christopher's sake. That beautiful man can't possibly be talking about himself.

Christopher has always been embarrassed by his mistakes during those two years apart. We all do foolish things—but what I am hearing is so unlike him that it's no wonder why he didn't want me to know. Grace was a shameless tramp that he drug home and sobered up night after night. He was so humiliated by her that I can't imagine him doing anything similar. Dear God, if he was worse ... How the hell did Eric's daughter, Ellen, come into play? Who are these other girls I have never heard of? No wonder why he's wanted silence.

"I only did it for your future," Grace begs through the monitor. "You know I never gave up hope for—"

Christopher smacks the laptop onto the desk. We all cringe at the force. "If you wanted Lilyanna and I together so badly why didn't you insist I stay with her and stand up to Paul, the perfect man who dumped you time and time again? My real father and his friends came to the rescue even when I hurt them. I was a huge disappointment with the way I acted like some big shot, throwing around money, getting into trouble, and hurting poor Ellen. She was actually getting me to shape up when I got shoved away like rotten garbage with not so much as a goodbye. It ripped her and Eric apart, and I thought it was that everyone was disappointed to the point where they had given up on me. Lord knows I was disappointed in meself! Now the real reason is bloody well clear."

Eric's reluctance in approaching Christopher makes me unsure if he is standing behind the laptop to back Grace or if he's afraid to get near the fuming beast. "You really have it all wrong. Grace wanted you to have a solid family, not be an outcast who didn't know where he belonged."

"Bloody bad job she did! I was always the outcast. I had a right to know the truth just as much as you had a right to tell me."

"Christopher, please. Just let me explain," Grace begs.

"We are done here!" With a *smack,* he slams the lid on his laptop, ending the call and leaving the rest of us in shock.

45

Eric stares out the window, looking to the sky for answers. Donovan sits with his head nearly in his lap, remembering his own parental betrayal and knowing that more looms around the corner, no matter what we learn.

Christopher doesn't deserve this pain. Never in the thirteen years I have known him has he ever lost his temper in such a wild fashion. This level of fire is uncharacteristic, and I worry for him. He sits shrunken in a reading chair. The red in his downturned face is slowly subsiding, yet his anger still smolders. Is the hiding of his face caused by shame for his actions or embarrassment that the truth has surfaced?

If I had moved to England, none of Christopher's problems would exist. Eric would still have his relationship with Ellen, and Mom may have left Donovan alone. A pressure simmers in my head as years of betrayal and loss are finally absorbed. Although my thought is irrational, it also makes perfect sense. "This is all my fault," I mutter. "Every bit of pain in this room is either my fault or amplified by my actions. I'm the problem."

"Darling, don't be ridiculous." A calmer Christopher puts a hand on my shoulder. I feel like his anger transfers to me.

"No!" I snap at him. "It's all my fault, beginning with Donovan and ending with Eric's problems with Ellen. I could have prevented them all."

"Lily!" Donovan jumps out of his seat before regaining his composure. "You know that isn't true," he calmly reasons. "Let's get you some air." He walks me out of the house. His heart is pounding, but his demeanor is cool. Inside the driveway we hide between two cars. "Lily, you know what you feel isn't true."

"I know," I say calmly and resigned to frustration. "I'm totally overreacting. A satanic inner voice says I'm a horrible person who causes suffering, and a big part of me feels you should just leave and have a normal, healthy life for once."

"I'm not leaving you," he says, insistently. "You know that. Especially now that we don't know what we're up against. I swear, every day something happens to rub my face into the fact that us breaking up was the biggest mistake ever."

"Donovan, that doesn't make any sense. How would staying together have stopped any of this?"

"Neither you or I would be swimming in a mess of everyone else's problems. I know it's selfish, but is it so wrong to want you back? To desire the level of happiness that I only get when you're in my arms? What I'm trying to say is, you are not someone who causes suffering. I made the biggest mistake of my life when I thought that way about myself. Don't let it happen to you."

The last thing I need is a dose of Donovan remorse, but he's right. "I'm just locked in a cell of my own guilt, and I have to get out. Obviously Christopher is in the same boat. We should become fitness junkies to burn off frustration." I pick up a rock and chuck it across the street. The act actually helps. "Didn't playing football used to help you?"

"Like that will ever happen," Donovan snorts. "Though I bet Christopher would be an entertaining disaster with tackle gear."

"Or maybe I could do—"

"Hmm … A runner. That would work for you."

"A runner? Yeah, I could do that. Damn it! This is all such a huge disaster. It's like everybody is on love drugs, and I can't stand it anymore. I need to tell Christopher the truth about us and Chuck Cunningham's room. I have to escape the bullshit somehow."

From out of nowhere, Christopher's voice resounds. "Who's Chuck Cunningham? Is everything all right?" Christopher appears as if every emotion he feels is a contradiction. His eyes stab me while his form appears weak, like he wants to release a furious scream before he's sick to his stomach. He was so much calmer inside a moment ago. What has set that poor man off now?

"He's an old TV character we use as a joke," Donovan says, sounding as deflated as I feel. "Lily's just got some anxiety brought on by lack of sleep. Can you give us a little more time?"

Something in Christopher's eyes as he walks away sends razor blades through my veins. Oh, crap. How much did he hear? "I've got to suck up my problems and get back inside. Christopher needs to know this changes nothing between us."

"Thank heaven our test results aren't here." Donovan sighs. "Since whatever we find is yet another dose of betrayal, let me get through Anna's rehab first. Now I need to get my daughter home to her own cold reality."

ॐ

Christopher stands at the patio door, watching his father play with the children. "You all right?" I ask, approaching him with trepidation.

"Let's go upstairs," he says sternly. "Today has given us much to talk about."

As Christopher shuts the bedroom door he firms his stance, flipping his hair aside to reveal his lovely eyes have grown darker and stormier than ever. A new side of Christopher is brewing, and I shiver at his glare. "I thought you might like to finish what was started."

My stomach twists. "What do you mean?"

"A few minutes ago the pin was pulled on our marriage. Would you like to throw the grenade or shall I do it for you?"

His words fail to register in my hazy mind, but his tone does. My only response is a blank stare. I pray he didn't hear Donovan's talk of our break up.

"All right, Lilyanna. If you can't admit the truth, I'll say it for you. It's time we had it out about those two years apart. Clearly you and Donovan have much to say about it. Do you care to share?" Christopher's glare is unwavering, making me feel there is no possible way I can squirm out of anything. His arms drop as he heads for the door. "Fine! If you want games you have them, but I am not doing to my children what my parents did to me. We no longer have ties. However, the children must never know our marriage is a sham. If you won't cooperate, I'm leaving and taking the children with me. I'll sue if I have to, but I don't think you'd want that."

My desire to rationalize with him is halted by his state of rage, fearing his senses are blind to all else. Instead I sit silent, unresponsive, and feeling imprisoned for a crime I didn't commit.

"Lilyanna, do you understand me?"

A nod is my only reply.

"Good! We will be out the rest of the day. Have dinner on the table at six. Bring your game face." The slam of the door behind him shatters my heart like splintered glass.

Full body tremors hit as I crumple to the ground. Even though it is ridiculous that my prior actions hurt Christopher, and may forever haunt my children should the bigots of the world learn and ridicule them, only my foolish irrationality is to blame.

Below me the garage door closes. Outside the bedroom window Christopher drives off with Eric and our children. My cries turn into blood curdling screams as my life abandons me.

ॐ

The kids run in, still excited from the wonderful time they had at Knox Berry Farm without me. Eric sports a grin that rivals those of my children. "Lilyanna, glad you are well. Christopher said you had a horrific headache and we would probably order take away for dinner."

It takes all I can muster to conceal my hurt. "Thanks, Eric. I'm much better now. Dinner will be on the table in ten minutes."

Christopher enters carrying a bunch of kitchy toys and looking knackered. He likely has the headache he claims I was suffering from. Serves him right for ditching me.

"Cracking. Need any help?" Eric asks as Antonia chases Graham around the kitchen for reasons completely unknown to me.

"If you would make sure the kids wash that would be perfect. Thank you."

Christopher gives me a luscious kiss with a beautiful smile. "Glad you are well."

"On it!" Eric chimes while chasing the children up the stairs to their rooms. As soon as they are out of view, Christopher heads upstairs, now appearing as if he's returned from a funeral.

"Rough day?" I ask.

"I think you know the answer to that," he mutters. Christopher lumbers up the stairs, and I feel that though his public actions were adoring, his private ones show he is really walking away, not only from me at this moment, but from our life.

46

I feel as if I am in a movie—in a scene where tension exists because the only sound comes from the ticking of an old clock—only here there is nothing but silence that tocks through me. The glow coming from the digital clock on the nightstand reveals it is two in the morning. When last I looked it was midnight. How did I manage to actually get a few hours of sleep? In the week since our blowout, scarcely a civil word has been uttered between Christopher and I that wasn't in public, and we've each accumulated less than a night's worth of rest.

This battle has to end.

Light seeps through the crevices of the adjoining bathroom's door. Stiffly I lie in bed, pretending to be asleep and watching the numbers on the clock morph as the minutes crawl past. At two thirty-four in the morning I rise, worried for Christopher who has been silent the entire time. Standing just outside the bathroom, my raised hand halts before knocking. Faint sobs travel through the door—the sound of a broken heart. Softly I knock. "Christopher, please, let's talk."

The *rip* of a tissue being pulled from a box comes to my ears, followed by a deep breath. After a moment, the door wildly swings open. Christopher emerges from the bathroom and storms past me. He seems to want me to think he has been stewing the entire time. "Christopher, we need to talk about this."

I follow him to the bedroom door that he slams behind him, halting my pursuit. From outside he mutters faintly, "I'm sorry," so softly I question if I actually heard it.

Back to bed I go. Another night, another dose of pain.

ॐ

High atop the Hollywood Hills, Robert and I stand in a majestic mansion resembling an old English castle. With the exception of modern luxuries woven into the façade everything about it screams antique. It seems fitting that we find ourselves here as tonight's party, celebrating the sixtieth anniversary of Anthem Records, will be filled with rock n' roll royalty from all of its eras.

Nestled in the corner of a large room lined in grey bricks and windows overlooking Los Angeles, we put the final touches on a cake. The full-sized replica of a Vox Super Beatle amp, seated in an original metal frame, stands tall and proud. Robert and I dote over little details that make it look so real someone may plug a guitar into it.

"Wow! That looks incredible!" Jenny exclaims on her approach. "Have you seen how much champagne they brought in?"

"Yeah, along with all the whisky," I add.

"Yeah, along with the hot delivery guys who carried that stuff in here," Robert says, fanning himself. "I would gladly drink anything those guys have to offer."

"Robert, that is vile!" Jenny laughs and gives his arm a little shove.

Robert gets pouty. "It's not fair that you get a tall, hot man and I don't."

My voice deepens and sounds lined with smut. "You mean that Jenny and I both got the tall, hot man and you never will!"

With a flick of his hand he walks off, leaving Jenny and I giggling. "Hey, Christopher!" Jenny yells as he enters the room carrying a couple of guitar cases. "Did you see this cake Robert and your wife made? It's amazing!" Christopher dashes over, his hair flowing with a lovely bounce. Seeing him is heartbreakingly beautiful. "Isn't it smashing?" Jenny beams.

Christopher's grin flows in response to her use of his vernacular. He then looks at the cake with a keen eye of appreciation, nodding his head as he strolls around the back and observing the fine details. "I wouldn't call it smashing. I'd call it absolutely perfect. Whatever gave you the idea to make a cake like this?" He puts his arms around my waist from behind. My hands grip his elbows, tightening the embrace.

"It was all Eric's idea. He even helped me chart out the details."

"Hey, Jenny!" Robert bellows from across the room. "Get over here and help me with these trays. I'm not the only one working today, you know." Jenny drops her shoulders with a sigh before dashing off.

"Do you really like it?" I ask.

"It's perfect," he says, maintaining the snuggle.

For the first time since our world went upside down two weeks prior, he continues to show affection once others have left. When I turn to him, I can scarcely look him in the eyes for fear he will run. "Christopher, please. Nothing here is so important that we can't walk away and talk. Don't you think it's long past time we faced the inevitable?"

Christopher's eyes downturn. His swallow is so deep it is audible. "No," he firmly states. His eyes pop up, and they start to storm the way they did the day this madness started, yet I sense what he thinks is irreparable pain leaks through his façade. "Not at all. After all that was revealed, what could we possibly say that would be in the best interest of our children?"

With a turn a quick as a snap, Christopher heads out the door, slamming its push bar down in disgust as he shoves his way through.

ꝏ

Now this is more like it! When the tough get shunned for three weeks, they start playing dirty!

I slink into the bedroom, wearing Christopher's favorite nightgown—a short baby pink number with little silk roses adorning the straps. It's barely long enough to cover my ass. If I sway my hips, a little bit of my bare butt peeks out, revealing my lack of underwear.

Christopher is already in bed, hugging the edge of his side, just like he's done every night since the day of revelation. If he really doesn't want me near him, he'll have to reinforce it while I'm flashing him.

I approach his side of the bed and deviously straddle over him, giving him a glimpse of my glory before I slink down and spoon him. My hand slides down his torso, headed for unfair territory. "The children are sound asleep," I say in my sexiest voice while nuzzling into his neck.

Christopher's eyes close me off, and I feel a barrier suddenly brick in his emotions. "Lilyanna, please stop. I don't know why you think this is fair to either of us."

I bring myself to sit, trying not to sound defensive as my heart fights his rejection. However, my pain has burdened me for so long that I can't help but feel like a part of me is attacking him. "Christopher, what do I have to do to get you to talk?"

Christopher's eyes tell me my concern was likely justified. He bolts out of bed and faces me, completely on the defensive. "If you want to talk, why don't you call Donovan? You always have so much to share."

The door shuts behind him with a cringe-worthy *slam* that reverberates pain in my heart, leaving me to another night of weeping. Even though I've never been certain how he would take the news of Donovan and I, never, ever did I think Christopher would be such an extremist. How can this man who holds so much compassion be willing to shred a heart over something he can't understand?

༼ༀ༽

One month. Exactly one month ago today disaster struck.

Some way, some how, no one is the wiser as to my situation. How I have kept it to myself is bewildering. Each day I rise, paint on a smile, go to work, come home, tuck my children in bed, then wash the smile away with tears.

Today that changes.

Christopher sits in the basement while the children and Eric play outside. Nervous energy jitters through me as I head down the stairs. This is it. I'm going to confess everything and hope I can do it in a way that keeps my marriage in tact. If I fail, I'll pick up the pieces and do what is best for my children, even if it means being exiled.

Christopher stands, looking through some music.

"Christopher, we are going to talk."

He tosses the stack in his hands onto his desk, forcing himself to stand tall and composed. "I suppose it has to happen eventually."

I stand strong, committed to the task. "About what was said that day—"

"Lilyanna, the truth is out. Until you find a way to convince us both that a problem does not exist, all we can do is put the children first and ignore the rest the best that we can, which we both know is bloody impossible. Now just play along and let everyone think all is right, though we both know it never will be."

"So you won't let me talk, and I'm supposed to spend my life ignoring the truth?" I can't do this anymore. I *won't* do this anymore.

"If that's what it takes, then yes."

"Well maybe you can live your life in denial, but I no longer can." Storming up the stairs, I head out to the garage with my purse, keys, and a resolution to fix my life.

47

The benefit of Anna's rehab stint was short lived. A few days after she was released, Donovan left the house on his own accord and dropped Sunshine off with Eric in another attempt to shelter her from reality. Donovan and I are rendezvousing at his motel to create a plan of action. He wanted time to give Anna an honest shot at rehab, and I've been trying to save my marriage. Thus, Donovan has no idea how Christopher has treated me, only that all has collapsed and I am done.

My veins become tingling rivers of happiness as I knock on the motel room door. Closing my eyes in anticipation, Christopher's image appears. Damn it! He said I could live any way I see fit. Since he won't even succumb to conversation, he certainly isn't allowed haunting privileges.

Donovan's voice carries through the door as he opens it. "And every time you hear it's getting worse you freak out," he yells into the phone. His smile radiates with a joy I haven't seen in years as he draws me through the threshold and into his arms. His unreserved touch brings my heart and soul into complete harmony with his. God, how I've missed him.

Anna fights the battle so boisterously I can discern every word. "Because there is no way you are going to stay with me. Why would a man like you want to be around a mutilated woman he doesn't even love?"

Call me cold, but if she would learn how to use a stapler properly, mutilation wouldn't be an issue.

"That's not true," Donovan says into the phone. "You know I love you."

"Not like you love Lily," Anna yells. "You told me right

after we met that she was the only woman you would ever love."

Wait, Anna knows about us?

Donovan kisses my forehead, then steps away. He yells into the phone, "And you told me that I was the only man you ever trusted, which is how we got together in the first place. Do you love me Anna? Have you ever loved me? Be careful how you answer, because I am going to make myself clear. Freak out one more time, or cancel that appointment next week, and I'm gone for good."

I beckon Donovan to accompany me on the bed, eager to rest my head on his chest. Judging by past experiences, he should have a week, two tops until she flips again.

Unwilling to wait a moment longer, my lips get lost in his neck as my hand slides into his pants. Holy God, he's not wearing any underwear. My action brings his grin almost up to his eyes, and everything south of my waistline tingles.

"Fine! Here's your answer," Anna screams through the phone. "You claim you care what happens to me? Fine, I'll get a mastectomy and suffer through chemo, but I won't do it here."

My breath freezes at the word that terrifies all women.

"Where else would you do it?" Donovan asks Anna as his eyes beseech my forgiveness for withholding her secret. "One of the reasons we came here was so you could visit the treatment center at UCLA."

I slip next to him so the phone now resides between us, making her words even clearer. "Anywhere but Southern California," Anna shrieks. "If I'm going to fight, I need to know you are in this with me. We either leave and forget Lily exists, or you let me go off to die. I will not be mutilated in front of her."

Dear Lord, please let me have heard that wrong. I can't steal the husband of a dying woman no matter how much of a banshee she is.

Donovan ends the call. His face reflects how he feels Anna's suffering. "That's what I wanted to talk about before we decide anything."

"Please tell me I didn't hear the M word. I can't even bring myself to say it."

"Yeah, and chemo. She should have done it over a year ago, but she wanted to try alternative medicine. It seemed to be working, but then things turned for the worse. Now she's without a choice."

"And she takes the resulting aggressions out on you?"

"Every drop of it," he says without reservation.

"And her diet?" I ask.

"A combination of macrobiotics and poor body image. Macrobiotics might have worked if she didn't have conflicting priorities. Lily, I've done everything I could to ensure she has access to every possible option. I'm in debt up to my ears. Through it all, Anna has become more and more of a monster. Though I've never been truly happy with her, at least I was content for a while. Now even that is gone. More importantly, I need to protect my daughter. Anna goes through great lengths to keep me around, but she fails to do the one thing to make me feel I can stay, which is to focus her aggressions constructively. She's a lot like Mom. Every time I think I've found a way out, she springs another trap. How much more abuse can I take before I flip again?"

I touch my hand to his heart and enquire about my selfish fear. "Do you think she's really serious about moving?"

"I know she is, and if you and I leave with Sunshine, I'm betting Anna will be gone from this earth before we are out of the state."

"So it's either we run off and she does what she does or you leave with her?"

"As of now, yes, which means we really need to stop and think about our actions, and we don't have much time to get creative."

48

It was only a matter of time.

Lying alone in a motel room, talking about our woes, the inevitable happened. I did what may have been the most foolish thing ever—told Donovan about Christopher's antics.

"What!" he screamed, nearly tossing me out of his arms as he jumped from the bed. His teeth were clenched so tightly I thought they would shatter. "Get home, right now, and have Eric take the kids to the playground. I'll be waiting down the street. The second they leave, I am going to lay that scrawny little bastard out."

I barely get them out the door before Sir Lancelot charges inside. "Where is that Mancunian snake?" Donovan's protruding eyes and flattened lips of steel confirm why I didn't inform him of Christopher's behavior earlier.

"In his studio," I respond. Donovan charges about two feet before regret creeps back, and I stop him. "I really don't know if we should do this."

He sneer reflects he is offended on the deepest level. "What happened to the girl who was subservient to no one? He has one chance to pull it together, else I'm reclaiming you and the five of us are out of here." Donovan's thundering footsteps as he descends the stairs remind me of the pounding of hells bells in double time—each step weighted with doom. I should have already called for an ambulance.

"I've had it with you," Donovan growls. "Lily filled me in on your behavior over the last few weeks. You have ten seconds to apologize and explain before I turn you into dog food."

To my shock, Christopher stands up to Donovan. He looks as if a turtle could threaten him more. "I wondered when you would finally show. Now maybe we can get to the bottom of things. I won't be threatened by your kind."

What the hell has gotten into Christopher?

Donovan slowly progresses toward him, bearing his teeth as he speaks. I no longer thought Donovan capable of deep anger. "What exactly is *my kind?*"

Christopher attempts to look unaffected—yet his eyes jitter. "Now I know why your mother turned on you."

Dear Lord, does he want to die?

Donovan's face tells Christopher's British teeth may soon be in need of American dental work. "If you don't straighten out immediately, Lily will have no choice but to leave you. You know there is no way she will go without her kids."

Christopher holds his ground. He must desire getting pulverized. "No court would ever grant her rights given the circumstances."

"What circumstances?" Donovan asks with a sneer.

"You're trying to convince Lilyanna to leave me so you can take advantage of her. I never believed your mother's suspicions until I heard your joke about me and tackle gear, love drugs, and pulling a runner."

"What the hell are you talking about?" I ask, shocked and confused.

"I may have gotten in deep, but I never used a rig," Christopher says in self-defense.

I'm astounded. "Who said you did?" My brain scrambles to grasp what he is talking about.

"Donovan sure thought the idea was funny. I see no humor in it."

"When?" I ask, turning to Donovan, who is equally perplexed.

"Out by the car the day the test results arrived. You accused me of still being on Ecstasy, only you used the code of love drugs, and said you were going to pull a runner."

All becomes clear, as I understand his backwards translations of English slang versus Basic English. "Christopher, again you don't understand us."

Anger still flares in Donovan's eyes. "Christopher, after what you did to Lily, you had better start talking. If not, Lily and the kids are leaving with me."

"Why? So I can look the fool and you can steal her away for your own use, just like your mother claimed."

"Do not push my buttons," Donovan warns.

"Christopher! You know those were ridiculous accusations."

"I know nothing of the sort. Of course you claim he is innocent. There is such a thing as Stockholm Syndrome."

With calm words and arms that are tightly wrapped around his own chest, Donovan lets him have it. "You fail to see who the real abuser is, and I won't let it continue."

I scream at Christopher. "Are you calling me a liar?"

"Either that or maybe you are just a whore."

Donovan slams Christopher against the wall, punctuating each point with little shoves that intensify the threat. "Lily does not deserve this treatment. She is an amazing woman who would do anything for her children, even suffer mental abuse for their well being. Go ahead, let the person who would sacrifice everything because she loves and believes in you slip away, and then see how you feel when your head hits the pillow every night for the rest of your life. You know deep in your heart there's not another woman in the world for you. If you fail to fix this now, rest assured you never get another chance with her." Donovan releases his victim. "Well, Christopher?"

Christopher stares at the ground, neither speaking up for me to stay, nor pushing me to go.

"He's right, Christopher," I warn. "Now or never."

His silence causes me to crash. I don't need a valiant fight, only to know that the real Christopher still wants us, but apparently he doesn't.

"All right, Lil. Time to get out of here," Donovan says, escorting me to the stairs. Anger is still pronounced in his face, yet a slip of a smile shows through. Christopher appears shrunken as I take the lead with the intention of tracking down Eric so I can get my kids.

49

"Lilyanna, please wait," Christopher solemnly requests, his eyes still to the carpet, red and welling with misery. "Something did happen between you two, didn't it?" he asks meekly.

Donovan steps up behind me, ready to catch my fall. "Yes, it absolutely did," I answer in no uncertain terms, suddenly feeling fifty-feet tall, yet fearing for my children where the shrapnel will fall.

"It was always obvious something was amiss with the two of you," Christopher chokes out. "When I returned to America, I noticed cologne on your pillows. The same scent came from Donovan's closet when you packed his things. Then I found that letter and the pieces fell into place. I wanted to believe it was comfort, but I was always concerned it was abuse. When my past emerged I feared it was only a matter of time until you left. For weeks I've hoped that if I could keep you from saying you were leaving, that you would stay. When you left today I knew we were at the end and that I had only forced it. So when Donovan arrived, I saw it as my only chance to have comfort that you would be safe.

"I feel so foolish, putting you through all of that," Christopher sobs. "Neither of you have done anything wrong. Honest actions are never wrong."

Donovan closes his eyes and turns away. Frustration blankets his face. He grabs my hand, "Come on, Lily. I think you and I have been through enough already."

Pieces of all of us are dying. The beautiful soul I love has returned, and we're breaking each other's hearts. Now I understand why. As much as I have every right to leave, I can't turn my back on the real Christopher. "Donovan, wait. Don't you see? All along, Christopher knew something happened with us, but he trusted me so much that because I had faith in you, he did too. Now, even though he fears our marriage is crumbling, he's willing to risk pushing it over the edge of a cliff to be sure that I am safe. He's pretending he misunderstood our conversation to get you to talk. It's not that he's not fighting for me, it's that he knows he screwed up. Even though he now feels forced to let go, he is trying to do what's best for me by making sure I won't be victimized." *Donovan, doesn't that sound at least a little familiar?*

Still, I need answers as to why Christopher is so hurt. Without them, I can't help him. "Christopher, what the hell happened during those two years that brought you so much shame you were convinced I would leave?"

Christopher's head drops to conceal his face. "When my trouble in school started, I realized I was a failure who left behind the person he loved most. I was constantly bombed, just like Mum was in America. Then I met Clara. It was never serious, but when she got pregnant, I planned to do the honorable thing. Mum stuck her nose in and paid Clara to get an abortion and leave. There hasn't been a night since I haven't prayed for forgiveness."

The skin around Christopher's eyes bunches as tears drip to the ground. "The whole mess sent me down deeper. Drugs helped, mostly because I handed them out freely to those who followed me. Ellen came back into Eric's life, and I got her friend, April, involved. Ellen was helping me pull it together when Eric tried to keep her away. She had already heard so many bad things about Eric from her mother that now she really believed the worst. Nothing was going on, though soon it probably would have. I thought the reason he shoved me aside was that he didn't trust me. Ellen hardly speaks to Eric now, all because he kept Mum's secret."

"What happened to Ellen?" I ask, inching closer. "Is she okay?"

Christopher's sobs deepen. His eyes press together

harder. Sometimes the greater the physical pain, the faster the emotional pain escapes. That seems to be his hope. "She's fine," he says. "When April started having problems, Ellen shoved my face in it and got me clean. April is mostly fine but she still has a hard time following verbal instructions and stammers for words. She hates herself, says she feels stupid all the time. It's my fault. I never should have gotten her started. It took me years to see that."

The magnitude of his words and depth of his pain seep in. It all sinks into my gut. What I have heard is frightening, but I know the real man, and I promised long ago to never lose sight of him. "Just because you were involved in the catalyst does not mean you are responsible for the outcome. You are not responsible for April's drug use just like Donovan wasn't for Mom's alcoholism." Finally I touch my hand to Christopher's cheek. "So where do we go from here?" I ask.

Christopher inches up his head. "You mean, after all you've heard, you are still willing to stand by me?"

I dare to inch closer. It's not Christopher I fear, but the pain I know this must be causing Donovan. "Christopher, in all the weeks you have treated me like shit, never once have I thought less of you because of the mistakes you made. Who you are is what is important to me, not your regrets."

Donovan's words snap my attention away. "I'll talk to you later, Lil," he says, sounding defeated before his focus turns to Christopher. "Hang in there, man. Call me later, and I'll set you up with help."

A bitter smile crosses Donovan's stony expression as he heads for the stairs. If I could split myself in two and hold on to Christopher while giving Donovan all he deserves, I'd do it without question.

Donovan's steps stutter before he storms back to Christopher. Anger reverberates in his eyes. "Hurt her again, in any way, shape, or form, and I'm coming after you. You haven't heard the last of me yet." He begins to walk away, and then turns back in resignation. "Or maybe you have, if

Anna has her way."

Everything inside me clenches. There's no way he's getting away from me again. I've had it with Anna.

50

Yesterday Donovan turned into the Incredible Hulk; today it is this Wonder Twin's turn. Attempting to keep my fury in check, I resist the urge to pound down Anna's door and opt to ring the bell. My head needs to maintain clarity, yet if my resolve lacks firmness, I'll crumble over her suffering, thus negating my mission.

When the door flies open with Anna looking disgusted by my presence, my charming smile hopefully disguises both my desire to rip her a new one and the tears I fight over her suffering.

"Donovan's not here," she barks. "He took Sunshine to get her away from me."

I try to smile off my annoyance while handing her an overstuffed shopping bag. "Actually, I'm here to see you. Eric went a little crazy and fixed a huge turkey last night. I thought you might like an escape from cooking dinner."

"In other words, you are trying to save Donovan from my alternative medicine diet. Yeah, I know he told you. Come on in," she says, dreading my acceptance of the invitation. Inside the well-lit house her illness becomes apparent. Without her make up, her face resembles a cadaverous raccoon.

Anna heads toward the kitchen while grumbling about being hospitable. I stop and tell it like it is. "I'm not staying where I am so clearly unwanted, but I am going to talk and you will listen." Anna takes a strong stance with folded arms. Something tells me that even in her weakened state the woman has the ability to wipe the floor with my ass. Still I press on. "I know about the ultimatum you gave Donovan. Make no mistake, if you move, you will go alone. If you persuade Donovan to leave with you, I will follow and lure him away. If you run off with Sunshine, I will hunt you down and take her, even if I can't do it legally. Donovan and I will raise her as our own. I don't care how much hiding we have to do."

Anna laughs at me like I'm vermin. "You would never leave Christopher."

I hold my ground and force myself to relish in the falling face of the woman who thinks she has the upper hand. It's the only way to push me through this. "A few days ago that was true. Not now. Donovan must have left a few things out. Apparently Christopher has known about us for a long time, so don't think that you have any power in the ability to tell him if Donovan leaves you. I've also discovered a world of information that has put my relationship with him hanging on a fraying thread, so I've nothing to lose. If you stay, you will continue to get professional psychiatric help along with medical treatment—a mastectomy, chemo— whatever it takes so you can raise your daughter like she needs. Optionally, you let me stand by you like a sister should."

Anna's expression softens. Her annoyance is further tussled by my closing words. "Anna, please let the people who love you help you."

Her eyes abandon me. "I'd think you'd want me out of the way," she mutters. "Aren't situations like yours easiest after people die? All I am is a roadblock."

"Goodbye, Anna," I say, closing the door behind me.

Tough love sucks.

༜

For hours, Donovan and I have sat woven together on the sofa in his office, our eyes captivated by society's potential stamp of approval that sits before us. My lips confess into his neck. "The bitter-sweet of it is, I have the life I always wanted. I love Christopher, and I want to be by his side to watch our children graduate college, get married, enjoy all their successes and love them through all of their mistakes. We know we can make it through this."

Donovan places his head onto mine, caressing my crown with his cheek. "Even though Anna chooses not to see it, I do love her. I want to help her survive and rediscover that person she fought so hard to be. I know she's in there. Whatever you said to her yesterday made her see it too." He brings my eyes to his. His falling tear follows the path of my shattering heart. "Last chance. Do we face whatever truth lies in that envelope with the acceptance that we have already made our decision, or do we open it knowing we may want to backpedal?"

"Some things we are still in together."

"Yeah, let's do this." Donovan snatches the envelope. Our interlaced hands clutch as we walk to the corner of his office. My head buries into his chest. I fear this is the last time I will ever relish in the rhythm of his heart, yet somehow I know better. He flips on the shredder. "Count of three?" he asks.

"Yeah," I barely utter.

"One," he says boldly. *For Anna and Sunshine.*

"Two," I add. *For Graham, Antonia, and the sweetest man in the world.*

"Three," we force in unison.

Our quivering hands communally lower the sealed envelope. Again our dreams will rip apart. Never will we let a stupid piece of paper dictate our lives. We were meant to be together, but everyone is hurting enough, and we won't let a legality tempt us into taking them down further.

Suddenly I yank back the slightly chewed envelope and hand it to Donovan. "You have to open this!"

"What? We just spent two hours deciding not to."

"Read it aloud," I insist. "You'd better sit, because no matter what it says your ass may hit the floor."

Donovan ignores my advice and rips the letter open. He gives me a grunt showing disapproval before reading aloud.

"The first set of tests show that specimens A and B are full siblings and the children of the hair strand test, specimen E." Donovan huffs, "Fine, so we're siblings." Then his face goes pale. "Wait, *first set of tests?*"

A slight dizziness swirls in my brain. My hands go clammy as they brace me against the desk. "Keep reading," I say, feeling I'm about to hurl.

"The paternity test shows that specimen F is—is the child of specimen B. What paternity test?" Donovan asks in a panic.

The news crawls through my veins like poison. If ripping them out would bring relief from my disgust over our indiscretion, I would have already sliced my skin. "Antonia," I mutter, gripping the desk tighter. "I would have told you sooner, but it was so unlikely, and I just couldn't bring myself to admit that no matter how I sugar coat it, I cheated on Christopher."

"Lily, this can't possibly be right," Donovan says. His words sound pleading. "We stopped almost before we started. That and her due date didn't match."

"I lied to you about her due date. Also, you had the same health teacher I did. Don't you remember that sperm seeps out before the big event happens? Contrary to popular belief, two people can conceive a child without either having an orgasm."

"That's depressing. Wait, if you were unsure, then you and Christopher must have … Gah! Before or after me?"

"Donovan! I know men freak out when these things happen, but don't make me feel like a whore!"

"I'm sorry. That was unforgivable." His voice mirrors my pain. He draws me close, wrapping me tightly into his chest to shelter me from the hurt. "Do you plan to tell Christopher?"

"No. Ridiculous as it may be, in some states the penalty for our consensual relationship can be a life-long jail sentence. Not to mention that if those test results ever come to light, the whole family will suffer. I can't imagine hating myself more than I already do. How could I have ever done this to that sweet man?" My sobs feel acidic.

"Hey, look at me," Donovan says, gently. "Really, really look at me. We're forgetting something incredibly important." Raising my chin, he delicately brings his lips to mine, allowing them to linger. "We've been given an angel, yet we barely did anything to bring her to earth. Doesn't that seem like God has bestowed his blessings? Lily, I promise that we will find our way. Some way, somehow you will be the pot of gold at the end of my rainbow. Until then, please be there to catch me when I fall, because the drop may be a tall one."

I bring my face closer so that my falling tears will find complacency with his. "We will make this work. I'm never leaving your side."

"I'm going to do everything in my power to save Anna, but if she doesn't make it, I'll never remarry. I'll always be at the ready. Meanwhile, I'm going to keep drinking mint mochas and staking claim on your hair."

"You want another lock of it?" Somehow I now see endless hope for our future in the ocean of his eyes.

"You know it."

"Trade you for another T-shirt."

"Anything for you, Lily. All you ever have to do is ask."

51

Unwilling to lose sight of my fortune, my gaze is locked on Graham and Antonia playing catch in our yard. Their grandfather runs after an ill-thrown pitch with a smile that is brighter than ever. At the kitchen table sits Christopher with his laptop, his fingers pressed into his temples while video chatting with Grace. After five weeks of tension, they seem at peace.

"Christopher, you were right in knowing I wouldn't return without you," Grace tells him. "You had been abandoned enough. In the end you did what you felt best for your family, just like I thought I did by not telling you about Eric. My prior actions cannot be changed. However, I can shape how I move forward in light of them."

While Christopher ends his call on a peaceful note, he's still a little prickly when he joins me at the patio door. "Better now?" I ask.

"Not as well as could be. However, if you can still face me, then I can, albeit barely."

"So those two years remain closed?" I ask. "It's really up to you."

"As far as we are concerned, yes, but to me they are a never-ending nightmare. So many bad memories have surfaced I can't stand to pass a mirror."

My hand glides through his locks, revealing a better view of his adorable face. "That's unfortunate, because you are still beautiful in my eyes."

"I don't know how you could possibly say that," he says, sounding heavy hearted.

As my eyes focus into his, my wedding vows ring stronger than ever, bringing forth drops of love from my eyes. "I will never lose sight of the amazing and sensitive man you are. I will be your strength when life fails you, laugh with you in good times and struggle with you in bad, and be the best that I can for you and our children, no matter where life takes us or what challenges lie ahead. I will always love you, and I will live in joy with you, for as long as God allows."

Christopher's eyes tear along with mine. "I promise to be everything to you that you will allow, to stand by your side, to respect every nuance of you whether I understand it or not, and to share every bit of my being. You bring out the best in me, and I will remain faithfully by your side and by the sides of our children for all of my days."

With a gentle kiss, he brings a smile to my lips. "Seems like we should have done that some place more formal," he says.

"That reminds me, there is a formality we should address."

"What's that, luv?" he asks, pulling my head onto his shoulder.

"Eric leaves in under a week, yet can legally stay another month. Let's work on a few surprises."

52

The sun's golden rays beam into the kitchen on a lovely late-winter morning. Christopher dances in, returning from the grocery store with supplies for tonight's party. His lack of grace makes for a cringe-worthy version of the waltz as he swoops shopping bags onto the table then swirls me around the kitchen. He nearly spins me into the breakfast bar before continuing his little jig and pulling two bottles of champagne out of the bags.

"Wow. You look radiant! Are those bottles still full?" I ask.

Christopher waltzes to the patio door and calls for Eric before gliding back to kiss me. "Grab some glasses, will ya luv?"

"What's all the commotion?" Eric asks.

With the *pop* of a cork, Christopher commences pouring. We follow his lead in raising a glass as he stands elongated, his free arm tucked behind him in a grand stand. "To Eric's wisdom and the idiots who don't follow it."

"Sounds bloody cracking to me," Eric says. "But what's the point?"

"I just got a call from Tyler Lane," Christopher says while bursting with pride.

"The guy from Spiral Lamb?" I search my brain to ask.

Christopher's arms fly up as he turns into my favorite marionette. "Really, Lilyanna, I'm thankful you don't have star lust, but this is a little much." Christopher's eyes return to Eric. "He felt bad about what happened with the tour, especially since we were so accommodating. He also said that Mike was released from his contract after sneaking items onto the merchandise tables, not only after repeatedly being instructed not to, but also without someone to sell them. Now the promoter is scrambling to find local acts to fill the remaining nights."

"That's cracking, Christopher," Eric happily states. "I knew that yob would hash it!"

"It gets better," Christopher adds. "The promoter was so pleased that we didn't cause a single headache, we've been asked to open for St. Screwdriver's Revenge when they hit the West Coast for the end of their tour. We can sell our merchandise and will receive a tiny per diem."

"That is excellent!" Eric says, hugging Christopher. "I am so proud of you."

"To Mancunian wisdom," Christopher sings, sounding like a cheerleader.

"To Manc wisdom," Eric adds.

"Hey, I feel left out. Can't we say British wisdom so I can be included?"

"Are you English, Lilyanna?" Eric asks. "I thought Beckett was German?"

"Yes, but my father's mom was English."

"Really? From where 'bout?"

Christopher lets out a groan.

"Islington. Near Liverpool." Hopefully now I won't get earache from two overtly proud soccer fans.

A gleam of camaraderie crosses Eric's face. "Really? My family was originally from just up the road in Everton. They moved to Salford a month after I was born."

Christopher is so busy rolling his eyes at my Scouser heritage that he remains oblivious. "Wow, Eric, that makes you a Scouser by birth."

"Yes, I guess that is just one more thing that we have in common."

Slowly Christopher's eyes widen, and his mouth drops into an adorable little O. I stick my grubby fingers into his open wound and rip. "Well, since I'm one-quarter Scouser, and Christopher is half Scouser and half Manc, that makes the children—"

"Noooooo!!!!"

&

My nerves feel torn and frayed as I open the front door. With an ear-piercing squeal, Sunshine bursts through, anxious to show Antonia her new toy. In the threshold stands Anna, pale, weak, and smiling. This is the first time since last week's ultimatum that we have laid eyes on each other. I risk bodily injury and give her a huge hug, completely catching her off guard. My face enlivens when the hug seems genuinely returned.

Donovan follows behind, carrying a medium-sized moving box and looking exhausted. "Oh, no," I tease. "You're not moving in. I'll take your daughter for a few days, but you're on your own."

He forces a smile. "I thought I'd bring this over now so it's one less thing to deal with Thursday night." With a nod to the stairs he whispers, "Follow me."

Inside Antonia's room, where Sunshine will stay during the first stage of Anna's recovery, Donovan drops the box in exchange for me. "How is she holding up?" I ask. My gut churns at the thought of the M word. "Any more flying fists?"

"She's fine," he assures, "else I'd have brought Sunshine's suitcase as well." A lock of hair from below my temple finds joy as he twirls it through his fingers. "As much as you and I being near each other is a challenge, I can't imagine going through this without you. Thanks for talking sense into her."

I bring a kiss to his cheek. "You and me, together forever."

Donovan lingers behind as I leave Antonia's room. His eyes scan the posters and chotskies that reflect who she is. He runs his hand over her pillow, as if brushing the hair out of her face while she sleeps. "You okay?" I ask.

"Yeah." His snicker is laced in irony. "Remember how

I've always said you would get everything you want? Seems like now I get some of that too. I can do this, Lily. Antonia being mine is what I wanted all along, and I've hidden that desire. Now it's a different kind of hiding. Nothing really changes, except now my heart is fulfilled. Let's go downstairs. I need to muster the courage to see her."

The beauty of the two-tier, flourless chocolate cake with Grand Mariner ganache I made for Eric pales compared to his radiance as we all surprise him in the family room. "I never expected anyone to remember let alone a celebration," Eric modestly says. "You shouldn't have."

"How could we not?" Donovan asks, handing Eric a present. Donovan's hooded eyes float to Antonia, still afraid to bring her into full view. Eric uncovers a tie that is tasteful, yet also as colorful and youthful as he emanates. Donovan's gaze slips back to Eric. "We thought a traditional Dad's gift was appropriate. It's nice to have a sane father figure."

Eric marvels at the tie like it is a rare gem. "Thank you. You have no idea what this means. I'll wear it proudly on all the best occasions."

"I foresee many of those in your future," Christopher says as he places our gift before Eric. Inside a shirt box, he finds a manila envelope decorated by the children. On the back, Graham has drawn a picture of our home with five stick figures—our family, including Eric. From inside he slides out a stack of government forms. Christopher and I hold each other along with our breaths, hoping we have not overstepped our bounds. "U.S. Immigration department?" Eric inquires. "Are you having me deported?"

"Quite the opposite," I say. "We hope you'll at least extend your stay, but we'd rather you made it permanent. Since Christopher is a dual citizen you can apply for an IR Visa. All of the paper work is complete except we need to re-run the DNA test formally. For good measure, Grace has signed an affidavit stating you are Christopher's birthfather and should be allowed to stay with your son."

I sneak a peek at Donovan, whose eyes again conceal a peer at Antonia. She stares at him with a crooked head, curious as to why he won't look at her.

Eric sits silent and still, staring at the papers. "We'd understand if you don't want to give up your life back home," Christopher nervously adds. "Hopefully you'll stay until we fly back to England for the birth of my cousin's son."

"Hopefully by then you will have named the poor kid!" Donovan chimes in.

"Actually, Christopher and I figured that one out when we were completing the paperwork."

Donovan shoots me his famous blinking eye roll. "Okay, which British rock stars did you rope in for this one?"

"Just one," I state. "Eric Christopher Taylor Eccles goes perfectly with our two middle name convention."

Eric's eyes fly to us. Understanding how much he is loved acts like a shot of adrenaline. Suddenly the man who feels he hasn't a place in the world anymore has a family who not only acknowledges him, but also is requesting he change his entire life to be with them. Eric's smile reveals more than his words ever can.

"What do you say, Eric?" Donovan asks. His eyes finally land on Antonia when she crawls into his lap. His voice hitches, and he keeps his eyes locked on the top of Antonia's head, concealing the dampness coating them. "Think you could put up with this pear-shaped family where you can never tell who lives where or which child belongs to who?" Donovan's eyes come to mine. They shine brightly, filled with hope.

"Cracking! Call me Yankee Doodle and hand me a pen!"

53

Aimlessly I stare into the refrigerator without appetite. Food serves as a diversion from the source of my feeling of futility.

"You're looking down. Something wrong?" Eric asks.

I gesture toward the papers that sit on the breakfast bar. "Either Mom played a cruel mind game or she spent years hiding the truth for reasons we'll never understand."

"I thought the blood test proved Donovan is your brother?" Eric asks as the doorbell rings.

"Yeah, but how do we explain the adoption papers? Donovan and I are going to put them in a safe deposit box and try to forget about them."

I open the door to Donovan, my Wonder Twin of Grumpitude. The bags under his eyes almost make me feel triumphant. Finally we have arrived upon a time when Mr. Perfect also looks battered from endless nights.

"Are you ready? Let's go," he says, motioning to leave. His car key is pointed and at the ready. I'm surprised he didn't leave the motor running.

Grabbing his shirtsleeve, I pull him toward me, encouraging him into an embrace. "No—yes—no," I reply, bringing forth a speck of levity.

"Come on," he says, smiling. "I need to get back to Anna. This surgery can't be over with soon enough."

"All right. Let me just grab—"

"Here! Here's your answer!" Eric screams from the kitchen. "She was a bloody lunatic!"

"Yay! New drama!" Donovan says, mocking childish joy. "Lord, what now?"

"Look at who the judge is that signed the papers," Eric

says while fuming as we dash in. "There's no way I'm believing this is a coincidence."

King Midas' finger points to a signature that reveals this paper is gold—fool's gold. "Can I see that and borrow your reading glasses?" I ask Eric. He whips them off like the Superman he is before storming out of his seat.

Donning the specks, not only does the signature become clear, so does the intent of the charade. "All those years of grilling me," I say in realization. "All those late nights watching her movies."

"You do know who that is, right?" Eric asks. "Because I find it highly unlikely Rhode Island ever had a judge named Anthony Wedgwood Benn."

Donovan's face is a ball of confusion. "Oh, come on! You know this!" I practically shout. "How many times did Mom watch *Pirate Radio*? Anthony Wedgwood Benn was the actual guy who led the bill that stopped offshore radio stations. She bitched he was British rock's biggest villain. Mom intentionally did this to hurt us!"

Oh you failed, Mom. Wherever you are, I hope you can see the nail you intended for my coffin just got thrown back into yours.

Eric looks like an angry father. "How could she have so convincingly faked those papers?"

Donovan scrutinizes the faux documents while looking over my shoulder. "Mom was a Litigation Paralegal when she met Dad. After he died she went back to work part time as a secretary in the same field. She knew how papers looked, but how the hell did she get her hands on the state seal?"

Even with Eric's glasses, the imprint is too faint to make out—almost like someone barely applied enough pressure for an indent to appear. Grabbing a pencil, I gently rub the side of the graphite against the paper. The image that appears makes my brain feel contorted in shame of its idiocy. "Take a good look at it now. It's the seal of Dad's Rotary Club!"

Donovan takes the papers, looking to them in resignation

of how much the woman he tried to help wronged him. "I can't believe she hated me that much."

"Why would your mum forge such falsehood?" Eric asks with fury. "She should be ashamed for not seeing who you are. I'd be proud to call you son!"

Donovan peers up at Eric. His eyes sag nearly to his knees, reflecting a painful truth of unfairness. "Thank you. My own father never said he was proud of me. At least Christopher has always known you and Grace love him. Well, one part of Mom's final mystery is solved. I doubt if the rest ever will be. I'll a—I'll take these to the office and shred them," he says, heading out the front door.

I follow him outside. With a soft touch to his arm, I stop him as soon as we are out of anyone's earshot. "Those are mine," I softly assert, looking at the sheaves of hatred. "They are why Mom squandered the opportunity to tell Christopher about us while on her death bed. Instead of risking his understanding, she threw gasoline on me, hoping I would strike the match. That judge's name was her way of saying I should have listened when she tried to pull us apart. If Aunt Audrey had died later, my name would be on these papers." Donovan's eyes lower, and I dip my face under his, recapturing his view. "These are proof that we are doing the right thing in standing by our families just as much as they are the reason why someday you and I are going to be together. Now go home and take care of your wife, so we can keep proving Mom wrong about us."

54

I rap upon the door of the Venice bungalow. I'm an unexpected, and hopefully not unwelcome, visitor on this drearisome day before Anna's double mastectomy.

Anna opens the door. Her pale skin and red eyes show her disease is getting the best of her. "Hey," I whisper, nudging my head to encourage her outside. With what I need to do, I'd prefer if Donovan didn't know I was here.

I give her a sly smile as she steps out, like we are about to get away with something. Forcing myself to think of this as a fun game and forget what I am really doing, I hand her an envelope with a little bounce and a forced smile that she sees right through.

"What is this?" Anna asks as she extracts the contents.

"It's a coupon book. Whenever you need something, you use it. Take a peek."

"One girl's night out," she reads aloud. "One home cooked meal, delivered. One night of babysitting. Boy, there sure are a lot of those," she says, her voice locking.

My guts feel they are about to hurl out. "You'll need them when you see what's at the end."

On the last page she finds a substantially sized Victoria's Secret gift card. The tears that have been welling in her eyes turn to gushers. It amplifies the pain I feel—pain for her, for her suffering, and for knowing what that coupon really means for her and for my soulmate.

"Why are you doing this?" she asks with a hearty sniffle.

My voice quivers as I fight my tears. "Because I've chosen you as my sister. No blood test on earth will change that."

I lose the battle over the waterworks, and we bring our

arms around each other in consolation of the other's misery. Donovan appears from inside, holding an electric razor. His head is completely shaven sans his eyebrows. We freeze, each not expecting to see the other. My insides turn to falling rain in new understanding of how real Anna's situation is. This is supposed to happen to other people, not to you, not to the ones you love.

Anna hides her face, not wanting to expose even more of herself. This is the last time for a long time to come that her beautiful hair will veil her discomfort.

My eyes return to Donovan, our hearts breaking anew. Stepping up to him, I impose myself. "Here," I say, reaching for the razor. "I'll hold this, you hold her."

Donovan guides a sobbing Anna to the bathroom. She looks into the mirror, and her fingers grip her scalp in hatred of her situation. No one should have to suffer like this.

Anna crumples as I plug in the razor, unable to face the mirror any longer. Donovan follows her down, taking her head in his hands. "You ready?" he asks. She gives a fast nod of approval, then cowers as I lower the razor. Donovan looks up at me, completely lost and unknowing how to help her. For once I am grateful that I am not the one in his arms.

Anna braves her eyes upward, her head still low. With one last look at Donovan I again start the razor, quickly spin to the mirror, and begin shaving my own head with the intention of leaving nothing behind but his favorite cluster of locks on each side.

Some things we are still in together.

55

Twenty-two Years Later

Donovan whistles as he comes up the stairs, carrying the last of Christopher's gear. On this eventful night, Christopher will partake in a concert celebrating the British Invasion by honoring the memory of his fathers.

"Here we are," Anna practically sings while handing out cocktails. "My special recipe for a special occasion. Shall we drink to the obvious?"

The four of us take pause with sadness welling in our hearts. Simultaneously we raise our glasses to the long-gone man we'd give anything to bring back. "To Eric," we all say.

The orange juice cocktail floods my mouth with an herbal tang. "Anna, this is fantastic. Does this have sage and gin?"

"I think there's honey, too," Donovan deduces.

Anna sighs. "I know I'm still not the best cook, but you would think that after all these years I could get something past you two."

"It sure leaves a tingle on the lips. What makes it orange?" Christopher asks.

"That's it!" My hands fly heavenward. "I truly give up! This is ridiculous, even for you."

Donovan whispers to Christopher, "That would be the same thing that makes it taste like oranges."

Christopher looks at the glass questioningly as we all snicker. "Oh, bloody hell! I officially surrender to the enemy," he states with a bold smile and a kiss to my lips.

"All right, let's get this amp loaded and get out of here," Donovan says, interrupting us.

"What's that doing here?" Christopher asks. "I loaded it first for a reason."

"No, you thought you loaded it. I found it downstairs. Old age must be setting in and your mind is slipping."

"Are you real? Oh, my giddy aunt," Christopher babbles, mostly talking to himself. "After all the trouble it's been giving me—"

Donovan cups his hand over Christopher's mouth. I think he's wanted to do that for decades. "Seriously Lil, what possessed you to marry this guy?" he asks, smiling.

"Love doesn't need to be perfect, it just needs to be true."

Donovan gives me an adoring smile. *Truer words were never spoken.* "All right, let's do this," he says, taking the amp.

"You ready, luv?" I ask Christopher.

"Really, Lilyanna. There you go, stealing my lines again. You can't just steal another person's lines."

"I love you, too." With an adoring kiss, we head out to the car.

&

My body waivers as I stare into the coffin. The image of my beloved Christopher is merely a blur from the haze of my tears.

Thirty-one years.

For thirty-one years we shared marital bliss, and I am so very grateful that I appreciated him for who he was, not casting him aside for who I wanted him to be.

It happened during the sound check, with all of us watching. As an impromptu jam lead Christopher into his best Pete Townsend impersonation, a jump and a swing brought him to the ground, straight to his knees, slumping over his guitar with a clutch to his heart. We all ran to him, but before we could make it he fell backward, all of his muscles going slack. Anna and Donovan tried to resuscitate him, but it quickly became obvious their efforts were in vain.

Tears streamed down Donovan's face as he realized the thrusts to Christopher's chest were useless. His eyes pleaded me for forgiveness when we saw that all hope was gone.

While the others tended to Christopher's empty shell, I stood as tall as I could, turning to the heavens. I felt Christopher looking down from above, as if our eyes were locking one last time, and wondered if we would ever meet again or if we had found the end of our rainbow. Reaching my arms to heaven, I cried, "I love you, Christopher Paul Eccles, and never will there be a day that I forget or stop loving you."

For thirty-one years we stood by each other as husband and wife, loving and supporting one another, no matter what transpired. We always accepted the other for who and what they were, all the while never doubting the special love we shared. My heart will be incomplete until I find him again.

In the week since Christopher's passing I've been without hope or complete thoughts. Try as my family might to enliven me, sorrow extinguishes all other emotions.

Cards and flowers continue to pour in as the news spreads and stuns. Much like for his father, Eric, people have come out of the woodwork with stories of how Christopher touched their lives.

I've scarcely left my room since the funeral. Instead, I cling to Christopher's pillow, asking God why. Everyone wants me to get fresh air, but I hardly see the point. Donovan drags me out of bed for a walk. My scraggly hair, mismatched sweats, and filthy slippers make me look an embarrassment, but people are lucky I am dressed. Foolishly, I've led us in the direction of the park where Christopher and I used to take the kids. Memories of playing with our children tear at my heart, and it is like losing him all over again. My knees drop into the middle of a sandbox, as my eyes become faucets of despair that refuse to cease flowing.

My time with Christopher was like living on a playground—one happy game after another. In the rare times when we fell and got scraped, the other was always there to kiss our wounds and lead us off to the next game. For all the madness and indecision in my life, my time with Christopher was nothing short of amazing.

One month ago, my soul was blighted by the loss of my beautiful husband—the man who retained his boyish charms and sweet voice until the very end—the man who never faltered in his love of life, music, or his family. Nothing spares me from the severe pain that haunts my heart.

My thumb slides over a nick in the railing as I ascend the stairs. Christopher put that nick on the banister while bringing up Graham's crib. This house was practically pristine when we moved in and almost every scratch and ding is a product of our family, thus making defects treasured memories.

"Damn it, God! Why did you take my Christopher?"

Two months after Christopher's passing I feel human again. It began while experimenting in the bakery. I've put Sunshine in charge of management duties so my only responsibility is to have fun. Sunshine never fails to amaze me with her business sense and creativity. In many ways, she is an unlikely extension of me.

I may not be ready to fly again, but I am definitely ready to take a stroll in the sun and face the blue sky, even if it brings forth tearful memories.

56

Readying to embark on a quest for the perfect ensemble for a night out on the town with the girls, the melodic chime of the doorbell shakes me from my nightmarish daydream of trying on clothes. On the way to the door, I detour by the bathroom for another look in the mirror.

"Oh, hell yes, I can still wear hot clothes!"

A second chime of the bell forces an end to my delirium, and I head for the door.

Donovan stands on the porch, clutching a bouquet of white roses. In presenting them, he reveals a black suit with a tie of deep blue swirls that make the dazzling orbs on his face wrap me in an ocean of beauty. Age is blessing him with a distinguished air. His specs of gray at the temples, and the few pounds gained over the years, do little to shame his allure.

"Wow! This is quite the surprise," I say, beaming while sniffing the roses and motioning him into the house. "Why are you so nervous?"

Flicking his hands out to the sides, his mouth goes slightly agape. "I can no longer get anything past you."

"Nope! Spill."

Without pretense, he dives into his mission. "I'm ready, Lily. I've been ready for years. When things changed, I wanted to give you time to heal and hopefully come to me, but I'm tired of waiting."

The moment Christopher passed, I stopped noticing other people existed, whether they were my friends, my children, or my soulmate. Three months later, reality is catching up to me, and Donovan's words snap me back to earth. "What about Anna?" I ask. My hands are clammy with discomfort. Why am I not throwing myself at him like I want to?

"Conveniently gone," he says, retrieving a sealed envelope from his jacket pocket. "At least I was able to hide that. She left a month ago. For the last year it was pretty obvious she no longer had any desire to be around me. I promised I would give you this along with her blessing."

My eyes crawl to the envelope placed in my hand as a thousand ants march up the back of my legs.

"Lily, the night I left for college you said you hoped we would be together in the end. I'll keep my distance while you recover, but when you're ready, I promise you'll never regret it."

Donovan heads for the door, hesitating at the threshold before leaving without looking back. The urge to pursue him is resisted, knowing that in my weakened state it would be a disservice to us both. Although I know our reunion is as near as a call away, I need every inch of the distance growing between us as he drives off.

With apprehension brought on by an unknown source, I sit on the porch to read Anna's letter.

Lily,

Donovan and I were a joke. We are victims who married for convenience; both thinking that having a family could make us normal.

It didn't.

After years of being exploited I didn't trust men, though somehow I knew Donovan would never abuse me. I was right.

My terms were simple. I asked him to marry me with the stipulation that he could return to you whenever opportunity arose as long as any children were provided for. However, he could not force an opportunity and I couldn't stop one.

I broke the rules; once by leaving notes trying to push you and Christopher together and again by trying to protect him from Lana's wrath as she died.

Christopher's passing is my exit cue. Consider this a deathbed confession. I'm killing off who I was in a moment of self-imposed strength. Since you and Donovan can never marry, I won't bother with the mess of a divorce. Sunshine will know how to reach me, but as far as Donovan is concerned, I'll no longer be in his way.

Thank you for helping me when I was ill. Funny thing is, the better I got, the more I realized how ridiculous my marriage was. It's long past time for me to move on, but after all he did for me, I needed to know Donovan would be provided for. Now that destiny has kicked in, we are all free.

You're poisonous, Lily. For years I've watched you weaken your victims. If someone consumes too much of you, or drinks of your tears, they are forever destroyed. Don't hurt Donovan any more than you already have.
Anna

℣

My attempt to shop for the perfect dress is thwarted. Thanks to Donovan's visit, my brain misfires at every minor ding in the road. Eventually I cave to whimsy and toss my credit card onto the sales counter. I succumb to buying an alluring, strapless little black number that I pray doesn't make me look like a decrepit tart. The frivolity continues as I book a limo filled with a boatload of champagne.

The mission for a carefree night is fiery until I ascend the stairs to my bedroom. Photographic memories line the stairwell and serve as a memorial to my years with Christopher. Frozen in time is a lone cupcake—the one with my engagement ring stuck in the top. Hesitation dominated me before I married Christopher. I was so afraid that I could never give him all he deserved. Despite my fears, we shared a beautiful marriage that was perfect in so many ways. I'd give anything to be able to tell him one more time that I love him.

Dispiritedness brings difficulties to my preparation for the big night out. I forgo much of the planned makeup, knowing it will smudge if I tear. As concern for my attire begins nagging, fate kicks in and the limo arrives. When I head out the door with a painted smile, Sunshine sticks her head out the limo's sunroof and catcalls at me, making me again rethink my dress.

Inside the car, the girls are merciless in their complements. Judging by the look on the face of Graham's wife, Betty, I'm not a harlot. If anyone would accuse me of being tarty, it would be her and the stick up her bum.

Once at the club, I sheepishly order a Martini. There's a crazy drink menu here, yet I've no desire to experiment. Where the hell is Lilyanna Eccles? She would be all over this menu and order the wackiest thing possible. Instead, some washed up old broad invaded me and ordered a standard Martini. I don't want to shrivel up and die because my husband did. I want to be like Eric, who lived to the ripe old age of ninety-four and never stopped thriving. Or like Grace, who passed on at eighty-eight and didn't try to be a teenager, even though she kept up with them. She was just herself, and she was inspiring.

My eyes go to Antonia, who forces a smirk, which slowly builds into a bold smile. There is a lesson in her eyes. While she was raised by an incredible man, she is the product of something greater—a force that clearly believes Donovan and I should be together. In a silent moment of defiance, I raise my glass and drink goodbye to the grieving widow who struggles to face each day. The Martini goes down smoothly and it makes the right of passage feel destined. Determined to spice up my life I order a Thai Chili Splash. I have little clue what's in it, but Antonia thinks they're divine.

I'm ready for the next phase. Something just fired my jet engines, and I won't shut them down. As the waitress brings my drink, Antonia gives me a wicked little smile that rivals that of her birthfather. I take that first sip and burst out with my new life.

57

A sonic boom set on repeat wakes me from slumber. I stumble to the window, and the source of the clamor remains evasive. Did I leave the TV on downstairs? I don't even remember getting home. How the hell did I make it up the stairs without falling onto my face and snapping my neck? A quick survey of the house brings me a big, fat goose egg of nothing, yet the intensity of the pounding increases.

Ah crap! I'm hungover.

I am grateful for the little man tap dancing on my brain. He exists not because I drank to forget, but because I drank to remember. Last night, I vowed to bring myself back into the land of the living, and I praise every dehydrating taste of life I had.

I plop myself down on the sofa in the family room and dare to let myself form thoughts about my future. Donovan's voice greets me with a hopeful tone. "You're up bright and early considering how much you tied one on last night. I got a full report a little while ago from Antonia."

I look to the phone in my hand as if it's diseased. I don't remember picking it up, let alone possessing the intention of calling Donovan.

"I'm moving," I state.

What? Who said that?

You did, Lily—loudly and clearly. You're moving.

"What? Where? Why?" Donovan's voice adds to my stew of emotions. "Lily, I'm sorry if I said something out of line yesterday."

"Donovan, we can't happen here," I spit out with urgency. "I'm buying us tickets for a long cruise to some faraway place so we can decide what to do next. How soon

269

can you be ready?"

"Lily, I've been ready for decades."

⁂

One week after I nearly place myself into an alcohol induced coma, Donovan and I are in Rome, ready to embark on a twelve day, Mediterranean Cruise. Once my foot hits the ship's deck, I'm Marco Polo reincarnated, ready to venture into a new world. In the middle of a crowd I stop Donovan to reunite our lips. "It's about time I could do that." Eager to continue, we race to our cabin.

Donovan motions for me to wait outside our cabin door. After bringing our bags inside, he swoops me over the threshold and onto the bed. Our kiss has the fluidity of Crème Anglaise as he slowly glides me downward. When his lips retract, his gaze pours his soul into mine in a moment of gentle surrender to the knowledge that there will never be an escape from the love that engulfs us. Emotions flood, causing a fury of passion to race over me. Like a NASCAR pit crew, I have his shirt on the floor before unfastening his belt so expeditiously the act almost feels violent.

Donovan touches the buttons on my blouse at a luxurious pace, savoring our passion. I insist on helping, nearly slapping his hands out of the way so I can rip off my skirt. These little necessities are but a time-sinking barrier to his embrace. Suddenly, Donovan pulls back, captures my eyes with his, and brings my engine to a skidding halt.

"Hey," he says, his voice low and soothing. "I've waited over thirty years to be with you again, and I plan to savor each moment. Lily, you are just as lovely as the day I first noticed you as the breath taking woman you are. I've never told you about that day.

"That summer there were so many things we wanted to do together. Then Mom and Dad sent us both off to camps. The day you left I felt hollow, like my heart had a hole in it. When Dad brought you home my heart skipped all over the place. Then I left for football camp and was miserable. It freaked me out how much I missed you.

"When I returned home, you had this amazing chocolate cake waiting, and we gabbed the night away on the sofa, just you, me, two forks, and that cake. I knew then that I was in deep for a girl I should never have anything but the most fraternal of thoughts for, but you were lovely and had a smile that launched me into orbit. That is exactly the girl who lies in my arms now, and I need to show her something."

He pulls back my long locks and nuzzles into my neck. "For decades I've longed to kiss this spot again." He presses his lips under my ear, making me throw my head back with a glorious sigh. "And that is why."

His lips linger down until they grace my upper arm, sending a universe of stars twinkling through me. "You used to have a black, satin blouse, and the edge of the sleeve came right here. I would play with it, subtly moving my finger up a little higher to touch more of you even though you were off limits. This was as high as I could go."

Sliding down my torso, his kiss nestles into my stomach. "This is where I laid my head when you were pregnant with Antonia. For a moment I let myself believe we had achieved the unthinkable, only to learn later that we were bestowed a gift." Skating up to face me, his eyes draw me into an abyss of tenderness. "We still have so much life ahead of us. Let's enjoy it to the fullest."

His consuming love sweeps me up and takes my heart heavenward as our lips meet. The glow emanating through the crack in the curtains glimmers upon Donovan's crown in a near angelic halo, making him appear as a deity above. Everything he does pleases me, whether it's the gentle nibble on my ear that etches paths of fire down my spine or his little sighs of pleasure that make me dizzy. Not a single bit of my being fails to cave to his very breath.

God, how I have missed him—how I have craved his caress. Seeing him like this, his chiseled body bare and feeling like velvet in my arms, makes me weak. His touch, his eyes, his fragrance—they all enrapture and consume me. No one can govern me like Donovan.

He wraps me in his embrace, and our legs entwine like vines. I become a blooming morning glory as he sinks into me at a deliciously slow pace. Again we transcend time and become one—the way we are meant to be.

My head rolls back in ecstasy at his touch. Feelings of love and longing overwhelm our souls, fueling our passion. How many times have our embraces been restrained? How often have we unjustly muted our words? The feeling of a soulmate inside you is like that of no other. With him I find completeness—in my mind, in my soul, and in my body—like an extension of me once removed is fused into place. He belongs right here, completing my void, electrifying my soul, and searing our duality into one.

Donovan's passion is unrushed, unrestrained—causing me to tighten around him quickly. When my eyes meet his, I'm transported back to our first time like this, when I looked into the eyes of my best friend, my lover, my soulmate, and the man I love so deeply it pains my soul. Just like before, it is there that my heart and gaze cannot leave until we share the greatest physical pleasure of all.

The product of his desires burns inside me, and the currents of my pleasure feel like an undertow, pulling his soul deeper into my vortex. Collapsing into each other's arms we surrender to the mercy of our fate.

58

Tucked into a booth in the far corner of the ship's dining room, Donovan and I each refuse to share the other with the world. My eyes are firmly locked on him as he bites into a croissant. "Gack!" he exclaims, and I release the laugh I knew was coming. "Why do people rave about the food on cruises?" he says, unceremoniously dropping the faux delicacy onto his plate. "I think I've actually lost weight."

"You're welcome," I sing in regard to my time spent refining his palate.

His eyes lock on the croissant in shame. "All those years I spent at the gym trying to work off the pastry I nabbed from your shop only to learn I should have just gone on vacation."

"Ooh! Good point!" Excitement nearly bubbles out of my pores. "We need to find some place with a gym nearby. That kills my idea of living in the middle of nowhere. Oh! We could buy a house with a basement and build our own gym." My fork drops onto my plate with a *clang*. "Let's install a home theatre, too. Then we never need to leave the house, and you can walk around naked all the time."

I don't get any reaction out of him. Instead, Donovan's eyes remain on the croissant, and his hand is tapping on his leg. "Hey, you okay?" I ask. "You look like you just ate moldy cheese."

"Yeah. I've got a lot on my mind. There is a lot to face once we board that plane home tomorrow."

"If that's all it is, then why is your wall suddenly up so high it violates air space? Are you having second thoughts about moving?"

He places his hand on mine. "Never. It's just that

sometimes when you dream of something for so long, when it finally arrives it becomes scary. Come on, we need to hurry or we'll miss our excursion."

☙

Donovan and I are part of what feels like an endless sea of tourists being herded through the Acropolis. Donovan fidgeted the entire bus ride here, only to come alive as we off-boarded and he sucked in the air, as if it holds magic. As we climb the hill to the Parthenon, Donovan points to an easily-overlooked that appears precariously perched above the city. Its lovely marble columns and unusual placement make me wonder how I, along with so many others, could easily have missed it.

Donovan pulls us as close to the temple as permitted. Tourists brush pasts as he wraps his arms around me from behind, and we absorb the gem that is a testament to the ages. "The Temple of Athena Nike has been around since 400 B.C. It was built to express Athens' ambitions to beat Sparta. It reminds me of us."

"Donovan, I hate to burst your bubble, but didn't the Spartans win that battle?"

"Look at the big picture. The Athenians were defeated, just like we were, yet today we stand in Athens, along with that temple. We are both a symbol of victory." Turning me to face him, something in his eyes conveys his words are supported by the ultimate power. "The big difference is, though someday that temple will fall, you and I are eternal. I truly believe that."

From his pocket, he removes a small box containing two rings; one with a large, radiant cut diamond, the other a band of tanzanite and sapphires. "In Plato's *The Symposium*, Aristophanes tells that humans were originally two complete people who were attached. Since humans had great strength, they were seen as a threat to the gods, thus Zeus split them in half to weaken them. It is said that when two halves find each other, they will know no greater joy than reuniting. If soulmates are two that come from the same source, how fitting are our birth circumstances? We really are victorious and blessed. I no longer feel like I screwed up all those years ago. I have everything now, that is if—" Donovan lowers himself onto one knee. "Lily, will you give me the honor of reuniting with my other half?"

The radiance of the sun on the diamond pales to that on Donovan's face. He looks twenty-one again, just like the last time we were together. It is like his life has been lived on pause in anticipation of this day.

Once upon a time, I had dared dream of this moment. When I did, love swelled in my chest and sent tears flowing down my cheeks. As emotional as it was, never did I imagine how intense the reality could be. My racing heart, my locked breath, my stomach of butterflies—every cliché swirls through me, turning me into a vortex of bliss. Rapidly I nod, fanning my face to disperse some of the emotions that overwhelm.

Standing tall and proud, high upon the hill for all to see, Donovan rises to place the rings on my finger. "I promise to love and stand by you," he vows, his words steady. "To honor and treasure you, not merely for all of my days, but for every moment of what is to come. Wherever God takes you, I will stay by your side, in any situation, and without shame. I will always love you."

How he could stay so grounded in this moment floors me, as I can barely start my words. "I promise to always be the one who never abandons you, to never let you down, and to be there no matter where God places us, no matter what the circumstances. I will always love you."

"You and me forever, Lily."

"You and me forever."

59

My eyes focus on the paper before me, unwilling to look up and face the kitchen and the memories it holds. My heart hears Eric sing as he cooks, the children laugh as they play, and Christopher's music traveling up from the basement. While signing the final page of the escrow documents, I exhale the last breath of my old life.

When I told my children they could have the house, looks of horror crossed their faces. It was then they understood my decision to move to Montana was final. Donovan and I have agreed to come here at least every Easter, Thanksgiving, and Christmas so I can continue to fix those meals and spend precious time with our family—giving us two worlds. As for the bakery, I signed that over to Sunshine last night.

I slide the papers across the table to Jenny, who finally discovered her calling as a realtor. Like mine, her smile is bittersweet. "I hope if my world ever crumbles I find your strength," she says, completely unaware of how strong I've always been. We're the perfect example of how two people can know each other yet hold secrets the other would never guess.

Donovan and Julian return after loading the last of the boxes into the moving van. "All set?" Donovan asks.

"Yep." My eyes scan the kitchen. I can't help but wonder how it will look when I next enter it on Thanksgiving.

"It's unbelievable how full this place is considering how much we loaded into the van," Julian muses at the furniture left behind. All I have taken are personal effects, some photos, mementos of Christopher, and my best kitchen supplies. This is the time for rebirth.

"We'll meet you outside," Donovan says, effectively pushing everyone out. My eyes must scream for a moment of privacy.

"Actually, we should take off," Jenny says. "I'm going to force my husband to spend the rest of however few free on-call minutes he has with me. Good luck, Lily." Jenny hugs me so tightly I feel she is trying to squeeze out my pain so that I can leave it all behind. The gesture moves me, and I dab my expression of love for Christopher from my eyes.

"Bye, Lily," Julian says, flashing his bright smile before hugging me. After the others leave, Julian stops just shy of the door. He selects his words carefully. "This may be out of line, but you told me a long time ago that Donovan never touched you in any way that wasn't welcome. Is that still true?"

"Julian, not all who have problems are abusive, just like not all who have unorthodox relationships are dysfunctional. Thank you for watching over me, but I've always been fine."

His smile warms me. "Be happy," he says, departing.

As I close the door, the house feels hollow, not just of my belongings but of all life. I expected to feel Christopher here, but he's moved on, just like I need to. On the descent to the basement, my vision becomes so blurred from sorrow it is hard to see the steps. My intent is to stand in the center of the room and feel the music one last time. Instead I halt at the bottom step and accept that even if I weren't moving on, this part of my life is forever gone.

"Goodbye, Christopher. Thank you for bringing me more joy than I ever thought possible. I'll always love you, and I will always miss us."

Fleeing the house, my tears leave behind a trail of love.

Stepping out the front door, the glow of the sun surrounds me, drawing me into the next life.

60

"Why are we doing this?" I ask Donovan as we move my belongings out of his room. We are so removed from neighbors we can make out on our front lawn in total privacy. There is very little pretense here. If we didn't fear these family visits, we would just tell all the locals we are married, like we do when traveling.

"Because we love our families and want to spend time with our grandchildren." Donovan grouses while grabbing a box of my things and heading off to stash them in my closet. "Remember how badly you wanted kids? This is one of those times when it comes back to bite you in the ass."

Grabbing another box, I follow behind. "God, I thought we moved to a remote enough area where no one would want to come. Maybe we should have left the country."

"I'm too old to learn another language," Donovan gripes as he sets the box in the closet.

"And I'm too old to lift these boxes."

Instead of taking my box, he steps aside to grant me closet access. "You're never too old to be in shape."

"And you're never too old to stop being a gentleman." I chuckle and shove the box into his arms.

"Touché," he says, placing it in the closet. "They should be here any minute. Your room looks normal. Maybe a little too clean though. Did you get a new frame for your wedding picture?" he asks, pointing to my nightstand.

"No, I just polished it. I like to do that occasionally."

"As you well should." Donovan kisses my forehead, and we move on to his room. Inside the open closet sits a laundry basket. The brightly colored lace garments in it make for a revealing display that sends me racing. "Crap! I forgot to remove my laundry. We don't need anyone finding dirty, lady undies in your room."

"Let them, it will add to my playboy image."

"Either that or they'll think you're a closet transvestite." I remove a pair of bright, blue panties from the basket, stroll to Donovan, and hold them against his crotch. "You being a cross dresser would explain a lot about why we've spent five years in hiding."

His eyes grow with mirth as he lofts me onto the bed. His lips attack my neck with a vengeance. "We both know there is no way they will think this hot hunk of man is a transvestite."

"Gee, D-boy, your ego trip is a bumpy one." His kisses send a twitter through my nervous system. "Oh, dear God. Are we going to be able to make it a week without this?"

"I don't plan to," he asserts.

"Donovan!"

"Please, Lil. I'm not that reckless. I have a little surprise." From his nightstand he grabs a motel key for the place across town. "We're checked in for the week, so we can make a lot of emergency trips to the, uh, grocery store. Oh, and the senior center has BINGO every Thursday. We can pretend we never miss it and have the whole day alone making dirty noises and keeping the rest of the motel entertained." His lascivious smile caves way for his lips to resume an assault on my neck.

"So that's why that flyer is on the fridge," I utter, breathlessly. "I feared senior dementia was kicking in. They are never going to believe we play BINGO, let alone be caught dead at a senior club."

"That's why I made it convincing and put together a bag of good luck charms for you to take when we go," he says while unbuttoning my blouse.

I stop undoing his pants to shoot him an incredulous look. "Me? Why do I get to be the crazy old person with the

BINGO fetish? Dare I ask what's in there?"

"Nothing bad, just a rabbit's foot, a few of Christopher's old guitar picks, a hand-rolled cigarette butt that you claim belonged to Johnny Depp, a blue-haired troll doll, and a miniature garden gnome."

My protest is halted by kisses that work their way down my navel. Seriously, he must spike his protein shakes with Viagra. Just as my moans confess I am melting at his touch, the doorbell rings. "Crap!"

"See this is exactly why I got us that motel room," he says, looking rather pleased with himself while getting off of me.

"You'd better not answer the door like that," I warn, pointing to the bulge in his pants.

He rolls his eyes at me. "I'll join you in a minute. Why can't Graham be late for once?"

After cramming the rest of the dirty undies in the washer, I fling open the front door to my two grandchildren who frantically scream about watching cartoons with their Grandpa Scooby. All of our family refers to us along with Christopher and Anna with grandparental equality. Graham started it when he explained to his son about the multitude of grandfathers he had through Christopher. To Donovan and I, it makes life all the sweeter.

"Mom, you look fantastic." Graham kisses me. The older he gets, the more he looks like Eric.

Betty chimes in, sounding unintentionally snobbish. "Yes, Mom, you seem to be glowing. I need to raid your medicine chest to learn your skin care secrets."

And that's another reason why we've been rearranging our lives. Betty is damn nosey! Unless my son is a Casanova like his uncle, this glow is out of her reach.

Antonia comes up the driveway. The bounce of her long black hair ironically reminds me of Christopher. "Hi, Mom!" Her hug clings to me in the way that people hug you when something is wrong. When she pulls back, she smiles uncomfortably.

"Where's Uncle Scooby?" Graham asks.

"It sounds like he's raiding the fridge," I reply, leading the way to the next room.

Donovan stands over the sink, pouring out the milk from a carton I bought two days ago. "Oh hey, Graham. I didn't hear you come in."

"Don't know how you could have missed the ruckus," Graham states as the grandkids attack Donovan. "Maybe that hearing is starting to go."

"No way! Aging is not an option around here." Donovan hands me the empty carton with a wink. "Looks like we need to buy more milk today. That one spoiled. Where's Antonia?"

"She's here somewhere." I head off, concerned at what may be troubling her.

Antonia stands inside my room, holding my wedding picture. Both of our gazes lock on the image of Christopher. "Your father was an incredible man," I say. The mist that forms in my eyes matches hers. Donovan passes by the room, then stops in the doorway.

Antonia's breath quavers. "Don't you mean, my father *is* an incredible man, just like my other father was?"

My insides lock while my eyes drift to Donovan. He enters the room and places a hand on Antonia's back. We stand transfixed, looking for a sign as to how she is feeling.

"Dad didn't know the truth about me, did he?"

"How do you know?" Donovan asks.

She swallows hard, still staring at Christopher's image. "I just ... do. You two sure go through a lot of trouble to hide. It's smart. Graham and Sunshine would flip out. You can't ever let them know."

"And you?" I ask.

Antonia nods. It's accented by a sniffle that turns to sobs. "You are both so happy. I'd give anything to be like you."

Donovan takes her in his arms. "You will be someday, sweetie. I promise, and my promises always come through."

"I was so afraid to say something. What if I was wrong?" she says, as Donovan dabs the tears from her eyes. "Will you tell me everything? From the beginning?"

"Of course, we will." I take Antonia's hand and sit her on the bed.

Donovan smiles to her before raising his eyes to me. "Just as I thought life couldn't get any more perfect. I'll be right back. I'm going to send Graham and crew out for that milk. Hopefully he won't get mad when he finds I gave him directions to the store in the next county."

I start our story with the intent of giving Antonia every last detail. She deserves the truth, regardless of how she may come to view her grandparents. Thus, I start with words that I know will bring forth a chuckle. "One day, somewhere among the roses and petunias, my sanity squirted out of my brain and fertilized the backyard."

61

A vertical line of pixels flashes with mockery. I feel it is telling me I am missing something of importance. I've been drafting my memoirs in a daring move to preserve who I am now for my future incarnation. It's a simple plan to register my story, along with Donovan's journals, with the Library of Congress. Upon our demises, the catalogue numbers will be engraved into our headstones without explanation to anyone as to what they mean. In the next life, we only need to remember our names and visit our graves. If we can do that, the rest will fall into place.

"How's it going?" Donovan asks as he enters our home office. Placing a cup of tea next to me, he smiles with remembrance. My lips mimic his nostalgia.

"It's been awhile since I've had tea."

"Me too. What was it with those two and tea?" he muses.

"Mine was British," I say, beaming at the memory.

"Mine was crazy," he asserts with wide eyes. "I'm still amazed she never went off the deep end. I constantly warned her doctors to be two steps ahead at all times. Every day it became a new game with her. Like when she tried to sabotage the stew on the day we built the playhouse, because she was lashing back at me for making her stop the notes. Then she wanted to steal your necklace because you stood up for me and ruined her purple dress, which she wore to punish me because I stopped her from cutting her arm, then wouldn't fight her when she hit me for it. The woman could be downright diabolical."

Lord, I haven't seriously thought of Anna since word of her suicide came through a year after we moved. She couldn't take that she had again fallen victim to cancer. She clung to Donovan like a sticky booger only to dump him once Christopher died. Her venomous letter overshadows the pleasant days we shared after her recovery.

"You didn't answer my question," Donovan says. "How's it going?"

"I'm done. I'm just making sure I haven't forgotten any details." That baneful bitch. I gave her years of support, yet she ended them with evil words. Calling me poisonous and drinking of my tears. What the hell does that mean?

"Where did you start?" he asks.

"When I almost smacked you into Mom's flower bed."

Donovan chuckles. "I don't know what would have been worse, the thorny rose bushes or Mom's wrath if I landed in her Lilies of the Valley. I seem to recall the petunias took a beating."

"Yeah, Mom would have killed us."

"She sure would have. I'm going to bed. Join me soon?" he asks with sparkles flaring in his eyes.

"You know I can't resist that look. Give me a few minutes."

Donovan scoffs on his way out, "Lily of the Valley. How ironic is it The Dragon Empress' favorite flower is so poisonous?"

Lilyanna Petula Beckett. I'm named after a droopy, poisonous, flower and a great singer with a goofy name. With a sigh I raise my cup, ready to drink to my mom and her madness. As the brim hits my lips, unsteadiness conks me over the head. The cup meets the desk so fast the tea slops. With fervor, I search the Internet for "Lily of the Valley poisonous." The results boil my bile, sending it up the back of my throat.

Lily of the Valley is a highly poisonous plant and can be deadly if ingested. Small doses over time can weaken a heart. A large dose, either eaten or steeped into a tea, can cause blurry vision, halo effects, vomiting, and alterations in cardiac rhythm. Larger doses will alter heart rhythm, thus increasing the likelihood of heart failure while under stress.

All that homemade tea Anna made for Mom …

No one ever questioned Mom's heart problems because of her illness.

My mind presses rewind on an imaginary remote control, and my life speeds backward. The picture freezes as I re-enter Mom's hospital room to find Anna feeding Mom juice, then adding water to the vase of Lilies of the Valley that had been steeping since the night before. If their water were added to the juice, Mom would have been drinking the Lily's tears.

Anna said she tried to protect Christopher that day. I thought she meant how she tried to keep him in the hall. Instead it was by silencing Mom.

I scramble to the closet and dig through a box of memories. I pull out Anna's letter.

It's long past time for me to move on, but after all he did for me, I needed to know Donovan would be provided for. Now that destiny has kicked in, we are all free.

With trembling hands the letter is placed back in the box. My stomach wretches, and I race for the bathroom. The walls spin around me in a blur. The sudden dizziness bringing me to my knees and puking into the toilet.

Images that I tried to repress for so long again burn in my mind. Christopher's heart attack—the sweating, the gasping, the clutching of his chest, all horrific memories that make me wretch. The burn reminds me of alcohol—the cocktails Anna made, Christopher's inability to taste the obvious orange, the tingle the drink left on his lips. Again I hurl into the toilet.

Oh, God. Anna, why? All so you could leave and Donovan wouldn't be alone?

Donovan hears my puking and dashes in to check on me. I can't face him.

"Poison!" I holler between heaves, my brow sweating. "Poison!"

"What?" Donovan kneels beside me, pulling back my hair and feeling my forehead.

I can't tell Donovan. He would never be able to live with himself for bringing Anna into our lives if he knew.

Again I hurl.

Donovan needs to leave before I break down.

"Food poisoning," my voice rushes out. "Go to the drug store. Get me something."

"Lily, I can't leave—"

"Go!" I scream, my head dipped down into the bowl so I can't see him. For years he protected me from a horrible truth; now it is my turn. My shock helps me ward off emotion until he drives away. Hugging the toilet, I hurl and scream.

62

"Mmm…" I mutter. Gentle kisses tap on my neck, and I wake with a demure stretch. Though I am now eighty-six years old, the heat of Donovan's passion still has my knees buckling. If it weren't for this sofa supporting my butt, my rear would hit the floor.

Smoothing my hair, and thus comforting my soul, he places a paper tiara saying, "Happy New Year" on my head. On the coffee table in front of us sit two flute glasses and a bottle. "What's with the tiara? Is that sparkling cider?" I ask.

"Yes, and before you go asking more questions, tonight I am rewinding the clock to the New Year's Eve when I stood you up. I've spent my life trying to make up for all the misery I caused, and this is the last thing on the list."

"Donovan, that was more years ago than I care to admit. I'm long past that pain."

"This isn't about letting go of the past, it's about embracing the present. I thought I had no idea what to say that night, but the truth is, I was just nervous about admitting it, so … Lily, as crazy and as wrong as this is supposed to be, I'm in love with you. Each morning when I see you, my faith in the world is renewed. When you pass by, a tingle enlivens me and makes me want to be a better person. The warmth of your smile comforts me throughout the night no matter what my troubles. You have always been the one person who loves me for whom I am, and I truly hope that when we are old, you are still sitting on the sofa with me, loving me as much as I love you. Happy New Year, Lily. You and me, forever."

"You and me, forever."

ဢ

Birds sing as the sun gazes through the bedroom window, greeting a new day. Donovan curls tightly around me then jerks back in horror of my cold and lifeless body. Looking down upon him, I witness his realization that attempts to revive me are in vain. My heart gave out a moment ago, and I have been fighting my natural instinct to move into the light. I need to convey one last time how deeply I love him.

He cradles me in his arms, then turns his eyes heavenward—locking with mine one final time. "I'll find you again, Lily. I promise."

We will be together again, Donovan. Through all of time you have been my light, my guardian, my love. I will plead our case so that we will no longer be enslaved to misery. We've had thirty-four glorious years together, and although they have been lived in the shadows, they have been nothing short of phenomenal.

With my final thoughts as Lilyanna Beckett-Eccles, I drift away from my grieving love. I force my spirit down the hall one last time, drifting past the photos that line it—photos of my happy childhood with Donovan, the amazing life Christopher and I shared, Graham, Antonia, and Sunshine's wedding pictures, their children and grandchildren, and all the love that surrounded Donovan and I in my final years. At the end of the line sits the two halves of the infinity symbol we carved into his old bedroom floor, reunited. Though this life had its rocky moments, I want to forever cherish every heartbeat.

The pictures fade from view, and I am drawn deeper into an enrobing white light. Before me a welcoming figure emits warmth and grace. He spreads out his arms, and my drifting ceases as his face becomes clear. My darling Christopher embraces me as only he can. "Hello, luv. I've missed you terribly."

Again I am filled with the warmth of his love and beauty.

"All this time you have waited for me?"

"Of course. As soon as I left my earthly body the memories flooded back. I spent hundreds of years stealing you from him. I'm not going to stop now. Come on, luv. Enjoy what we've got for tomorrow never knows."

Epilogue

On this warm summer's day, something in the serenity of the clear, blue sky makes me long for the crashing waves of the ocean.

A moving truck cruises past as I walk home from the library. It's likely the people who bought the house across the street. Hopefully, they don't have any bratty kids like the last ones did. Then again, I could use the baby-sitting money.

The truck stops where I anticipate. It's followed by a sedan. A middle-aged couple exits the car, looking tired yet eager to start their new life. They stop in front of the house and lock their arms around one another. Together they look ahead with dreams of the future. I want to be like them someday. Actually, I think I once was. I've been having some really strange dreams lately. Sometimes they make me lose sight of what is real.

A slightly battered sports car parks behind the sedan. From it emerges a heart-stoppingly handsome young man of about my age—tall, dark haired, and completely gorgeous. Though he looks to be athletic, nothing about him screams that he is a pathetic jock. A grade-school aged girl with a family resemblance bounces out of the car and runs to the couple, who is seemingly their parents.

I capture his sight. *I know you.*

Of course you do. You would never forget.

Automatically we walk to each other, forsaking his beckoning sister. "Hi," he says. His green eyes pull me in to a field of eternity.

"Hi. You must be the new neighbors."

"Yeah, I'm Brayden. The brat is my baby sister, Cammi. She drives me crazy," he says, rolling his emerald orbs while blinking them in pleasant annoyance.

"I'm Amara," I offer. "Are a—are you still in school?" A gentle breeze blows tresses of hair across my face. Brayden tucks them behind my ear, threading them through his fingers as he goes.

"Yeah, I'm entering my senior year. You?"

"Me too," I reply, suddenly realizing that a boy I've never seen touched my hair as if he has done it a thousand times before. "I guess we'll run into each other a lot."

Brayden's sister runs toward him, screaming, "Come on, Brayden. Dad says you get first pick of the rooms, and I want to know which one I get." Cammi yanks on Brayden's arm. She's cute, but his patient smile is a little forced. "I hope I get the one that looks onto the backyard."

"Ok, I'm coming," he replies. Cammi runs back to her new home with anticipation. Brayden's smile is wicked. "She can have the best room in the neighborhood as long as mine is sound proof. Nice meeting you, Amara. I'm sure Mom will send me over soon to borrow some eggs or something."

Now that gives me an idea. It's time to make those chocolate-mint brownies I've been craving. Something tells me I have the recipe to steal Brayden's heart.

More by Diane Rinella

The Rock and Roll Fantasy Collection
Scary Modsters…and Creepy Freaks
It's A Marshmallow World
Queen Midas in Reverse
Voices Carry
Moonlight Serenade

Something to Dream On

ABOUT THE AUTHOR

Enjoying San Francisco as a backdrop, the ghosts in USA Today Bestselling Author Diane Rinella's 150-year old Victorian home augment the chorus in her head. With insomnia as their catalyst, these voices have become multifarious characters that haunt her well into the sun's crowning hours, refusing to let go until they have manipulated her into succumbing to their whims. Her experiences as an actress, business owner, artisan cake designer, software project manager, Internet radio disc jockey, vintage rock n' roll journalist/fan girl, and lover of dark and quirky personalities influence her idiosyncratic writing.

You can visit her website at www.dianerinellaauthor.com and on Facebook at https://www.facebook.com/DianeRinellaAuthor